MOTION
FOR
MURDER

a Jamie Winters mystery

Kelly Rey

To Bob. For knowing how my mind works and staying with me anyway.

CHAPTER ONE

———

I knew right away that it wasn't going to be a typical day at the law firm of Parker, Dennis, and Heath. For one thing, there was only one client waiting in the reception area when I got to work, a huge man in a ketchup-stained T-shirt with a pelt like a squirrel and work boots that spoke to days spent hiking in landfills.

For another thing, that client was holding a gun.

I saw only three ways to handle the situation. Three became two when I saw I had a dead cell phone. My next option was to approach him calmly, discuss his issues coolly, and dispatch him to the nearest police station quickly. Or make a hard left, flee to the kitchen, and hide behind the refrigerator until braver souls took charge. That's why I was hugging the SubZero when Missy Clark came in the back door. Missy had been a secretary with the firm for a lot of years, and she'd seen a lot of things. But a colleague cowering beside a major appliance wasn't one of them, and it stopped her in her tracks.

"Hey, Jamie." Her right eyebrow lifted. "What're you doing?"

"Ssh." I cocked my head toward the reception area and put my finger to my lips in the universal gesture for *Be quiet— can't you tell there's a kook with a gun out there?*

Missy tiptoed over to squat beside me. "What's going on?"

I pointed. "There's a gun out there with a house attached to it."

She took a peek. "Adam Tiddle." She sighed. "He's harmless. He's mad because we didn't take his case. He thought it'd make him a millionaire. He's been showing up ever since

Dougie turned him down." She shook her head. "I told him it was going to bite him in the briefs."

"I don't think biting is what this guy has in mind," I said. "Unless chewing and swallowing are involved. I'm not going out there until he's gone."

Missy shrugged. "He's not as bad as he looks. He was in a car accident."

"I've seen him," I said. "No car accident did that."

"His neighbor was changing a flat, and Adam was holding up the car," Missy said.

I nodded. "And the jack broke?"

Missy looked puzzled. "What jack?"

Oh.

"That's the problem. There's no negligence there except for his own. He just doesn't get it." She pushed herself up. "I should call Dougie and warn him."

Dougie was Douglas J. Heath, Esquire, commonly known in secretarial circles as Dougie Digits for the creative and offensive use of his eleven fingers. Thank goodness the eleventh was only an extra pinky finger. I shuddered to think of the damage he could do with another thumb. Dougie had a penchant for spandex and a predilection for ogling secretaries in sundresses. He was the approximate weight of a garden gnome, with a perpetual swagger, and arms that formed two hairy parentheses to his torso. Dougie had once sued a Chinese restaurant for causing a stress disorder because its fortune cookie had predicted grim tidings, and that pretty much tells you all you need to know about Dougie.

Before Missy could pick up the phone, the gnome himself burst through the back door, all pink and flushed with the effort of hustling the six feet from his Mercedes. Everything left Dougie pink and flushed. He broke a sweat lifting his bottle of vitamin pills. Dougie wore the most expensive shoes, the most beautifully tailored suits, and the priciest haircuts, and he still looked like the sleaziest personal injury lawyer in town. He was holding a DVD in one hand that was either a memorialization of his weekend escapades or a copy of his latest commercial. I've seen his commercials. I wasn't sure which would be worse.

His eyes narrowed when he saw me and widened when he saw Missy. All men reacted like that to Missy. Probably because she was five-nine, and five of it was legs. "I don't see any computers in the kitchen, ladies. And it's too early for lunch, Winters."

A flush of embarrassment started at my belly button and washed upward. "You're probably wondering why I'm hiding next to the refrigerator," I said, but Dougie wasn't paying attention. He was too busy looking at Missy. "That top does amazing things for your cans, Clark."

Missy didn't even flinch. She gave me a sidelong look that might or might not have included a wink, tore a paper towel off the roll, and handed it to him. "Here. Clean yourself up. You've got someone waiting."

Dougie brightened and blotted. "A new client?"

"Hold on, you probably shouldn't—" I said.

Missy ignored me. "Yep. Sounds like a live one, too."

"Hot damn, and it's only Monday." Dougie swiped the towel across the back of his neck and dropped it on the counter beside his video. "Teeth?" He peeled back his lips for Missy's inspection.

"Teeth," she agreed.

His lips snapped shut. He adjusted his tie, straightened his lapels, ran a hand through his hair, and patted Missy on the backside. "Make me a protein shake, will you, doll? I'll be right back."

"If you're lucky," Missy muttered, yanking open the refrigerator.

I just sat there, feeling like I should be doing something, as long as that something wasn't following Dougie into Adam Tiddle's orbit. So I measured a half cup of Dougie's protein powder into the blender for Missy while ogling the bare-chested model on the label—he was probably a louse, too. A stench rose from the blender, and I clamped the lid on to stifle it. Judging by the odor, Dougie's daily protein shakes tasted like Adam Tiddle's boots.

Missy had gotten as far as slicing a banana when we heard a shout and the clatter of Bruno Maglis in the hallway, and then Dougie was back, panting, sweat running down his artificially bronze cheeks. His eyes were a little wild. "You could've told me Tiddle had a gun," he said to Missy. "I can't believe you didn't tell me Tiddle had a gun. He could've killed me out there! Do you really hate me that much?"

She probably did, but Missy didn't confirm or deny. She dropped the banana pieces into the blender and hit a button, serene as the Virgin Mary, and watched Dougie's protein shake slop around for a few seconds.

He turned to me, hands propped on his hips. "Did you know Tiddle had a gun?"

"I didn't know it was Tiddle," I said, which wasn't quite the same thing.

"Christ." He shook his head, snatching the glass Missy offered him. "You broads are too friggin' much. Good thing he forgot to load it."

That explained the yelling. Probably Adam Tiddle, out of frustration. As slippery as Dougie Digits was, you didn't get too many shots at him. So to speak.

Dougie drank half the shake in one motion, let out a ripping belch, and left his upper lip unwiped. Between the protein shake and the makeup, his face looked like a color wheel. "I threw the dumb country fuck out," he groused. "Next time he sets foot in here, call the cops." He fixed me with the death stare. "That means you, too, if you can stop humping the refrigerator long enough."

"There's nothing going on between me and the refrigerator," I said hotly, but Dougie had gone back to his protein drink. Probably a good thing. There was a cheesecake in the fridge that might say the fridge and I had something very real. But that was for another time. I got out of the kitchen before Missy had the blender rinsed out.

My desk was squeezed into the reception area with Missy's and the firm's third secretary's, Paige Ford, who hadn't graced us with her presence yet. Probably got lost on her way to work. After all, she'd only been with the firm for six years. I dropped my handbag beneath my desk and sat staring at Adam Tiddle's empty chair while I pondered the meaning of life. I'd like to say I arrived at some stirring realizations in those thirty seconds, but I'd be lying. Instead, I noticed the small white envelope propped against my computer monitor and forgot all about Adam Tiddle. It was an invitation to the senior partner's house for the annual firm barbecue. According to Missy, Ken Parker held the affair every August in his private Xanadu, nine rural acres complete with rolling hills, stables, and an in-ground pool with Jacuzzi. Since I'd only worked at the firm eight months, this was my first invitation. I tucked the invitation in my bag and suspended all thoughts of resigning for the moment. I was just shallow enough to want a glimpse of how the other half lived before I slunk back to my downscale apartment and rued my decision not to attend law school.

Also, I wanted more of that cheesecake.

I switched on my computer and sat back to admire my surroundings while it booted up. It wasn't an unpleasant place to work, once you got past the lawyers and the staff. The partnership owned the building, a rehabbed Colonial within walking distance of the courthouse and all the downtown power restaurants. Lawyers upstairs, tucked safely out of sight from bill collectors and disgruntled spouses. Secretaries downstairs in the line of fire. Basement reserved for closed files and Dougie's gym equipment. According to Missy, Ken Parker's wife had done the decorating. Lots of navies and burgundies and creamy whites. And for the lawyers, lots of mahogany and leather. Ken Parker and Howard Dennis had wanted to create the impression of understated wealth, dignity, and integrity for their practice. If you overlooked Dougie Digits, they'd succeeded.

Thing is, Dougie Digits was hard to overlook. Believe me, I've tried.

CHAPTER TWO

———

I hefted an expandable file off the floor beside my desk and settled in for an exhilarating eight hours of typing Answers to Interrogatories. Interrogatories are written questions that have to be answered by both plaintiffs and defendants, things like: What were you looking at two seconds before you tripped over that crack in the sidewalk and fell four years ago? This is the glamorous side of being a legal secretary. Because I was the rookie, the less desirable jobs like typing multi-paged motions and Answers to Interrogatories fell to me, and I let them fall. I like to think it was because of my emotional maturity, but I suspect it was because of my lack of assertiveness. My sister, Sherri, always exhorted me to open my mouth for something other than eating, but when you're five-three and weigh only ninety pounds, you can't afford to waste that much energy. I know what you're thinking: such a problem to weigh only ninety pounds. Let me give you a different perspective on it. I'm thirty-three, and I still wear training bras.

Before too long, Paige showed up, grunted hello and disappeared into the kitchen for her coffee break, having exhausted herself from the three mile commute. That was all the conversation I could handle from Paige, so I stayed where I was, typing away diligently, until my interoffice phone line buzzed and I was summoned to the conference room.

The whole staff was there when I arrived, their expressions reflecting varying degrees of pain, the reason for which soon became apparent. Dougie had connected his laptop to the flatscreen and was punching keys with that gleam in his eye that signified the unfurling of a new commercial spot. Usually after one of his commercials appeared, we were overrun for the next week by lunatics with dollar signs in their eyes. I wasn't looking forward to it. Dougie's existing clients were scary enough.

Ken Parker, the elder statesman and founder of the firm, had been given the seat of dubious honor in front of the flatscreen. Ken was slipping into old age with a grace reserved for the very rich. Tennis and sailing preserved his trimness, daily naps preserved his stamina, and hair like a Samoyed, thick and white, preserved his handsomeness. He had the reputation around the county for being a few degrees short of plumb, but he had more integrity than anyone I'd ever met and the sort of gentlemanly good manners most women have only heard about in rumor.

The third partner, Howard Dennis, was standing by the window, punching numbers into his cell phone and looking self-important while the firm's associate, Wally Randall, openly adored him. Howard was built like a bathtub with fangs, and he kept them sharp chewing on the secretarial staff. If I had to choose between a night with Howard and a night in hell, I'd start shopping for a fan.

Wally was Howard's pet lawyer, and he was kept on a choker. Wally didn't use the bathroom if Howard didn't rubber stamp it first. He was tall, dark, and awkward, with wrist bones like radio knobs, and knees that clicked and popped like castanets. You heard Wally coming well before you saw him. He claimed this was due to college football injuries, but I knew better. I knew it was from crawling around behind Howard.

The bookkeeper, Janice Iannacone, was closest to the door, looking like she might make a run for it. This was her usual post during office meetings. I used to think it was Dougie's commercials that made her so sour, since she knew better than anyone what they cost the firm. I came to learn she was sour because she detested everyone and everything. Including her ex-husband, or maybe because of him.

I spotted an open seat beside Donna Warren, the overworked paralegal. Donna was sitting at the table with an open law book in front of her, scribbling on a legal pad and trying to disappear. I knew how she felt. I'd rather be typing Answers to Interrogatories myself. You couldn't describe Donna.

To describe her would be to describe the air. Such was her ability to vanish into her environment.

"Okay, we're all here," Dougie said, unnecessarily. "Got the new spot here. Let's take a look, shall we?"

All the blood drained from Ken's face as the screen flickered to life, and Television Dougie appeared, shellacked and pancaked, looking more like a cadaver than a representative of one of the county's wealthiest law firms.

"It's a different world today," he intoned with appropriate somberness. "Car accidents. Slip and falls. Medical mistakes. At any moment of any day, you could fall victim to someone else's negligence, and who would pay the price?"

Ken glanced up. "A little heavy-handed, isn't it?"

Television Dougie was steamrolling on. "Has someone you love been unjustly arrested for drug possession? Have you suffered the indignity of losing your license for driving under the influence?"

Ken did something that sounded like a moan.

"For Christ's sake," Howard said. Only he said it into his cell phone, with his back turned to the television.

"Keep watching," Dougie said, implying it was about to get better.

It didn't.

"Don't suffer one more day. Call the law office of Parker, Dennis, and Heath, and let us help you get every penny you deserve." TV Dougie slammed his fist down on the table, and all of us jumped. All of us except for Howard. He was too busy listening to his voice mail. "We'll get justice for you," TV Dougie vowed. "Someone must pay!" An oily smile, a flash of gum, a lurid wink, and the firm's phone number mercifully appeared over his face before the screen went black.

Dougie powered off the flatscreen. "Pretty good, huh?"

"You might want to think about whitening strips," I said. He frowned at me.

Ken shifted in his chair, sighing heavily. "I've told you before, we partners should approve these scripts. I can't say I think much of your lottery approach."

Dougie's eyebrows drew down, making him look more perplexed than usual. "Melissa? What do you think?"

Missy swallowed hard. "To tell you the truth, Doug, I agree with Ken. It's not very...classy. It could use a little..."

"Class," Paige said.

Missy looked at her. "Right."

Dougie's lower lip pooched out. "Well, my wife liked it."

"I hate it," Missy said.

"I hate it, too," Paige said.

Dougie blinked in open surprise. "Donna? What about you?"

Donna pulled her face out of the law book, her cheeks the color of burgundy wine. "I, um, didn't really–"

"Why're you asking her?" Wally practically yelled. "Who cares what the *support staff* thinks?"

Donna glowered at Wally before disappearing back into her legal research. Instantly her expression smoothed out and became placid. I envied her ability to escape with such ease.

"Well, I like it." Dougie gathered up his laptop. "It'll start running this Friday night, during Springer."

"Naturally," Ken said. "Are we quite through here? I have a meeting with Dr. Forchet." He pushed himself to his feet and left the room without waiting for an answer. One day I hope to have that much self-confidence. I won't even walk out on the cleaning crew.

"Did anyone make coffee?" Paige asked the room at large. "We're out of coffee. I need a cup of coffee."

"Dunkin Donuts made some." Missy tapped my arm. "Let's go, Jamie. We've got work to do."

She pushed me along with the force of her anger, and when we got back to our desks, I said, "Are you okay? You seem a little irritated. I'm sure Paige can make her own coffee."

"*My wife liked it.*" Missy shuddered. "That guy should get a clue. I think all those dumbbells have gone from his hands to his head."

I watched her savage her computer mouse for a few seconds. This was interesting. Missy's usual reaction to the TV spots was more benign "So what do you care if his wife liked it?" I said finally. "Someone has to."

"I don't," Missy said, jamming a sheaf of paper into her printer tray. "I don't care at all. Those two deserve each other."

Uh-oh. I was leaving that one alone.

"Hey, Winters."

I looked up to find Wally hovering over my monitor, holding something that looked suspiciously like Interrogatories. "You wanna type these up for me real quick?" He did something with his lips that resembled a smile.

I didn't, but I couldn't think of a polite way to decline, and Missy didn't seem to be volunteering for the job, so I grabbed the pages and tossed them on the desk.

His lips flatlined. "I need them by two o'clock."

"You'll get them," Missy said, "when she gets around to them."

I nodded. Wally went white with indignation and stomped off to find Howard. Missy gave me an encouraging smile and bent her head to her own work while I resumed typing the Interrogatory answers. I wasn't sure what Missy's problem was with Doug, but it was between the two of them. The truth is, I would've run shrieking from this job in the first week if it hadn't been for Missy. I'm still holding that out as an option if my paycheck ever bounces. Not that I expected that to happen. All the partners drove Mercedes, and Wally had a baby Beemer. Even Janice had managed to save enough to buy a used Lexus. As much as everyone hated to admit it, this was probably due to Dougie's shameless commercial spots. The spots brought in every hothead within the viewing area with an axe to grind, but they also brought in a seven-figure revenue stream, according to Missy. It made me feel a little sorry for Ken Parker. He'd founded a dignified solo practice and would retire from a three-ring circus with Dougie Digits as the head clown.

CHAPTER THREE

—————

The next day, Paige demonstrated remarkable planning skills by showing up with a giant cup of Dunkin Donuts coffee. She settled at her desk, and the three of us did what legal secretaries do, keeping the firm afloat with little or no recognition. Every now and then, Wally showed up to drop files on the floor by my desk before running back to Howard's side. Janice stopped by Paige's desk to rifle through her client ledger sheets and growl at us. Donna floated past with her nose in a law book. I kept an eye on the clock so I wouldn't miss lunch. It was pretty much business as usual until my skin began to prickle, and I looked up to find a gorgeous blonde woman standing in front of my desk. All three of us stopped typing simultaneously. Or maybe the power cut out from her force field.

"I'd like to see Mr. Heath. My name is Victoria Plackett." She gave me the sort of smile that opened doors and wallets alike. I wondered if she practiced it in front of the mirror. It just wouldn't be fair if that came naturally.

Across the room, Paige hung onto her desk with bared claws and practically fell off her chair to get a better look.

"Do you have an appointment?" I flipped through the Law Diary's calendar pages until I got to the right date. At least I think it was the right date. This woman's perfume was smothering my synapses.

"I'm sure he'll see me," she said, smile still firmly in place. "I have an interesting case for him."

"I'm afraid he's very busy," Missy began, when Dougie thumped down the steps cradling a Playboy magazine, which pretty much killed that notion.

"Winters, the toilet upstairs is clogged, and I want you to—" He stopped in mid-sentence, his mouth still open. "Well, hello." He oozed up next to the blonde with one hand out and the other tucking the magazine behind his back. "I'm Doug Heath. How can I help you?"

The blonde let Dougie fondle her hand for a moment before taking it back, while the smile ratcheted from brilliant to dazzling. Any more charm and I'd need sunglasses "I'd like to speak to you about a case, if you have the time. Your girl here says you're busy."

I thought I heard a hiss coming from Missy's direction.

Dougie flung the Playboy onto my desk and pretended to consult the calendar while digging banana remnants out of his incisors with his pinky. He bared his teeth at me. I nodded briefly. He nodded back and straightened. At least I think he straightened. She had about six inches on him in bare feet, and her feet were not bare. They were strapped into dangerous-looking spike-heeled sandals.

Missy cleared her throat. "Doug, aren't you supposed to—?"

"No," Dougie said, not taking his eyes off the blonde.

"But I'm sure that the luncheon is—"

"No," Dougie said again. "That's next week."

"Okay," Missy said, a little frosty. "But the Nobel committee will be very disappointed."

Dougie did an Elvis thing with his top lip and escorted the blonde to the stairs with one hand at her elbow, probably to keep from tripping over his tongue. Missy watched them with more venom than a cobra. Paige stuck out her tongue at their backs and was touching up her makeup before the blonde's heel hit the first step, since Paige tended to run about as deep as a puddle.

I had enough of my own neuroses that I didn't need to share theirs, so I went back to work. One of the skills I'd acquired in my time with Parker, Dennis, and Heath was the ability to type kindling-dry legalese without actually reading it. This came in handy whenever Howard Dennis presented me with one of his excruciating product liability Complaints. While Dougie's Complaints used words like "outrageous" and "pomposity," Howard's used lots of "wherefores" and "hereupons." It was the difference between reading Tolstoy and reading Jackie Collins. Jackie was entertaining, but she wasn't going to expand your sphere of knowledge. Anyway, the ability to slog through the legalese while planning your weekend was a skill useful in waiting rooms, where you could pretend you were reading the Wall Street Journal while eavesdropping on the people around you.

I was almost finished with Wally's emergency desk clutter when I came across something undecipherable. Squinting at it didn't help, so I took it over to Missy and pointed. "Can you tell what this is supposed to be?"

She looked up from the letter she was working on, said, "No clue," and lowered her head again. Guess she was still miffed at Dougie.

I glanced over at Paige, who was hard at work trimming her cuticles. "You want to take a stab at it?"

"Whose is it?" she asked, as if that made a difference.

"Wally's," I said.

She shuddered. "No, thanks. That boy should've been a doctor with that handwriting."

Now I had to track down the boy genius. The best place to start would be Howard's office, since Wally liked to sit quietly in there and soak up the atmosphere.

I stomped up the stairs, legal pad clamped to my chest, and peeked through doorways. Janice's office was the first at the top of the stairs. She snarled at me when I poked my head around the corner. Dougie's door was closed, and I saw no good reason to open it. Predictably, Wally's office was empty, as was Howard's.

Ken Parker's office was at the end of the hallway. Ken had a standing open-door policy except from three to four each afternoon, when he eschewed good interoffice relations for a daily nap. It was open now, so I thought I'd stop in to thank him for the party invitation.

"Damn it, Ken!" Howard's bluster stopped me in my tracks. "His goddamn commercials are making us a laughingstock!"

Howard and I didn't agree on the color of paint on the walls, but I couldn't argue with him there.

Ken said something I couldn't hear, but I heard Howard just fine. "Then we should get him the hell out of here! Is this the sort of practice you want to have?"

I'd heard enough. I wasn't comfortable eavesdropping on them, because I didn't want to risk getting fired but mostly because I couldn't hear Ken. Besides that, Wally was just coming out of the restroom rubbing his palms on his slacks while he clicked along on those rickety knees, and he zeroed in on me like a laser-guided missile. "What are you doing up here?" He was practically glowering with righteous indignation. Wally liked to keep the second floor unsullied by the riffraff secretarial staff downstairs. Since it seemed he didn't wash his hands in the restroom, he apparently wanted to sully it himself. "You got my Answers?"

Silence fell in Ken's office, and I bit my lip, wishing I'd had the good sense to eavesdrop when Wally was in court. The little non-hygienic weasel had a knack for showing up at just the wrong time. "I need an interpretation," I said, borrowing the blonde's bright smile, because everyone knew any man could be won over with charm and a bright smile.

Any man except Wally. "I knew you didn't belong in the legal field," he muttered, snatching the papers from my hand. I swallowed a "Same to you, fella," and waited while he frowned at his own handwriting.

Howard Dennis strolled out into the hallway while I was waiting. I tried hard not to glance his way, afraid I'd look as guilty as I felt. He was sporting the casual look, which for Howard meant his coat was unbuttoned, and his puffy little hands were thrust into his pants pockets. He came right up behind Wally and peered over his shoulder through half glasses, reading from the legal pad. I could have sworn Wally leaned back against him, but I was probably wrong. Probably Howard just blew in his ear.

"Good work, son," Howard told him.

Wally beamed.

Howard looked at me. "What are you doing up here?"

"I just asked her that," Wally said. "She can't do her job without help."

I waited for him to stick out his tongue at me. It wouldn't have surprised me. "I do need help, Howard," I said agreeably. "He gave me an emergency project, and I can't read his handwriting, and it's delayed my getting to work on your Complaint."

Wally's smile disappeared at the same time as Howard's, for an entirely different reason. "No," he snarled, shoving the pad back at me.

I stared at him. "You're not going to decipher it?"

"N-O," he said, enunciating so exactingly I could count the veins in his neck. "It says 'no.' Can't you read? It's perfectly clear to me. And by the way, the toilet's clogged. Call a plumber."

"After you type my Complaint," Howard added.

And Wally said, "Of course, of course."

"But didn't you just use the bathroom?" I asked.

"There's no need for insolence," Wally said. "Go. Type. Call."

He'd make a fine dictator one day. I left the two of them stewing in their own grandeur while I fled back to the safety of the secretarial pool. By the time I got there, I was hungry from the stress of the second floor. I kept a box of Tastykakes stashed in my desk drawer for moments like this, so I hauled out a package of Butterscotch Krimpets. Nothing wrong with me that a good sugar fix couldn't cure.

Missy looked up when she heard the crinkle of the wrapper. "Uh-oh. Everything okay?"

I leaned my elbows on Wally's legal pad with a sigh. "What are the chances Wally will get fired by five o'clock?"

"Not good," she said. "He cleans Howard's pool on the weekends."

I grinned. She grinned back.

"You shouldn't eat those," Paige told me. "They'll go right to your hips."

"I can only hope," I said. If they did, it'd be the first time in my life I had hips. I finished the first Krimpet and eyed the second.

"Don't do it," Paige warned. "It's all fat and sugar."

"Your lipstick's smeared," Missy told her, and Paige retreated to her mirror in alarm.

"Don't worry about your hips," Missy said, even though I wasn't. "And don't worry about Wally. I'm going to put a box of Midol in his Christmas stocking this year. You'd be better off worrying about Dougie. His wife's on her way here to have lunch with him."

The Krimpet stuck halfway down my throat, and my breath stuck halfway up. I'd met Hilary Heath a few times, and those meetings had been only marginally more pleasant than a gynecological exam. The best word to describe Hilary was *sharp.* She had a body like a letter opener and the sort of eyes that could perform x-rays. More importantly, she had Dougie, and she protected her investment through unannounced inspections and merciless interrogation of the support staff. Hilary trusted very few and liked no one. Rumor had it that she'd once had a secretary fired for laughing at one of Dougie's lame comments. Hilary thought it indicated an unacceptable level of intimacy.

I shot a wild look at the clock. "You think we could take lunch early today?"

"You could," Missy said, "but why miss the fun when Hil finds Dougie up there with Bambi?"

"She's right," Paige said. "This'll be good."

It did have a certain appeal, but Missy seemed to be looking forward to Hilary's arrival a little too much.

"I don't know if I have the stomach for this," I said. "It might be too much confrontation for one day."

Missy shrugged. "Leave if you want, but I'm not going anywhere. Dougie's got this coming. *My wife loved it.* Huh."

Paige and I looked at each other.

"Besides," Missy added, "I'm skipping lunch today. I'm seeing Braxton tonight."

Braxton Malloy, the pharmacist Missy kept penciled-in on her Daytimer for a Monday night playdate. The relationship kept Missy in discounted prescriptions and qualified as a weekly aerobic workout at the same time.

Being the inveterate list maker that I am, working out has been on my to-do list for years. I just never seem to be able to find something I liked enough to stick with. At the moment I was trying to practice yoga, but because I had the flexibility of a two by four, that wasn't going so well. And I had a little trouble achieving oneness with the universe, since the universe was always conspiring to cheat me out of the finer things in life, like patience, wisdom, and a good parking spot at the mall.

Maybe I needed a Braxton. But first I needed to escape Hilary Heath.

CHAPTER FOUR

———

Women were put on this earth to be mothers. This is what I'm told by my own, whenever she's feeling out of sorts over having no grandkids, which is pretty much all the time. It seemed I'd experienced the allotted lifetime quotient of monthly periods without putting my uterus to better use. I think my father wants grandkids, too, but he's willing to wait for the husband first. My mother interviews potential sperm donors in the supermarket. Last Christmas she gave me pacifiers, baby booties, and a box of Pampers. I figure the Pampers will come in handy in another fifty or sixty years.

Fortunately for my mother, my little sister Sherri came along. Sherri's thirty-one and desperate for a husband, and she looks under every available rock to find one. As far as I'm concerned, she's a born mother. She's been telling me to wash my hands and wear clean underwear since she was five. She has childbearing hips and a good attitude about the whole baby thing, and I give her a lot of credit. It's not easy balancing my mother's desperation with her own. It couldn't be easy dealing with her own masochism, either. For the past two years, she'd been working at Williams Bridal selling wedding gowns to prospective brides.

Sherri and I get together weekly for lunch out of our mother's orbit, mostly so she could grouse about her Saturday night date, and she was waiting for me when I got to the Lincoln Diner. The Linc was your typical New Jersey diner, lots of vinyl and mirrors and chrome, and noise. It wasn't the Four Seasons, but the food was good, and the booths were clean. I slid in across from her, noticing she looked especially morose.

"It's never gonna happen for me," she'd announced before I'd picked up my menu.

I'd heard this before. "Sure, it will," I said, which is what I always said. I believed it. Sherri was pretty and curvy and could convincingly pretend she liked sports.

"No." She shook her head at the silverware. "No, it won't. You should've met the guy I went out with this weekend." She rolled her eyes. "And I thought pocket protectors went out of style."

I looked at her over the menu. "You went out with a professor?"

"Nah." She shook her head. "A student."

We paused while the waitress delivered a basket of rolls and two glasses of water, and then I said, "You might want to try dating men."

"He's a forty-seven year old junior," Sherri said. "He went back to college after his wife ran off with an engineer. He decided he was going to make something of his life. I think he wants to be a proctologist or something."

Jeez. I put down my menu and picked up a roll. "Listen, Sher, I don't think he's the one for you."

"No kidding." Sherri stared into her glass of water. "I can see it now. I help put him through medical school, and he leaves me for someone younger. It's a classic story."

Except the classic story wasn't about a doctor who graduated right into retirement. I buttered my roll and kept my mouth shut.

Sherri lifted her shoulders and sighed heavily. "So I saw the new commercial today. That Doug Heath isn't too bad-looking."

The waitress came back to take our orders. Caesar salad for Sherri, fettuccini with meat sauce for me. It was shaping up to be a stressful week, and I wanted to be fortified.

"Dougie's already got kids," I said when the waitress had moved on. "Two, possibly more." I'd been surprised the Ice Queen could bear children, but maybe she'd been warmer earlier in the marriage. I know if I were married to Dougie, I'd be a glacier after eighteen years.

"He could have more," Sherri pointed out. "It's easier for men. Tony Randall had kids when he was in his seventies." She sighed again. "It's just not fair."

I agreed with her there.

"Mom wants to set me up with Frankie Ritter." She picked up a roll, looked at it, and put it back in the basket. "I don't know. Frankie *Ritter*? He wet the bed until he was eighteen." She picked up the roll again. "He does have blond hair, though."

Sherri had always had a thing for blond hair. As a kid, she'd thrown out all of her brunette Barbies and kept the blond PJs. She wouldn't even look twice at George Clooney, which gives you some idea why she's still single. "Frankie Ritter's built like a tuba," I said.

Sherri blinked. "I hadn't noticed."

Right. The blond hair must have distracted her.

"I don't know." She tore a chunk off her roll and tucked it in her cheek. I buttered a fresh roll. Between us, we emptied the breadbasket in ten minutes flat, and by then our meals had arrived. After Sherri had salted and I had cheesed, she said, "So about that commercial. I thought it was kind of…"

"Low class?"

"Compelling. Persuasive."

Oh. Sure.

"I mean, every penny I deserve? That's good stuff. Makes me want to go fall down somewhere." She speared a lettuce leaf and thought about it. "I want to meet a Doug Heath," she said finally. "A blond Doug Heath."

"No, you don't," I said. "He's scum. He lies. He cheats on his wife. He cheats on his girlfriend."

"Yeah, so why are you working for him?"

That stopped me cold. I cut another quarter of my fettuccini and thought about it. "Well, the job market's tight," I said finally. "Besides, there's two other lawyers in the firm—"

"Blondes?" she asked hopefully.

"One's sixty-eight and one's fifty," I said.

She gave me a look. "Like that matters. Tony Randall, remember?"

"Maybe those Hollywood types are friskier in their old age," I said. "I can't see Howard or Ken having sex." And I didn't want to see it. Just the thought of it was enough to make my eyelids slam shut. "Can we talk about something else?"

"Suit yourself. Mom wants us to come over to dinner on Friday. She's making meatloaf."

Dinner at my mother's. It was four days away, and I wasn't hungry already. Except her meatloaf could make Betty Crocker jealous. One thing about my mother, she didn't let inconsequential medical findings about, say, cholesterol and fat content alter her recipes. Lots of eggs, lots of shortening, and no lean anything. After dinner at my parents', you weren't hungry for the next forty-eight hours. It's probably why my father had been eating one meal a day for fifteen years

Sherri shifted uneasily. "She's inviting Frankie Ritter."

"I can't make it," I said immediately. "I have to work late."

"You have to help me. I need to get married, Jamie. I want to have a baby. I want to quit the shop."

This was news. I looked up from my dish. "Why?"

"It's like torture." She jabbed at a crouton. It skidded across the plate and onto the table. "Nothing but happy engaged women—girls—day after day, and I have to stand there and smile like I'm glad for them. Well, not that I'm *not* glad for them, but I want to be glad for me someday, too, you know?"

"You will be."

"I'm thirty-one," she said. "If I'm going to have a baby, I have to do it soon."

"That's not true. You have time. Nowadays women have babies in their forties."

Sherri snorted. "Not women who have to work for a living. What, I'm going to go to my kid's high school graduation when I'm sixty? I don't think so."

"It's been done," I said.

"Not by me." She gave up on the crouton and poked at her salad. "I might as well go out with Frankie. How bad can he be?"

I put my fork down. "You are not dating Frankie Ritter. I'll help you find someone."

A light went on behind her eyes, and she sat up straighter. "You will? Really?"

"Sure." I swallowed. "How tough can it be to find a decent guy?"

"Blond," she said. "And it can be pretty tough. Thanks, Jamie. You know you'll be my maid of honor, right?"

Like I needed one more hideous bridesmaid's dress. "Let's find the guy first," I said. "Then we'll worry about the wedding."

"And the baby. Jordan. Boy or girl, it'll be Jordan." She reached across the table to squeeze my hand. "I feel a lot better just knowing we're in this together. And I'm buying."

"In that case," I said, "I feel better, too."

CHAPTER FIVE

———

I was lucky enough to miss Hilary Heath and her traveling Inquisition. She was gone by the time I got back.

Missy wasn't at her desk, but Paige was, more or less. She was pale and shaken, staring into space with her fingers twisted in her lap, her shoulders slumped. She seemed even less aware of her surroundings than usual. I rushed over to her. "Are you alright? What happened?"

She flinched and turned her head to look at me, but I'm not sure she saw me. "Water."

I hurried to the kitchen to pour her a glass of water. Hilary's visit must have been even worse than I'd imagined. Paige's hand shook hard enough to slop water over the edge of the cup. "It was awful," she said in a croaking whisper. "She saw Dougie with *her* and..."

Oh, no. I looked around for a trail of blood.

Paige shook her head. "Hilary wouldn't believe me. I tried to tell her Bambi was a new client, but she wouldn't believe me." One hand dropped to the blotter and came up clutching a computer-generated sheet. "I have the CFA right here. She never got to sign it."

CFA meant Contingent Fee Agreement, the document that proscribed Dougie's percentage of any recovery in a case. He didn't lift a pencil without a signed CFA in the file. No exceptions, no negotiations. His brand of legitimized theft had bought him a house once featured in *Contemporary Living Digest*. Of course, the photo layout had omitted the indoor/outdoor swimming pool in the master bedroom, probably because Dougie had been too busy *schtupping* the photographer to show it to her.

Paige's eyes glazed over. "Hilary told him she wished he was dead. It was ugly. Even Howard ran for the back door." Followed by Wally, no doubt. Paige dropped the CFA and the empty cup. "I think I might quit. That woman scares the hell out of me."

"You don't want to quit," I said, although I couldn't think of a single reason why. Quitting sounded pretty good.

"That's easy for you to say. You haven't even dealt with her a year." Paige shuddered. "Maybe I can put my desk in the basement. No one would bother me in the basement."

"There are no windows in the basement," I said.

"I don't need windows."

"Plus there are spiders."

"Maybe the basement isn't a good idea," she said. "Do you think they'd let me move upstairs?"

"I don't think so," I said. "Look, how angry could she be? They went out to lunch, didn't they?"

Paige shook her head. "She stormed out of here alone, screaming about going to see a divorce lawyer. Dougie left the building with that Bambi person to try to smooth things over." She caught my frown. "Victoria Plackett."

Oh. "So where's Missy?" I asked.

Paige rolled her eyes upward, which either meant heaven or the second floor. Since I didn't think Hilary was quite that powerful, I took it to mean the second floor, so I headed upstairs, taking the steps two at a time. I half expected to find Missy curled up in the fetal position in a corner somewhere, but instead I found her in Dougie's office, rifling through his desk with an urgency unmatched since Dougie's ill-fated experiment with sushi.

I hesitated in the doorway, watching her slam the kneehole drawer shut and yank open one of the side drawers. Papers rustled as she rummaged around inside then pulled out a single blue sheet. It looked like the sort of inexpensive faux-marbleized stationery available at any office supply store, but it was clearly something more than that to Missy. She took a second to read it over before folding it in thirds, her mouth drawing downward.

I was wishing I'd stayed downstairs at my desk, or even in the basement with the spiders, when Missy noticed me. "Jamie!" She slid the drawer shut with her leg, her cheeks reddening a little. "Boy, did you miss a show." She tucked the sheet into the pocket of her skirt.

"So I heard." I leaned against the doorframe. "Paige is still recovering."

"She got the worst of it." Missy came around the desk "Hil was in rare form today. Come on, let's get back to where we drones belong."

"What were you looking for?" I asked.

"Huh?" Missy glanced back at the desk, then out the window, then down at her feet. "Nothing. I wasn't looking for anything."

"Okay. Then what'd you find?"

"Just something Dougie wanted me to follow up on. No big deal." She flashed a weak grin. "There's nothing here for me," she said, and I got the feeling she wasn't talking about Dougie's desk. "Let's go."

I followed her toward the stairs thinking Dougie Digits sure made life complicated for a lot of people.

CHAPTER SIX

———

The rest of the day was business as usual. Howard came back from lunch and left fifteen minutes later for a two o'clock deposition with Wally in tow. Ken's door closed shortly afterward and stayed that way until four o'clock. Dougie's two-thirty appointment came in and left a half hour later, followed shortly by Dougie. All of which left the three of us free to get our work done in peace. It was just like a normal office, if you forgot about Adam Tiddle and Hurricane Hilary's visit and Dougie's new commercial debut. If you couldn't forget about those things, it was just the calm before the next storm.

At four-thirty, Donna crept down the stairs clutching a sheaf of papers. Not exactly a storm, more of a mournful breeze. "I'm awfully sorry," she said to none of us in particular, "but could someone tell me where the Biederman file is? I can't find it anywhere, and Mr. Biederman wants a status report."

Paige lifted her head. Her eyes were still a little glazed over, but at least she'd stopped twitching. "What?"

Donna hugged her papers harder. "Biederman. I can't find it."

"I don't know where it is," Missy said without looking at her. "It's not one of my files."

"It's Doug's case," Donna said.

Missy narrowed her eyes. "I don't know where it is."

I made it a point never to be caught playing computer games during work hours, so I closed my game of Solitaire before I stood up. "I'll help you find it."

Donna's little squirrel face brightened.

"We'll go look in Dougie's office," I said, slipping Missy a sideways glance. Missy was engrossed in the effort of looking engrossed in her work. All afternoon her teeth gnashing had been distracting me, and now she was playing it like she was expecting a gold watch on Secretary's Day. I still thought her issue with Dougie was between them, but I wasn't liking my idea of what the issue was. It smelled like an affair to me. Missy's anger, the paper she'd taken from Dougie's desk, it all fit. Of course, I'd been wrong before. Accepting this job was one example that sprang to mind.

"I hope he isn't coming back today," Donna said as we climbed the stairs. "He makes me kind of uncomfortable."

"He's a teddy bear compared to his wife," I said, trying to ease her anxiety.

But to my surprise, she said, "Oh, I don't mind Hilary. She's not so bad."

Which just went to prove how wrong I could be.

"I've been working on a brief in support of his Motion for Trial *De Novo* for a solid week," Donna said, standing aside so I could enter Dougie's office ahead of her. In case there were booby traps or something. "It went through four rewrites. I was researching citations until midnight last Friday. And today I heard him tell Ken he whipped the thing up in one day."

I made a laser line for the desk. Maybe there was more of whatever Missy had confiscated tucked away in there. "Isn't that just like a man?" I said, wondering why she was telling me this. "He was probably trying to earn brownie points with Ken."

"I could see Wally doing something like that," she said. "He could use all the help he can get. But Doug?" She shook her head. "I expected better from him."

"For God's sake, why?" I watched her thumb through the files on the floor beside Dougie's sitting area. Plain and breakable, Donna made me look positively voluptuous, so I sat beside her whenever possible at office meetings, but beyond that, she was the brains behind Dougie's operation. I'd always thought she preferred to remain behind the scenes, churning out erudite legal documents in contented anonymity twenty hours a day. Who knew she wanted to jump from scriptwriter to starring role.

"Where do you think *Doug* was on Friday night?" she asked me. "Not here, I can tell you that."

Probably not with his wife, either. "You know the partners don't work those kinds of hours anymore," I said. "That's why they hire people like you and me. And Wally."

She squinted up at me. "You don't understand."

Not the first time.

"He takes credit for everything I do," she said. "He didn't even tell Ken I had written the brief. Don't you think that's wrong?"

"Why don't you tell Ken yourself?" I said. "You know, work it into the conversation casually."

"Conversation?" She pushed her glasses up her nose. "I don't have conversations with Ken. I don't have conversations with Howard, either. He just leaves notes on my desk, what he wants me to do."

"But you work for all three of them," I said. "You must talk to them at some point."

She shrugged and clambered to her feet, taking a second to smooth out her dress. "That's what e-mail is for."

It seemed to me e-mail was for the rampant proliferation of ads for erectile dysfunction treatment and low-rate mortgage offers, but then I worked on the first floor so maybe I wasn't privy to its more intellectual applications. I went back to nosing through Dougie's desk drawers before I said something stupid. Like this: "I'll be happy to mention it to Ken next time I talk to him, if you want."

I could be wrong, but it looked for a second like she levitated right off the floor. "You'd do that for me?"

Sure, I could fit in right between finding a husband for my sister and a new location for Paige's desk. "You deserve some credit around here," I said, and I meant it. I just wasn't sure I was the one to get it for her. I didn't have Missy's seniority or Janice's personality or Paige's looks, but hey, I could always type a note and slip it under Ken's door

Just when I was feeling virtuous over the whole thing, she said, "Then this afternoon he dropped the bomb."

Uh-oh. I stopped snooping in Dougie's desk and waited for the proverbial other shoe to drop. Now that I'd evidently committed myself without all the facts, it was probably about to drop on my head.

"You know I sit in on all of Doug's trials," she said. "I help him locate documents, keep exhibits and witness lists straight, that sort of thing." She sneaked a glance at me, so I nodded. "Well, Lezenby's set for next week." Her toe dug into the carpet. "He told me he doesn't want me in the courtroom anymore. He said my looks are a liability with the jury."

Jeez.

Her eyes lifted to meet mine, and I had to work hard to keep sympathy off my face. "What's wrong with my looks?" she asked.

In a perfect world, there was absolutely nothing wrong with her looks. She was bright and capable and very professional, even in her long-sleeved, high-necked, floor-length granny dress. And with her hair drawn back so tightly into a bun that her eyes were slitted. Okay, so she had a little work to do in the looks department. But that shouldn't have kept her out of a courtroom, and it certainly shouldn't have any effect on a jury. My guess was in Dougie's world, without benefit of makeup and push-up bras and the brazen flashing of skin, she was a piece of furniture. My skin prickled at the injustice of it.

"I can't answer that," I said, which was true enough. "But I think Dougie's being very short-sighted not recognizing your value to this firm."

A small, resigned smile flitted across her lips and was gone, swallowed up by a massive sigh. "Story of my life," she said. "Look, I don't think the Biederman file is here. I'll just find it tomorrow. Thanks anyway."

I circled Dougie's desk, my ransacking intentions forgotten, and caught up with her at the doorway. I've always had a soft spot for underdogs. "Are you going to be alright?"

She seemed a little surprised, maybe even touched by my concern. "I'm always alright," she said. "But I'd be better if Doug would fall down the courthouse steps someday."

Which is when I began to like Donna a whole lot more.

CHAPTER SEVEN

I haven't carried too many childhood traumas into my adulthood. Long ago I came to grips with the fact that I couldn't cook like my mother, I didn't yearn to give birth like my sister, and I wouldn't ever preside over a diversified and profitable retirement account like my father. I didn't hold a college degree. I was single, and I lived in a shoebox. Some people would call this failure. I called it opportunity. I lived on a street in a town called Mapleton that was lined with trees and filled with bungalows, some of them expanded to two stories. My shoebox was on the second floor of a bungalow owned by Curt Emerson. It had lots of lawn, beige vinyl siding and a brown roof, and Curt kept the lawn mowed and the leaves raked, which was good enough for me. Curt was a package delivery driver by profession, a confirmed bachelor by preference, and a landlord by sheer luck. Mine. If I earned an actual living wage, I'd have to come up with reasons not to buy a place of my own, and I liked spending my evenings on Curt's deck enjoying the view. Of Curt. He was finer than any caricature I could watch on my television upstairs, alone. Plus, he fed me. Sherri once suggested that I had a thing for Curt, which was patently ridiculous. He was full of annoying habits, like keeping up on his laundry, keeping his cupboards stocked, and keeping his property tidy. I could never fall for anyone like that.

Since I hadn't been grocery shopping since the Bush administration and hadn't inherited the Winters women's genetic ability to create culinary masterpieces from a can of peas and chicken broth, I hadn't cooked dinner for myself. I'd been lounging around on the deck hoping Curt wasn't working overtime. He usually brought home Chinese takeout on Mondays, and I don't like to eat any later than seven o'clock.

He rolled in about six-fifteen carrying a brown paper bag and wearing his uniform, which stretched nicely across shoulders well developed from hard days spent tossing fragile packages haphazardly onto porches. Not that I noticed that sort of thing. The uniform, I mean. I was too busy noticing the Good Luck Wok logo on the bag. He spotted me as he came around the corner of the house and was smiling before he reached the deck.

"Hello, dear," I said. "How was your day?"

He held out the bag. "Got caught in the middle of a high speed chase during a hostage crisis. Same old, same old."

I blinked. "Really?"

"Nah. I got a speeding ticket." He tipped his head toward the bag. "Garlic beef. Kung pao chicken. Take your pick."

I arranged the little cardboard containers on the table. "You'll make a fine husband some day."

His eyes narrowed. "And you'll make a lousy wife. When are you gonna learn how to cook?"

"I can cook." I tore the lid off the egg drop soup.

He raised an eyebrow. "Cap'n Crunch isn't cooking."

Damn. "Besides, I have no intention of getting married. I'm leaving that madness to my sister." I dug the plastic utensils out of the bag.

"Madness is such an ugly word. Can't we just say insanity?"

I shoveled a few spoonfuls of soup into my mouth and sighed with bliss. "We can say anything you want, as long as this keeps coming home with you."

He chose the beef, and I had the chicken. We ate in silence for a few minutes while the day slid into night, and lightning bugs began flashing out in the yard. Curt got up and lit the citronella candles scattered along the deck railing. Even covered up in a uniform, he looked like an athlete, and he was. Every day he ran three miles and practiced aikido for a half hour while I sat upstairs and tried to contort my limbs into pretzels for five minutes before calling it a day. I had a lot to learn about persistence.

When we were finished, Curt took the leftovers inside. When he came back five minutes later, he was wearing shorts and carrying two beers. I took the beer and refused to gawk at his legs as we moved over to the loungers. I only took a peek or two.

"So what's the latest at Parker, Dennis, and Heath?" he asked. He always asked me that, although like most people, Curt couldn't abide lawyers and had developed a particular dislike for Dougie Digits. Probably it was based on my slightly biased office gossip, but he'd also run into Dougie a few times and had come away unimpressed. Dougie had that effect on a lot of people. His wardrobe had a better reputation than his legal acumen.

"Funny you should ask." I held out my bottle. He twisted the cap off and handed it back. "A client with a gun came in this morning looking for Dougie."

Curt gave me a sharp look. "You don't say."

"He forgot to load it."

"Now that's a shame." He took a long pull on his beer.

I gave him a sidelong look. "Aren't you going to ask his name?"

"Nope."

"You know I was in grave danger," I said.

"Were you?"

I studied the label on my bottle. "Well, I could've been."

"Why don't you quit that place? Find a job where people with guns aren't coming after you."

"Technically, he wasn't after me," I said.

"Technically, you could still be dead," Curt said, and I couldn't think of anything to say to that, so we let the silence hang over us while we drank half our beers.

My mind was flitting from one topic to the next like a moth around a light, and suddenly it settled on Friday. "Hey, how'd you like to come to my parents' for dinner on Friday?"

His look made me squirm. "Are you asking me out on a date?"

"Of course not." My cheeks felt warm. "I need a buffer is all. My sister will be there, too, and my mother invited Frankie Ritter."

"Ah." Curt nodded. "The blond hair."

Okay, so I'd divulged a few family secrets. It had been purely in the interest of finding a husband for Sherri. "She's making meatloaf," I said. "She makes a terrific meatloaf. One of the best meatloafs I've—"

"As long as it's not a date," he said.

"No date," I assured him. "I'll even get my mom to pack you a doggy bag."

"There's no need for threats," he said. "I said I'd go. But as long as you're getting things, you should get yourself a better job."

I should have quit while I was ahead. This was starting to feel like a night with my mother.

* * *

Curt and I had a deal, and it went something along the lines of him providing dinner and me providing dish-washing services afterward. Not long after this inspired piece of negotiating, I tried to run an end-around by stocking up on paper plates and plastic forks. In response, Curt had cut off the food supply for a week, and that's why I found myself a half hour later standing at his sink, elbow deep in Dawn and garlic sauce.

"So about this guy with the gun," Curt said from his seat at the table, where he was drinking a beer and ogling my backside. Or so I'd thought. I wasn't sure whether I was relieved or disappointed to find out he'd actually been thinking.

"Adam Tiddle." I swatted at an itch on my nose and deposited a soap bubble there that left me cross-eyed. "He's a client of Dougie's."

"Naturally. Did he point this gun at anyone?"

I uncrossed my eyes and looked over my shoulder at him. "Does that matter? He was holding a gun, and he was looking for Dougie. He should be arrested, don't you think?"

"Can't arrest everyone who does that," he said. "Might be easier for you to find another job."

I let out an exasperated sigh. "I don't want to find another job. I like my job—"

"No, you don't."

"—and I work with nice people—"

"No, you don't."

"—and the money's good—"

"No, it isn't."

"—and..." My voice trailed off. I'd run out of new ideas, and the ones I had left weren't very good. Curt sat there with a smug little smile, as if he could read my mind. Lucky for him he was good to look at, because I hated attitude almost as much as I hated washing dishes. I knew he would do some digging, and I knew that he knew that I knew it. That should have been good enough, but it had been a bad week, and I was wound too tightly. "You think I want to quit working and find myself a sugar daddy?" I snapped. "You sound just like my mother."

He smiled, showing irritatingly perfect teeth. "I don't know why you still feel the need to impress your parents. You'll meet a real guy when you stop looking, and then you can trot him home to make them happy."

"You're a real guy," I said, then because I realized how that might sound, I added, "Sort of."

"There's no 'sort of' about it, honey," he said. "I'm as real as it gets. And stop looking at me like that."

"I'm not looking at you," I said. "I'm cursing you silently. And spare me the 'I'll make you glad you're a woman' shtick. I'm not trying to impress my parents—I'm trying to shut them up."

He took a sip of beer and chuckled. "First off, your sister will eventually hook some poor schlub who'll make your parents very happy. Second, I wouldn't waste my time. You'll never be glad you're a woman. And third, what's that on your nose?"

I stuck out my lower lip and blew upward to dislodge the Dawn bubble. "What's that supposed to mean?"

"It means you've got some sort of—"

"Not that," I said. "That crack about womanhood. For your information, I'm perfectly happy to be a woman."

"Sure you are. That explains...that." His gesture encompassed, presumably, my entire body.

I slapped the dishrag down, sending bubbles skidding along the countertop. "What exactly is wrong with me? I'm in perfectly passable shape!"

"I'll have to take your word for it," he said. "Considering I never see your shape."

"Where," I said frostily, "is this conversation going, exactly?"

He shrugged. "You brought it up."

"I certainly did not. First you asked about Adam Tiddle, and then you started talking about the poor schlub my sister is going to drag home. Only one of those things is any of your business. Guess which one?"

"As long as I'm not the poor schlub," he said, "both."

"And I will not indulge your sick fantasies about womanhood," I added.

"Good. Because my fantasies are completely healthy."

I rinsed out the last glass and looked around for the dish towel. Drying wasn't part of the deal, but my hands needed something to do other than wrap around Curt's neck. Also, I didn't want him backing out of dinner at my parents' house. "Just so you know," I began mauling a plate with the towel, "I am perfectly happy to yank on pantyhose and jam my feet into high heels in the name of womanhood."

"Good for you," he said. "Now what's that on your nose?"

"Nothing." I scraped my forearm across my nose until the bubble popped. "You're not planning to be this disagreeable on Friday, are you?"

"I'm not planning to," he said, "but it seems like a hell of an opportunity."

* * *

After Curt and I had called it a night, I went upstairs to my apartment and sat at the kitchen table going through the day's assortment of bills and sales circulars. No inheritance checks or sweepstakes prizes. Plenty of opportunities to invest in retirement homes, Medicare supplemental insurance, and Rascal scooters. Looked like I'd be reporting to work tomorrow.

I sat back and took a look around, wondering what I'd do if I had some money. Not much. Curt had remodeled when he'd moved in, and while my apartment was small, I had new tile in my kitchen and bathroom, and a new wall-to-wall Berber in my living room. The walls were white, the carpet was beige, and the drapes were hand-me-downs from my mother. Maybe I could spruce it up a little, but I didn't see the point. Not when I was driving a junkyard reject. I'd have been safer on roller skates, or so my mother told me. And that pretty much answered the what-would-I-do-with-money question.

Dreaming the improbable dream left me with the inexplicable urge to straighten up, probably attributable to the three bottles of beer I'd had. I'm not much of a drinker, but I am a realist; I considered beer a dietary aid. I wanted to gain a few pounds. Plus my apartment was a mess.

Fortunately, since my place is tiny, straightening up didn't take too long. Pick up the old newspapers, swipe a few surfaces with a dust rag, wash my morning cereal bowl and spoon, and it looked good as new. The Chinese food was long gone, and the effort of cleaning had probably burned up all the beer calories, so I helped myself to a chunky peanut butter sandwich when I was done. Then, because peanut butter went so well with chocolate, I ate two chocolate cupcakes for dessert.

Neither the cleaning nor the chocolate eased my financial worries, so I popped a yoga DVD in the player and hauled out my yoga mat and props. A good half hour of stretching and twisting and bending usually cleared my mind, but for some reason it wasn't working this time. The events at the office—not to mention the idea of Curt's completely healthy fantasies—had left me unable to concentrate, so around ten o'clock, I showered and changed into an oversized T-shirt, unfolded my bed and tucked myself in to watch the news. Since it was the usual glut of murder and mayhem, it didn't take long before I started thinking about the office again. Dougie had created his own mayhem today, and not for the first time. I could understand Ken and Howard's displeasure with Dougie's way of doing business. I could understand Hilary's tantrum, even though for once it had been misguided. I could even understand Donna's wounded pride.

What I couldn't understand was Missy's vengeful attitude. It made me all the more curious about the paper she'd taken from Dougie's desk. I didn't condone snooping and snitching, but I thought I might get into work early and see if I could find that paper in her desk. Assuming she didn't shred it or take it home with her. Which she probably didn't, since her dates with Braxton Malloy, the Wonder Pharmacist, tended to be all-nighters. Then again, there was absolutely no reason for it to mean anything to me, other than that Missy had been acting out of character, so probably I should just mind my own business and roll into work fifteen minutes late like I usually did.

That sounded like the better plan, so I turned my attention back to the TV as the news went off the air and was asleep before the infomercials began.

CHAPTER EIGHT

———

Adam Tiddle was waiting in his parked car when I got to work the next day. I didn't notice him until he came up behind me while I was looking for my keys. By that time I had nowhere to go. There was a sameness about him that should have been comforting. Same stained shirt—mustard this time—same muck-covered boots, same deranged expression. What was different was the knife. "I couldn't buy bullets," he said when he saw me looking at it. "They wouldn't sell me bullets. This state." He shook his head at the sorrowful condition of a state that refused to sell ammunition to psychopaths. "I figured this was the next best thing."

For boning a steer, maybe. "It's lovely," I said. For lack of anything else. "But I can't let you in the office. It isn't open yet." I made a show of fumbling with my key ring. There wasn't much acting about it; my hands were shaking like a leaf in a hurricane. I wasn't a dummy. I knew Tiddle wasn't after me personally, but maybe he'd take what he could get. And what he could get was me. But I wasn't ready to die, not yet, not when I hadn't put my affairs in order, or said good-bye to my loved ones, or had a decent cup of decaf.

While I fumbled, I considered my options, which didn't take very long, since I only had one. I could spray Mace into his eyes, except the closest thing I had to Mace was a bottle of Visine, and that would only give him clearer vision while he chopped me into little pieces.

Damn the talk show safety experts; I was on my own. And in a flash of inspiration, I decided if I bumbled around long enough outside, someone would show up to save me. Or take my place. Just my luck, Wally had decided to pick Wednesday as his day to stop warming up Howard's seat for him.

"So," I said brightly, while I hunted for the office key among the four keys on my ring, "I guess you'll just have to come back a little later on. I'll be sure to tell Mr. Heath you stopped by."

"I can't come back later," Tiddle said. "I gotta get a root canal at eleven."

"Oh, that's a shame." I shook my head, full of sorrow and compassion. "Toothaches are just awful, aren't they?"

"Not as bad as bunions," he said. "Bunions are the worst." He scratched his back with the tip of the knife.

"Bunions are bad," I agreed. "Bunions, corns, calluses, hammer toes, just the scourge of podiatry everywhere."

"What's podiatry?" he said.

Huh.

"So you can see why I gotta kill Mr. Heath as early as possible," he said. "Onaccounta it's a fifteen-minute ride across town to the tooth doc. I don't wanna be late. I gotta pay for it whether I make it or not."

"That seems unfair," I said. "You might want to consider suing them to change that policy. We could handle that for you."

"You people can't handle crap," he said.

I had to disagree. We'd handled plenty of crap over the years. "Think about this," I said. "If you kill Doug Heath, you'll go to jail. Maybe for life. Now wouldn't that be a waste?"

"What're you, my mother?" He waved the knife around a little and glowered some. I got the feeling he'd heard about life wasting before. "Why would you want to kill a lawyer, anyway?" I asked. "They sue people for you, they get you money, and they keep you out of jail. They're good people."

He narrowed his eyes at me. "You ain't too bright, are you?"

"Dumb as a doorknob," I said.

"Mr. Heath lost my case. You got any idea what I'm gonna do to Mr. Heath for losing my case?"

I had some idea. "He loses lots of cases," I said, dangerously close to babbling. "It's a wonder he keeps his license. He's the worst."

"That ain't what he said on TV," Tiddle said, accusing. "He said he'd get justice. He'd get me all the money I deserve."

"And you actually believed him?" Oops.

"Open the door, girlie," he said, pointing with the knife. "So's I can carve him up like a Christmas goose."

I jabbed at the lock with the key. I wasn't sure it was the right key. Or even the right door. "I never had goose," I said. Jab, jab. "My family always ate turkey for the holidays. Well, spaghetti once, but that didn't go over so good. My father got gas from the sauce, and my sister spilled the meatballs, and—"

"I'm gonna do this," he said, and made a few samurai nunchaku sort of moves with the knife. Then suddenly he stopped. His face went white, and his eyes rolled up in his head, and he crashed to the ground in a dead faint.

Which, when I saw the bloody slice he'd put in his own finger, is exactly what I did, too. Except I hope I did it with a little more grace.

* * *

I was still in a fuzzy fugue state when I heard Paige say, "Is she dead?"

I opened my eyes. Paige, Donna, Howard, Wally, and Janice hovered over me with varying degrees of concern. A misty rain laced itself around us. My head hurt. And Donna's shoes didn't match her outfit.

"I guess not," Wally said. He might have sounded disappointed.

"We should get her inside," Howard said, without making a move to actually do it. "She may be bleeding on the walkway."

"No, we shouldn't move her," Donna said. "She may be injured."

"Well, she can't stay here," Howard said. "What will the clients think?"

Dougie Digits for a partner and he was worried about what the clients would think?

I rolled my head to the side. Adam Tiddle and his knife were gone, and so, as far as I could tell, was his fingertip. I closed my eyes briefly in relief and vowed to the universe that had saved me that I'd never be the first into work again.

"Look, she's passing out!" Donna said.

"Get her some water," Howard said.

"Here," Janice said, reaching out her hand. I managed a weak smile and reached for it. She took my keys. "I'm moving your car," she said. "You're parked in my spot."

CHAPTER NINE

———

"They think they'll be able to save his fingertip," Missy said a few hours later. I'd been scraped off the pavement and dumped behind my desk, with my transcribing headset somehow strapped to my ears and a new word processing file blinking in anticipation on my computer. Missy was back after chaperoning Adam Tiddle to the hospital on Howard's directive. Howard wanted no lawsuits against the firm. Dead secretaries didn't sue, so he wasn't concerned about me.

"That's nice," I said, though the fate of Adam Tiddle's finger meant about as much to me as the color of Paige's lipstick. My head hurt, and I was cold and wet. Howard had thoughtfully provided a box of tissues to dry myself off, and I had wet tissue bits clinging to me everywhere. I looked only marginally better than when I'd gotten out of bed that morning. But it could've been worse. At least Missy wasn't gloating over her X-rated night with Braxton Malloy.

"What a night I had." Missy wrapped her hands around a mug of coffee and smiled. She looked radiant, if not well rested, buoyed by her role in the salvation of Adam Tiddle's finger and other less noble things. "I swear. Braxton Malloy ought to be cloned. What a man. Did I ever tell you he likes to—?"

"No," I said.

She blinked. "You poor thing. Here I am going on about my love life when you've had a morning from hell. Is there anything I can do?"

"Well," I began, and she said, "I'm seeing him again Friday night. I don't know if I'm up to it."

"I'm sure you'll manage," I said.

"So." She blew off the steam curling up from the mug. "What'd you do last night?"

I shrugged. "Had a few beers with my landlord. Cleaned my apartment."

She grimaced. "That doesn't sound too exciting."

"It got more exciting this morning."

"Oh." Her cheeks were pink. Maybe it was the steam. "I guess it did. I'm sorry. Hey, at least he didn't have the gun again."

At least. I had to get away from this stifling compassion. I got up and went to the kitchen for a piece of cheesecake. It was as good as I remembered. I polished off that piece and cut another, eating it while standing at the counter. It almost made me forget my head hurt. Outside, the rain had started falling harder.

Missy came in when I was rinsing my plate, and since I was heavily fortified with all that fat and sugar, I decided to make a preemptive strike. "Listen, about that paper you took from Dougie's desk yesterday."

"Oh, that." She rinsed her mug and put it on the drain board. "That was just something that belonged in a client file and had gotten lost."

"In his desk?"

"You know Dougie." She smiled toward the door. "Speaking of which, would you look at what the cat's dragging in? He's here."

No self-respecting cat would sink a claw into Dougie Digits. He was wearing Spandex jogging shorts and a muscle shirt, and he was bulging out of both. Either he'd been out running or he was auditioning for *Lawyers in Lust.* Raindrops were sluicing through his chest hair and had beaded like car wax on his head.

"Ladies." He stopped and stared at me. "Jesus, you look like crap."

"We had a little problem here this morning," Missy told him. "Adam Tiddle came back."

Dougie backed up a step. "Is he still here?"

Missy shook his head. "He's at the hospital, getting his finger sewn back together." She patted my shoulder. "Jamie here fought him off."

"With what? A machete?" Dougie slammed his briefcase down on the table. It popped open, and a dog-eared copy of Penthouse slid out. "You cut off his finger? For God's sake, Winters, he'll probably be lawyered up by the end of the day. And not by one of us!"

"I didn't cut off his finger," I said. "*He* cut off his finger. But thanks for your concern."

"He cut off his own finger?" Dougie snorted back laughter. "Dumb country fuck." He shoved the Penthouse back in his briefcase, slammed it shut, and hefted it. "Hey, what'd he have? Scissors? Letter opener?"

I rolled my eyes. "A knife. He had a knife."

"You don't say." Dougie scratched his armpit. "Wasn't maybe a Ginsu Knife, was it?"

"I didn't inspect it," I told him. "Too busy trying to avoid it."

He waved that consideration aside. "This might be a hell of an opportunity," he said. "We could sue the manufacturer."

"Dougie—" Missy began.

"Obviously that blade's a hazard. They fail to protect dumb, country fucks from chopping off their own fingers." Dougie was growing happier by the minute. "We'll do a letter this morning, or maybe we should go see him. What do you think?"

"He doesn't want—" I began.

"Whatever you think," Missy said.

"A letter it is." Dougie nodded, satisfied. "Offer to represent him. It'll give him a little time to cool off. Wouldn't want him coming after me, would we?"

It was enough to make me want to kill him myself.

"Make me a protein shake. Will you, doll?" he said to Missy. "I'll be in my office, laying out a plan."

Missy began assembling the ingredients for his protein shake. "He really looks on the bright side of things, doesn't he?"

Uh-huh.

"I really admire that." She sliced a banana into the blender. "And he's up to running four miles a day. He doesn't look too bad for nearly fifty, huh. Uh-oh." She tipped Dougie's can of protein powder from side to side. "He's running out. I've got to finish Ken's motion before ten. Do you think—?"

"I've got to do something for Howard," I said quickly. Wash his feet. Something. "Why don't you ask Paige?"

Missy shook her head. "She's likely to come back with the wrong thing. I don't think she knows how to read." She sighed. "Maybe I'll ask Donna. Nobody will notice if she's gone. You hardly ever see her anyway." She picked up the wall phone and punched in Donna's extension. A few minutes later, Donna had been dispatched to the nearest health food store and I'd made a narrow escape.

I didn't think Dougie's exhibitionistic entrance boded well for the morning, but the next hour rolled past as peacefully as a Sunday in church. We cranked out the required documents to keep Ken, Howard and Dougie in business, and they managed not to alienate any of the clients who came and went in a steady stream. Donna returned with the can of protein powder and disappeared into her office again. If things kept going like this, I wouldn't have any new stories to tell Curt on Friday. Well, except for the tale of Adam Tiddle and his Ginsu Knife, but I wasn't sure I wanted to relive that one.

At two-thirty, an elderly man with a thatch of white hair and heavy black-rimmed glasses shuffled in and over to Missy's desk. "I'm here to see Mr. Heath about my case."

I glanced at him. Despite the aged elegance of his suit and tie, his thinness was evident. His glasses magnified his eyes into marbles, and his hands shook ever so slightly. I instantly felt sorry for him.

"Just a second." Missy picked up her phone to alert Doug. A second later she put it down and stood up. "Let me show you to his office, sir."

The two of them set off at a slug's pace for the stairs while I went back to work. I had a deposition to schedule, which gave me an extraordinary opportunity to demonstrate my lack of efficiency. A deposition is the civil equivalent of a criminal interrogation, only without a police presence and occasionally with more civility. Scheduling one required the concordance of attorneys' calendars, witnesses' availability, and court reporter's notification. Then, after spending a half hour on the phone accomplishing the impossible, and another fifteen minutes producing a written Notice of Deposition to be mailed out, someone would inevitably cancel the whole thing because he'd forgotten to put it in his Blackberry. Happened all the time.

It still beat typing Answers to Interrogatories.

Missy came back a few minutes later, her eyebrows drawn down to the bridge of her nose. "Anyone know who that was?"

Paige stopped typing. "I thought you knew him."

Missy shook her head. "He says he has an ongoing case, but I don't think I've ever seen any paperwork."

"Maybe you have," I said, "and you just don't remember the name."

"Maybe," Missy said. "Or maybe his case is with someone else, and he only thinks it's with Doug."

"Old people get confused like that," Paige agreed. "My Aunt Trudy once bought me a jockstrap for my birthday."

Missy gave her a look.

"Sharp dresser, though," Paige added. "His suit doesn't fit right, and no one wears ties like that anymore, but it's quality stuff. He must have money."

Missy brightened. "You think?"

"Either way, he seems like a sweet old guy," I said. "Very grandfatherly."

"Yeah, he does, doesn't he?" Missy's expression softened. "He told me his wife died of cancer, and his son died of an overdose. All he's got is his cat. It's such a shame."

Paige nodded. "You're so right. Cats are lousy company."

"Makes you wonder," I said.

"Wonder what?" Paige asked.

"Why it is some people go through so much, and others..." I let the sentence hang there, pregnant with poignancy.

"Others what?" Paige asked.

I ignored that and returned to the Notice of Deposition flashing on my computer. Somehow I'd managed to find an agreeable date for five attorneys and it had only taken me the better part of an hour. One of these days I'd do what Missy does, just pick my own date without consulting anyone else, and move on. Seemed like a good life philosophy, too.

Footsteps pounded on the stairs, and Dougie burst into our office, pale and fidgety. He'd exchanged his *Lawyers in Lust* outfit for a traditional gray suit without the jacket and his sneakers for Bruno Maglis, but from the looks of his face and his underarms, he'd done it without benefit of a shower. "I need the Ramsey file," he told Missy.

Something in his voice made me sit up a little straighter. Paige noticed it too, because she glanced our way.

"Which Ramsey?" Missy asked. "Nicole or Roberta?"

"Mack." Dougie rested his right hand on the corner of Missy's desk and wiped his forehead with his left hand. "Mack and Constance."

"Mack and Constance." Missy shook her head. "I don't think we have a Mack and Constance Ramsey file."

Dougie looked at me.

"Sorry," I said. "I've never worked on it."

"Me, either," Paige said as she thumbed through the client expense ledgers. "And they don't have a card, so you haven't spent any money on their case."

"That's impossible." Dougie leaned more heavily on his hand. "Look again, Paige."

"I've already looked twice," she said waspishly. "There's nothing there."

"Oh, shit," Missy said, and Dougie nodded his agreement.

"So you lost the file," I said. "It's got to be around here somewhere. Maybe Ken or Howard took it for some reason."

Dougie brightened. "Maybe. Why don't you call upstairs and find out?"

"Excuse me." Mack Ramsey had shuffled up behind Dougie unnoticed. He stood there swaying gently. "Do you folks happen to have some water handy? I'm feeling a little sickly."

"Oh, Christ." Dougie pushed himself upright in alarm. "Should I call an ambulance?"

Mr. Ramsey pressed a gnarled hand to his stomach. "No need for that. Water will be fine. And maybe a quiet place to sit for a spell."

"We've got that." Dougie sprang into action. "Paige, show Mr. Ramsey to the kitchen and give him a glass of water."

"Are you alright, sir?" I asked him as he passed my desk. He turned his huge eyes my way and gave me a small nod before disappearing down the hallway behind Paige.

When he was gone, Dougie said, "We have to find that file."

"I don't think there's a file, Doug," Missy said quietly.

"There's got to be a file." His voice was suddenly strident. "If there's no file, then I blew the goddamn statute!"

"Mr. Ramsey didn't seem too upset," I pointed out.

Dougie gave a dismissive wave toward the kitchen. "He was a farmer. He's not bright enough to understand."

I didn't think that was fair, but I didn't want to argue with Dougie in his present condition, so I kept my mouth shut. While Missy and Doug rifled through the client ledgers again, Janice came through the front door, smiling and swinging a set of car keys from one finger. Until that moment, I hadn't known Janice had teeth.

Dougie glanced up when he heard the jingle of the keys. "Janice!"

She froze, her smile disappearing.

"You ever write any checks in Ramsey?" he asked her.

She frowned. "Nicole or Roberta?"

He sighed. "Mack."

Janice thought about it. "No."

"You're sure?"

She gave him a look that would have gotten her fired if it had words behind it, but Dougie seemed too upset to notice. I didn't pay much attention to it, either, because I was busy looking at the key fob dangling from her hand. I recognized the BMW emblem from across the room. "You bought a new car?" I asked her.

She jammed the keys in her pocket. "I traded in the Lexus, if you must know. And don't scratch my paint when you leave. I had to park next to that heap you drive."

"You parked that heap I drive," I pointed out. "While I was lying on the sidewalk."

"You should've taken me with you." Paige was back without Mr. Ramsey, which spoke volumes for Paige's grace as a hostess. Evidently she'd left the poor old guy alone and forgotten in the kitchen. "I could've gotten you a better price."

Janice smirked. "I doubt it." She stomped upstairs without looking back.

"What a gem she is," Paige said.

I picked up the phone to buzz Ken and Howard. I had no intention of scratching Janice's paint. Not when I could dent the door instead. I'm not ordinarily the type to begrudge people success, but part of me wanted to forget the Ramsey file and investigate how a divorced mother of a college-aged son could afford Lexuses and BMWs. Parker, Dennis, and Heath didn't pay *that* well. I had the heap to prove it.

When Wally answered Howard's phone, my grip tightened on the receiver. It was almost a reflex. "Doug was wondering if Howard had the Ramsey file in his office."

"Which Ramsey?" He sounded distracted. Maybe I'd interrupted Howard's backrub.

"Mack," I said.

He sighed. "Hold on." I heard papers rustling and files shifting and then he came back. "It's not here."

"Okay," I said. "I'll check with Ken."

"What's the problem?" he asked.

Go figure. Usually Wally treated me like a telemarketer; today, he wanted to chat. "No problem," I said with phony cheer. "We're just trying to locate it."

"You broads screwed up again, huh?" I could hear the smugness in his voice, and I might have heard Howard chuckle in the background. It set my teeth on edge. I really might have to start shopping for a new job. A Wally-free job.

"No one screwed up, Wally," I said tightly. *Except possibly Dougie,* I thought, but I didn't say that. Dougie seemed to have enough trouble without the Boy Wonder smirking over his shoulder.

Turned out I didn't have to say it. "Whose file is that, exactly?" he asked.

Oh, no. "It's Doug's," I said, and Dougie turned around, hopeful as a dog waiting for a treat. I pointed at the receiver and shook my head.

"Figures." Wally must have covered the phone, because I heard muffled voices, and then he hung up on me.

"Screw you, too," I muttered. I punched in Ken's extension while Dougie continued to watch me, clearly hoping for a miracle. He didn't get it. I shook my head when I disconnected from Ken. He leaned both hands on Paige's desk and hung his head.

"It's alright," Missy told him, putting her hand tentatively on his back. "We'll go explain it to Mr. Ramsey. I'm sure he'll understand."

"You do the talking," Dougie said. "I'll just stand there, looking sorry."

Easy enough.

"I've got a better idea," Missy said. "You go back upstairs, and I'll tell him you got called out of the office."

That didn't sound fair. That sounded like Dougie the Weasel was going to run away and let Missy take his punches. And what's worse, she seemed willing to do it. Maybe if someone held Dougie accountable once in awhile, he wouldn't be the type to send his secretary into battle with a big wet kiss right in front of Paige and me and Wally, who'd sneaked down the stairs to perform reconnaissance for Howard.

I blinked and looked again. Yep, Dougie was kissing Missy, and Missy was kissing Dougie, and now I knew why Bambi had caused so much friction. My stomach sank all the way to the soles of my feet. I didn't know if I was more disappointed in Missy or disgusted by Dougie's ardent passion. But I could see now why Hilary Heath always seemed to be in a bad mood. Dougie's technique left a lot to be desired.

I couldn't take much more of the whole debacle, so I decided I'd go check on Mr. Ramsey myself. Only when I stepped into the kitchen, it was empty. I peeked out the back door in case he was getting some fresh air on the patio. He wasn't. He'd up and left, and probably it was the smartest thing he'd done since coming to see Dougie in the first place. Mentally

I wished him luck. With Dougie as his attorney, he was going to need it.

CHAPTER TEN

———

Generally speaking, the job of legal secretary is more prestige than pay. The only people making money at Parker, Dennis, and Heath were Parker, Dennis, and Heath. There also wasn't much opportunity for overtime unless one of the lawyers was on trial and needed documents typed for a morning court appearance. Since Missy usually had a date, and Paige evaporated at five o'clock sharp, that left me to fill the role of emergency secretary. I didn't mind. The extra three dollars in my paycheck came in handy when the rent was due.

Which is why on Wednesday night, I was elbow-deep in typing up some of Donna's research for Wally to use in arguing a motion the following morning. Sadly, I wasn't alone. Dougie was downstairs in the basement gym, working out. Primal grunting and the clanging of the weights carried into my office through the heating vent. Wally was alternately hovering, waiting to snatch the final page from the printer, and watching CNN upstairs on Howard's television set. Everyone else had been gone for two hours or more.

I was on the final page of notes when the phone rang. In a flash, Wally was in front of me. "Aren't you going to answer that?"

"Huh-uh." I mistyped a word and stabbed at the backspace key. "Voice mail will pick it up."

"It might be a million-dollar case," he said. "You never know." He pointed to the phone.

"Jamie!" It wasn't a million dollar case. It was my mother, and she was going to cost me a half hour. I scowled at Wally. He shrugged and headed back to the evening news. "I've been trying to reach you at home but you didn't answer."

"I'm working late." I turned to the monitor to find my spot.

"You shouldn't have to work late," she said. "You should have a husband to pay your bills for you."

"I like paying my own bills," I said. If only I could.

"I want both my daughters to find good men." I could practically see her clutching a wet hankie to her bosom. "Is it asking too much to want grandchildren?"

There it was. *Tortfeasor.* I resumed typing, propping the phone between my ear and shoulder. I'd heard the grandchildren argument before. It didn't carry any weight with me. Not when my sister was so anxious to pair up and turn into a broodmare.

"So I invited Frankie Ritter to dinner Friday," she said, oblivious to the clicking keys. "I ran into his mother at the drugstore, and we decided Sherri should meet him. What do you think?"

Like that mattered. A crash thundered up through the vent followed immediately by a string of four-letter words. I put my hand over the receiver.

"What was that?" my mother asked. "I heard something."

I sighed. "Dougie's here working out." She could hear a spider crawling in the attic but she couldn't hear my reasons for wanting to stay single.

"Oh, good, you're not there alone. That Dougie's a good man. You should find yourself someone like him. A nice man who'll work and let you stay home with your babies. A woman should be at home with her babies. Aren't there any single male lawyers working at your office?"

The same as the last time she'd asked. "One," I said. Wally. "But he's already got a girlfriend." Howard.

"Oh, that's a shame. Well, I won't hold you up." Since there were no unattached men handy, her work was done. "I just wanted to get your opinion on Frankie Ritter."

I thought it was the worst idea since Vanilla Coke, but I wasn't about to tell my mother that. Instead, I said, "Let's just see what happens."

"Yeah." She sounded pleased. "Let's see what happens."

"Jamie."

I glanced up and dropped the phone. Dougie was standing in front of me in spandex shorts and no shirt. I'd been there, and I could have done without the replay. His chest was heaving, sending sweat running down his torso. I had an imagination, but I didn't have to use it. I could see everything.

I heard my mother say "Jamie?"

His hair was plastered to his head, and in the forty minutes he'd been in the basement, he'd grown a heavy five o'clock shadow. He almost looked hot, except he was Dougie. And, of course, the spandex thing.

"What do you think?" he asked, flexing both biceps. "Some guns, huh?"

"Jamie!" my mother yelled.

"Um," I said, hoping for Wally's return. No such luck. Lawyers were never around when you needed them.

Dougie spun around to give me the back view. His anatomy showed itself in high definition. "Not bad, huh?" he said over his shoulder.

"Jamie!" my mother shrieked.

I scooped up the phone and dropped it in the cradle. She'd have to learn to deal with rejection.

Dougie turned around and used all eleven fingers to cup his genitals. "We got any mineral ice? I think I strained my groin."

He'd better not offer double-time if I put it on for him.

CHAPTER ELEVEN

———

"Okay, I've been giving this some thought." Sherri brought her three-wheeled shopping cart to a shuddering halt in the produce department. The perfume of forty different fruits and vegetables assailed us. I generally avoided the produce department, since it made me feel inadequate. Too many things I didn't recognize. Starting with Sherri.

She sized up the area. "They say vegetables are very sensual, so maybe I should hang out here for awhile. You know, feel up some cucumbers or squash or something." She took a look around. "What does squash look like?"

I tugged down the sleeves of my sweatshirt against the arctic blast of the supermarket air conditioning. I was only shopping for some food, not for a man, so I had no need for the heavy artillery. Sherri, on the other hand, was wearing her nightclub finest, a black leather miniskirt with a black bustier and high-heeled knee-high boots. She looked like an escapee from a sex dungeon.

I'd heard rumors about Thursday singles night at the supermarket being wildly popular, but I'd never seen proof of it. Probably because my shopping policy was get in after the crowd, make a direct hit on the ice cream case, and get out fast. Looking around now, I didn't exactly see Chippendale dancers stocking up on cat food and Wonder Bread. I saw eighty-something couples inching along clinging to their carts and harried single moms tugging litters of three-year-olds behind them. The produce department was desolate. I suspected Sherri's chance for success was as well.

"Why don't you try going up and down the aisles," I said. "I don't think too many single men hang out by the squash."

"Maybe the beer," Sherri agreed. "Which aisle is that?"

I sighed. What could you expect from a thirty-one-year-old whose parents did all the household grocery shopping? "They don't sell beer in supermarkets. That's illegal in New Jersey."

"Well, that's stupid," Sherri said, apparently overlooking the fact that this entire exercise was something less than bright.

I edged away. "If you need me, I'll be in the..." I fled down the nearest aisle. Fortunately, it was the cake mix aisle, and Duncan Hines was on sale. Anyone could whip up a box cake, so I dumped a lemon, a French vanilla, and a chocolate into my basket and went looking for canned frosting. It wasn't on my list or on sale, but it didn't have to be. I picked up two cans anyway. I didn't know about Sherri's success, but I was beginning to think my guardian angel had led me to Aisle Eight.

That's when I rounded a corner and noticed my sister over by the prepackaged cold cuts, chatting with a blond man. I ducked behind the end cap and peeked around the bottled soda for a better look. I couldn't say much for her execution. She was holding the biggest cucumber I'd ever seen, letting it rest suggestively against her jawline, a living trailer for Sherri Does the Supermarket. I cringed watching her. She had to be rescued from herself, but I hated to barge in when this one seemed to have potential and the right hair color. Tan slacks, navy blazer, even a tie. Respectable. Standing so close to Sherri in her leather getup, he looked like a vice cop.

Sherri nodded and said something and smiled into the cucumber, and ten seconds later I found out that's exactly what he was. He reached back into his waistband and whipped out a pair of handcuffs that glinted nastily when he slapped them on her wrists.

An elderly couple with matching silver hair stopped in their tracks beside the kielbasa case to watch with horrified expressions. I could practically hear them thinking that here was incontrovertible proof that the neighborhood had gone completely to pot.

"Oh, hell," I muttered, and stepped around the end cap with bright smile. "Sher! I've been looking for you. I—"

The man whipped around to size me up with a death glare. It didn't take him too long to decide I wasn't a threat. Or a hooker. Fortunately, I'd worn a pair of shorts I'd cut from old sweatpants, my dingy Keds, and a moth-eaten sweatshirt to ward off the store's chill. Looks-wise, I was as far removed from Sherri as Pam Anderson was from Janet Reno. "Do you know this woman?" he demanded.

"She's my sister."

Sherri seemed to have shriveled inside her leather casing. "We're just here to meet single men. Tell him, Jamie."

"Well, that's not exactly true." I approached in baby steps in case he had a gun to go with those handcuffs. "I'm not looking for a man. I'm just here for some cake mix." I held up the basket as proof. No reaction. Guess he didn't like cake. "But my sister here, she was looking for a date—"

"I got that much," he said. "You can meet her downtown. Come on, ma'am."

"I'm not a ma'am," Sherri protested, struggling against the cuffs. "I'm a Ms. Or Miss."

"She wants to be a Mrs.," I said helpfully. He was decent looking enough, if you overlooked the hostility of the handcuffs.

"That's true," Sherri said, brightening. "Would you happen to be married, Mr....?"

"Detective. And it's none of your business." He glanced into her cart. "You don't seem to be shopping for much in the way of food, ma'am."

"Hey, I tried to find the squash," Sherri said. "Bigger is better, right? A cucumber was the best I could do."

Behind us, I heard the old woman gasp, and then I heard a thump that I hoped wasn't her hitting the floor in a dead faint.

"She's not much of a shopper," I said. "Can't you see this is all just a misunderstanding?"

"I think I understand," the detective said, and I smiled. Finally. "Your sister made a pretty lewd offer concerning that cucumber," he said, and my smile disappeared. I heard the faint squeak of shopping cart wheels as the old man edged a little closer. This was good stuff to the Lawrence Welk set.

"Oh, come on." Sherri stuck out her lower lip. "All I said was you should see what I can do with a cucumber that big."

I rolled my eyes. The squeaking stopped, and I heard another thump and a low curse. The old man had plowed right into a display of packaged pepperoni. Served him right for being lascivious.

"Exactly," the detective said. "You think I don't know what that means?"

"It means a big salad," Sherri said. "Lettuce. Carrots. Cucumber. A salad."

"It means solicitation." The cop snatched the cucumber in question from her. "By the way, this is evidence."

"Look," Sherri said, "don't you think you're taking this too far? I mean, I can't help it if you're insecure about your manhood."

The thing about Sherri was she never knew when to quit.

"Let's go." He gave her shopping cart a shove with his foot. "You can explain it all to the judge in the morning."

"Maybe the *judge* will be reasonable," Sherri said pointedly. "Only you have to tell me now what time I need to be there, because I'll have to set my alarm. I can't wake up early without an alarm."

The detective looked at me in disbelief.

"It's because she watches Letterman," I said. Nothing. I swallowed hard. "Uh, Sher," I said. "I think you're going to jail tonight."

"Jail! I can't go to jail!" She turned to him. "I can't go to jail! Have you ever tried to sleep in a leather bustier? It can't be done!"

"Sorry," he said. "You should've thought about that before you propositioned me." He took hold of the crook of her arm to steer her through the store.

"Hey!" she yelled. "Wait! You don't want to arrest me. My sister here's an attorney and she'll sue you for everything you've got!"

He narrowed his eyes at me. "That true?"

"Not exactly," I said. "Actually I work for a lawyer. A good lawyer."

He looked unimpressed. "What's his name?"

I swallowed again. "Douglas Heath. Esquire."

It was hard to tell who started laughing first, but I think it was the old man behind me. Evidently he'd seen Dougie's television commercials. While the cop's cheeks were turning red, and he was busy searching for a tissue to wipe his eyes, Sherri motioned me closer with her head. "You've got to help me," she begged in a not-quite whisper. "Don't tell Mom about this. Or Dad. Just get one of the lawyers from your office and come bail me out, okay?"

With what? I had a basketful of cake mixes and frosting I could barely pay for. But I nodded anyway. "I'll be there," I promised. Just as soon as I could go borrow some money from someone. Or sell a kidney or something.

"Just one thing," she added as the cop wadded up the tissue and stuffed it into his blazer. "Don't get Dougie."

* * *

"So you and your sister don't look too much alike." Wally glowered down at me with his arms crossed.

"Well, you'd never catch me trying to carry off that outfit," I said, deliberately playing dumb. I'd heard remarks like that all my life. Hey, we can't all have legs like a giraffe.

"Does she wear clothes like that all the time?"

"Only when she's looking for a husband," I said nastily. That should do it. Nip this fantasy right in the bud.

He wasn't at all daunted by the H word. "Do you think it would be alright if I gave her a call sometime?"

In a second my life passed before me. Friday meatloaf with Wally. Thanksgiving with Wally. Christmas with Wally. I was all for Sherri finding a husband and getting married, but I drew the line at this. "I don't think so," I told him. "She's sort of seeing someone."

His shoulders drooped. "Is it serious?"

As an arrest. "Looks to be," I said brightly. "If you'll excuse me."

"I'm still waiting for that fee," he yelled after me as I fled down the stairs. By this time Missy was at her desk, and Donna was at mine. She leaped to her feet the instant she saw me, her plain, pinched face perking right up. "I heard Ken has a dep this morning. I was wondering…"

Damn. I'd promised to talk to Ken about her brilliance as a paralegal. What with Sherri being arrested and all, I'd completely forgotten about it. "I'll catch him this afternoon," I said. "Things have been a little hectic today."

"Thanks, Jamie." She smiled and scurried away. I squatted beside my desk to see what awaited me in the stack of files there. A few letters for Howard, a Subpoena duces tecum for Ken, a set of Form C Interrogatories to be printed up and sent out for Dougie. Nothing too difficult. This was shaping up to be a pretty good day.

Then Dougie got back from court.

CHAPTER TWELVE

———

It began casually enough, as catastrophes sometimes do. Dougie had gotten back just before one o'clock, tossing his briefcase on the kitchen table and mumbling something about the judge buying her robes at Walmart. Ken's deposition was still going on in the conference room, and Wally was hunkered down wherever Wally hunkered.

I was at the kitchen table slogging my way through a meatball sandwich I'd ordered in because I felt guilty about my late arrival that morning. Paige had ordered a turkey sub, and she was eviscerating the roll across the table. A little mound of lettuce shreds and hot peppers was growing on her paper plate. I was thinking those hot peppers might be kind of tasty with my meatballs when Howard and Dougie came into the room, and I stopped thinking and started trying to make myself invisible. Howard and Dougie together in the same room was never a good idea.

Howard began brewing himself a cup of Lemon Zinger tea, his mouth pinched tight. Clearly he had something on his mind. Dougie rolled up his sleeves and began assembling the ingredients for a protein shake. I lowered my head and watched him gather the can of protein powder, a handful of frozen strawberries, vanilla frozen yogurt, and an egg. He cracked the egg and dribbled it into the blender with some shell fragments still in it.

Howard pulled his mug from the microwave, dropped a teabag into it, and said, "I got a call today from Ronald Plackett."

Dougie scooped some frozen yogurt in on top of the egg. "Who's Ronald Plackett?"

Paige pulled a thread of lettuce from her sandwich, dropped it on her plate, and ignored both of them.

"Victoria Plackett's husband." Howard stabbed at the teabag with a spoon.

Dougie popped open the can of protein powder. "Who's Victoria Plackett?"

Paige glanced up. "The blonde."

Dougie froze in mid-measure. "Oh." A small smile played across his lips. "Her." He scooped out a level cup of protein powder and dumped it on top of the frozen yogurt.

"Somehow," Howard went on, his voice icy, "Mr. Plackett was under the impression that you made inappropriate, offensive, and sexually-related remarks to his wife. He was incensed. I wouldn't be at all surprised if he files a complaint with the Ethics committee."

Dougie shrugged, eyeballed the mess in the blender, and added a little more protein powder.

Howard yanked the teabag out of his mug and flung it into the sink. I cowered behind my meatball sandwich, and Paige stopped disemboweling her sandwich. "It might be helpful," he said, "if I knew something about her case in the event he makes good on his threats. I assume you took her case."

He assumed right. Dougie took every case.

Dougie capped his shake with the handful of strawberries and punched the Whip button on the blender. "She tripped," he yelled over the racket, "On the sidewalk outside a convenience store. Broke the heel of her four hundred dollar shoes and wants to sue. Tells you something about what kind of broad she is." He hit the *off* button.

"It tells me more," Howard said, "about what kind of lawyer you are. Was she injured?"

Dougie pulled open the cabinet in search of a glass. "No meds to speak of. Purely an economic loss. The shoes."

Howard glanced over at us with fire roiling in his eyes. Paige and I both busied ourselves immediately studying our respective sandwiches.

"That is not a case," Howard told him.

"In fairness," Dougie said, "you should see this broad. Tell him, girls."

We girls weren't telling him anything. Paige had given up on her turkey sub and was gathering her trash together, and I was flabbergasted that Dougie would jeopardize his license to practice law over a broken shoe because it came with a pretty blonde.

"That's it." Howard gripped his mug tight enough to crack it. "I've had enough of you, Heath. Do you know how many times I've had to defend this firm because of your antics? And those insipid commercials..." He shuddered. "No more. I'm meeting with Ken this afternoon about buying you out. I will not practice with an attorney of your caliber another day."

"You can't do that," Dougie said, finally pouring his protein shake into a glass he'd pulled from the sink. He sounded remarkably calm. They say the eye of the hurricane is remarkably calm, too. "I'm the bankroll behind this operation, and you know it. If it weren't for those insipid commercials, you'd be slaving away as in-house counsel somewhere, punching a time clock, and hoping your retirement account survives the recession." He dropped the blender into the sink. "You need me. Hell, I gave this firm a license to print money." He lifted his glass in a mock salute to Howard, who was standing thin-lipped and rigid, then drained half of it in one long guzzle.

"You'll regret this, Heath," Howard hissed at him. "I hope you burn in hell."

Paige and I looked at each other, and I could tell from her expression she was thinking the same thing I was: *This is getting really ugly, and we should probably find some help right now.* Or maybe: *Is my lipstick smudged?* With Paige, it was hard to tell.

As it turned out, it didn't matter what her expression said, because almost immediately after he'd taken his drink, Dougie collapsed against the kitchen counter, his face twisting into a horrible caricature of itself. The glass slipped from his hand and shattered against the floor a second before he landed among the shards and went still.

CHAPTER THIRTEEN

———

Hours later, when the police and medical personnel had come and gone, taking Dougie's shrouded body with them on a gurney, we gathered in the conference room. I couldn't shake the image of the gurney rolling past Dougie's Mercedes and into the waiting ambulance. It didn't seem possible that he wouldn't be coming back. I think we all felt that way. Even Howard, who'd added a dollop or four of whiskey to his Lemon Zinger. He clutched the mug with one hand and the fireplace mantle with the other as if he was afraid one or both would slip away and leave him adrift.

"The medical people think it was a massive heart attack," Ken said. He'd wrapped up his deposition at the first police siren and was now at the head of the table pretending he knew what to do. At least he'd dispensed with the pretense of tea and had the whiskey bottle itself in front of him.

"That doesn't make sense," Missy said. Her eyes were red and puffy, and she had a wad of tissue balled up in her fist. "You know how much Dougie was into fitness. How could he die of a heart attack?"

"Fitness doesn't mean anything," Paige pointed out. "Plenty of fit people have died. Maybe he took steroids."

"He did not," Missy said hotly.

I didn't know about the steroids, but I tended to agree with Missy. I kept seeing Dougie drinking his protein shake and collapsing, and I didn't think a heart attack had anything to do with it.

Wally had been leaning against the wall behind Howard. Now he pushed himself upright, taking a look around. "Did anyone call Hilary?"

"Oh, Christ." Howard drained his mug and left it on the mantle. "By now the police have probably notified her. Beautiful."

Ken sighed. "I'll give her a call. One of us should tell her we're sorry."

Which wasn't exactly the same thing as actually being sorry. I watched Ken let himself out to make the call.

"What were you two fighting about, anyway?" Missy ripped a tissue from the box in front of her. "You were always finding fault with Doug. He wasn't as bad as you thought, you know."

That was true. He was worse. Even Donna had had Dougie's fingerprints on her backside at some point. I sneaked a glance her way. She looked as shaken as the rest of us, but her eyes were dry. Her gaze flitted over to me and bounced away almost immediately.

Hm.

"He made this firm look ridiculous," Howard said flatly. "On television and in the courtroom. He was unprofessional. At times, incompetent."

"Guess you won't be delivering the eulogy," Paige muttered.

Missy dabbed at her eyes. "You could have stopped those commercials. You didn't have much of a problem with the money they brought in."

Ouch. Howard's lips thinned out even more than usual. "He hit on a client," he said. "We'll be lucky if we don't face an ethics complaint over it."

"Plus, he didn't bring in that much money," Janice said. "He'd lost his last three trials. I'm still paying expenses on two of the files."

My ears perked up a little. Janice didn't seem to be having much trouble referring to Dougie in the past tense, although he'd been gone less than four hours. I wasn't finding it so easy. I was half expecting him to come strutting into the meeting like usual, with his laptop in his hands and dollar signs in his eyes.

"So he was losing money." Howard grabbed Ken's bottle of whiskey and poured it into his mug, straight. "Perfect."

"What client did he hit on?" Missy asked.

"Victoria Plackett," Wally said. Evidently Howard had filled him in.

"You know, The Blonde," Paige added. She actually said it that way, with emphasis on Blonde. Paige could hold a grudge like nobody's business. Even now, she was squinting into her water glass, trying to catch a reflected glimpse of herself. I could have saved her the trouble. She looked like hell. We all did. It was hard to absorb a death in the family while maintaining perfect mascara.

"She broke her heel," Howard said, his voice dripping sarcasm.

"Oh." Missy seemed subdued. "Her."

The door opened, and Ken slipped back into the room. "Hilary will be stopping in before the end of the week."

Everyone took a moment to reflect on that. Everyone except Howard and Wally, who'd already huddled together to plot a strategy to keep them out of the office for the rest of the week. Even I began wondering how many sick days I had left.

"Well." Ken rubbed his hands together briskly. "What say we all knock off early today? I don't know about the rest of you, but I'd like to get home to my wife."

Wally thrust out his chest. "By all means, you go on home. I think I'll stick around and wrap up a little paperwork first." He attempted a smile that looked more like a grimace. "It helps to keep busy," he added. I couldn't argue with him there. The thing was, I planned to keep busy in my own apartment, far from Parker, Dennis, and Heath.

Missy was still sitting there staring at the box of tissues with a vacant expression that was a little scary. I'd seen that look before, on documentaries about psychotic killers. "If Wally's staying, I'm willing to stay, too."

"Well, not me," Paige said, springing to her feet. "Strawbridge's is having a sale on Clinique, and I want to get there before they sell out of my shade of lipstick. Come on, Jamie, I'll walk you out."

I felt the weight of Donna's gaze and knew she must be somehow still expecting me to laud her to Ken before I left. I handled that by ignoring it. I said my good-byes, gave Missy one last look, and followed Paige out the door.

CHAPTER FOURTEEN

———

I took the long way home, which meant I spent the next three hours sitting on a bench in Voyager Park, breathing in good clean New Jersey air, and watching moms and their kids playing amid the swing sets and sliding boards and seesaws, while pondering the tenuous nature of life. I didn't have a grand epiphany; I didn't even have a good idea how this could have happened. I felt sick and hollow inside, and I just went with it. I owed Dougie that much.

When the park started to empty out and I started attracting curious glances, I plodded back to my car and drove home, not feeling much better but at least having a good excuse to spend the night eating junk food and watching trash TV.

I was just about to open the door when I heard Curt at the bottom of the stairs. "Jamie? You okay?"

He was standing at the trash cans, holding a green drawstring bag. It reminded me I had something else to do today, when all I wanted to do was soak in a steaming bath and curl up under a blanket and stop thinking.

"I'm fine." I gave him a little wave and pushed open the door, hoping to avoid conversation. No chance. Curt's instincts were finely honed, and he was up the steps and on the landing beside me in three seconds flat. Smelling like pizza. My stomach gave a little growl. "What's the matter? You didn't even stop to mooch dinner."

"I'm not hungry." I ignored my stomach's opinion on the matter and stepped inside. Curt stepped in right behind me. "Wait a minute. Now I know something's wrong." He took my handbag and put it on the kitchen table along with the day's mail. Then he pulled out a chair with his foot and guided me into it. Ordinarily that kind of alpha male behavior would rankle me, but he did it while pretending not to notice my unmade sofa bed, so I cut him some slack. "Talk to me. Bad day at work?"

I meant to brush him off, but what came out was a sob, and then another, and then I was blathering and hiccupping on his shoulder, which I generally tried not to do. Curt's clothes were seldom ironed, but they were always dry.

By the time I'd soaked his collar, I'd managed to tell him all about Dougie's death. He disengaged me from his shoulder and moved around my kitchen, finding cups and spoons and heating water in the little apple teapot my mother had given me one Christmas in a paean to my alleged domesticity.

"So Doug Heath's dead," he said when I stopped blubbering. "Huh."

"Huh?" I stared at him. "Huh? My boss drops dead right in front of me, and all you've got to say is 'huh'?"

"No, that's not all," he said. "Where's the coffee?"

I stomped over to the cabinet and yanked out a tiny jar of Folgers. "You are a cold man."

He spooned crystals into both cups. "Dougie was a parasite. He's what made lawyer jokes possible. You didn't like him any more than anyone else did."

Maybe not, but my mother had always taught me to have a healthy respect for the dead, no matter what their profession. And part of me actually did like Dougie, I think. Sometimes he reminded me of the skinny, geeky kid who tried too hard. I don't even know if he was a good lawyer despite the rumors, and it almost didn't matter. He was dead, and his kids were fatherless, and Hilary—

"Oh, God." I couldn't think about Hilary. I accepted a cup of coffee and blew off some steam. "I wonder who'll be at the funeral."

"It'll be the usual turnout, I'm sure." Curt spooned sugar into his cup and stirred. "The bench, the bar, the poor, the downtrodden."

"Not funny," I said. Suddenly I thought of Adam Tiddle. Now Adam wouldn't need to think of any more inventive ways to kill Dougie.

Maybe he'd already succeeded.

"You need to stop thinking about this," Curt said, which would have been funny if it hadn't been ridiculous.

"I don't know how." I sniffled once, for pity.

"You do it the same way you always do," Curt said. "You eat. Why do you think they have meals after funerals? Now where do you keep your soup?"

I blinked. "Soup?"

He sighed. "Broth. Noodles. Meat. You do keep some in the house, don't you?"

"Oh." I took a sip and hid behind the column of steam. "I think I'm out at the moment."

Curt gave me a look. "You should've bought some food at the supermarket instead of helping your sister get arrested."

My mouth fell open. "You know about that?"

"Honey, the whole county knows about it." He grinned. "My brother's a cop, remember? I heard she looked kinda cute, for a hooker."

"My sister is not a hooker," I said, indignant. "She was just looking for a man."

"Like I said."

I took another sip of coffee and my stomach growled again. He was right; I should have bought some food. "Do you have any pizza left?" I asked.

He rolled his eyes. "I'll go grab a can of soup downstairs."

"I'd rather have pizza."

"Veggie okay?" he asked, and I rolled *my* eyes. It was like talking to my mother, only sometimes my mother listened. Lucky for Curt, I liked vegetable soup. I also liked sitting there at the table while he ran downstairs to get it, then sitting there watching him heat it up for me. It made me feel pampered and cared for. He'd brought half a loaf of bread, too, and he toasted two pieces, buttered them, and put them on a little plate, then stuck the rest in the fridge beside a container of nonfat yogurt that had seemed like a good idea three months ago. I squinted and thought I saw green fuzz on the yogurt container. But then the door swung shut, and I decided I was wrong.

He pointed. "Eat. Or you won't get your dessert." He held up a giant bag of Peanut M&Ms and flashed his dimple at me. You'd think we were married, the way he could push my buttons. Anyhow, I ate, and he tore open the bag and put it in the middle of the table, and that's where we were a half hour later, full of coffee and Peanut M&Ms and good feelings. He was right about the eating; it did take my mind off Dougie. Or maybe it was Curt's company that did it. Either way, I was finally able to relax.

Finally, when it became clear that he had no more surprises in his pockets, I got up to put my dishes in the sink. "You're a good landlord," I told him, squirting the remnants of my dish detergent in the empty soup bowl.

"Remember that on the first of the month," he said. He put his hands on the small of his back and arched gingerly, then stood up. "Listen, you want some company for the funeral?"

That was like asking a dog if he wanted food. I ran the dishcloth around on the dishes while I thought of a graceful way to accept. Then I decided I didn't need grace. I needed company. "I'd love it," I told him. "I take back what I said about your being cold."

"Don't." He put his cup on the counter. "I'm doing it for you, not for Heath. Get some sleep, will you? You look like hell."

"Good-night, Dad," I yelled after him as he walked out the door.

"Lock this," he yelled back through the closed door. I pulled a face and stuck out my tongue, and he grinned and vanished down the stairs. As soon as he was gone, I hurried to the door and threw the deadbolt.

* * *

Sherri called while I was lying in bed debating whether to watch Leno or yet another rerun of *The Breakfast Club*. "I've got an idea."

Uh-oh. Sherri's ideas usually ran along the same synaptic path that led to the invention of the Edsel. Witness her recent arrest.

"Bowling," she said into my silence. "We'll go bowling Friday night, after dinner. You're coming alone, right?"

"Well—" I began.

"They turn off all the lights at eleven o'clock," she said. "And you can swap lanes with anyone you want. It's kinky."

"But I'm not coming a—"

"I think I'll wear my hot pink sundress. What do you think about my hot pink sundress?"

I thought if she wore that bowling on Friday, I might have to bail her out again on Saturday. "That won't look too good with bowling shoes," I said instead.

"Yeah, you're right." She fell silent.

I said, "I'm not coming to dinner alone."

"Shut *up*!" she said, which really meant: Tell me everything.

I snuggled down into the blankets and hit the Mute button the remote. Jay Leno converted instantly to pantomime. "Don't make a big deal out of it," I said, "but I'm bringing Curt."

"The guy that lives in your basement?" She sounded dubious. "He's sort of hot. Is he blonde?"

"He's not hot," I said. "He's my landlord."

"Why's he live in your basement?"

Patience. "He doesn't live in the basement. I have no basement. He lives on the first floor."

"Well, that explains a lot." Not to me. She went quiet, considering. "I mean, he's always there," she said.

"He owns the house," I snapped. "Look, he's only coming as a favor to me, alright?"

'Why?"

That was a good question.

"What about Frankie Ritter?" I asked. "I thought he was on the short list."

"Mom's short list," Sherri said glumly. "My friend Rea Khrys ran into him at the CVS, and she told me he dyed his hair black. She said he looks like Marilyn Manson."

And she was worried about eating with Curt.

"So? He's still the same guy," I said, without much conviction.

"That's what I'm afraid of," Sherri said. "Maybe I'll meet someone at the Headpin Friday."

I didn't think hugely successful men spent their Friday nights at the Headpin Bowling Alley, but what did I know. I tended to date the type of men who considered Taco Bell gourmet cuisine.

Sheri's sigh crept through the line. "Lookit, they say you should try to meet men in church or social functions. Bowling's a social function."

"So's food shopping," I said. "And look how that turned out."

"It wasn't so bad," she said. "I met a perfectly lovely inmate who—"

"Okay," I said. "I'll go. But we'll have to stop here first to drop Curt off. I'm not subjecting him to a night of rental shoes and lane swapping."

"You're a good sister," she said. "Just let me know if there's anything I can do for you. I mean it."

"You could let me tell you about the day from hell," I began, but she'd hung up. I shook my head and put the phone back in its cradle and said a quick prayer that when I woke up, I'd be living in Sherri's world.

CHAPTER FIFTEEN

———

I didn't get much sleep that night. What little I got was tainted with dreams of Dougie, most of them featuring spandex. When I woke up, exhausted and bleary-eyed, the last place I wanted to be was the office, so I called in sick. When I got the answering service, I thought maybe the others had called in sick, too, so I went back to bed with a clear conscience and stayed there.

By four o'clock Friday morning, insomnia seemed preferable to Dougie dreams. I finally hauled myself out of bed and did twenty minutes of yoga by candlelight, drawing deep lavender-scented breaths. When my mind was marginally quieter, I headed to the kitchen, walking lightly so as not to disturb Curt, to fix myself toast and hot chocolate. I sat staring at it with glazed eyes while the silence of the early morning hours roared around me. Don't be fooled by the yoga; I've never been a morning person. Since I got tired around nine o'clock at night, I wasn't much of a night person, either. That left about five good hours a day, which probably explained why I was still single and unaccomplished.

But I didn't think I was going to have even five good hours today. Dougie's presence still filled every nook and cranny of Parker, Dennis, and Heath. His office had to be cleaned out. His files had to be reassigned. His clients had to be notified. Plus Hilary was supposed to pay a visit.

By six o'clock, I'd managed to finish off the toast. I dumped the remainder of the hot chocolate down the drain and added a bowl of Puffed Wheat to the toast. When I was still hungry after that, I added three more bowls and another slice of toast. Light eating only works to a certain point. Today I needed calories.

I stood motionless in the shower until the water began to run tepid, then plowed through the usual routine of face washing and mascara application and tooth brushing. Wardrobe selection was slow and painful. I wanted to look appropriately somber under the circumstances. We were an office in mourning, after all. No bright colors, no short skirts, neither of which was a problem since hiding my knobby knees was a religion, and I liked to blend in drab blues and greens. Finally I picked a dark green pantsuit, threw on a black T-shirt under the jacket, tied my hair in a ponytail, and headed for the office.

Dougie's Mercedes was still parked in its usual spot per the pecking order, third closest to the door after Ken and Howard. I avoided looking at it on my way to the door. Everyone else was already inside. I found them assembled in the conference room with Howard presiding this time. He had a legal pad in front of him and was checking things off as he went down his list, occasionally glancing at us over his glasses, a gesture I generally found intimidating, but now found pompous. Wally sat alertly to his right, nodding his approval. Ken was to his left with his chin on his chest and his eyes closed. Apparently Ken and I were getting the same kind of sleep.

There was a pitcher of orange juice in the center of the table next to a stack of paper cups and a tray of Danish that looked untouched. Missy motioned for me to sit beside her and poured me a cup of juice.

"Did I miss anything?" I whispered as I slid into the chair.

"Wally's getting Doug's office," she whispered back.

"That was fast." And not all that surprising, since Wally worked in a linen closet.

"Howard's not exactly drowning in grief," she said with a tinge of bitterness. I blinked at her over my juice cup. Above the table, she was giving Howard her polite attention. Below the table, her fingers were shredding a napkin to bits in her lap. If that napkin had been Adam Tiddle's gun, I wouldn't have given Howard long odds.

My gaze wandered around the table. Besides Missy's agitation, Wally's adoration, and Ken's apathy, there wasn't much to see. Paige was focused on her inventory of Clinique products.

Janice and Donna both seemed disinterested and anxious to return to their routines. There were only two people who appeared affected by Dougie's death, and Dougie was one of them.

"That brings us to the support staff," Howard announced, glancing up at said staff, who at the moment were being less than supportive. "As you know, this office has been functioning with a secretarial pool. Doug introduced that practice. I never cared for it."

My eyes flitted to the odd pinched look on Wally's face.

"I've devised a new system." Howard left a dramatic pause for effect. When it had none, he cleared his throat and moved on. "I've decided to dispense with the secretarial pool. Each attorney will have his own girl. Melissa, since you've got the most seniority, you can choose whom you'd like to work with." He drew himself up and straightened his tie. Wally glanced up at him and straightened his tie, too. Ken began to snore gently.

"I'll work for Ken," Missy said flatly. Howard and Wally deflated.

"Guess I belong to you," Paige told Howard. "Don't go getting any ideas."

Like she might actually work or something.

I felt a sinking sensation in my stomach. This corporate version of Spin the Bottle left me paired with Wally, but since I had the least seniority, there wasn't much I could do about it. Maybe he'd mellow as he aged. Or quit.

"Then that's settled." Howard put down the legal pad, capped the pen and slid it into his breast pocket, and took off his glasses. "Finally, I'd like to discuss the funeral." He paused for a dignified moment of silence, during which Ken continued snoring. Howard frowned in his direction. "Of course, we should all be in attendance. I'll be saying a few words at Hilary's request. The wake is Monday night and the funeral, Tuesday. We'll close the office, naturally. I've asked my wife to arrange for a luncheon at Darrow's afterward. Please dress appropriately." He seemed to direct this to me, although I couldn't see why, since Paige's skirt was presently doubling as a belt while I'd taken the time to dress in respectful mold tones. I'd never been to Darrow's, but I knew it was a favorite haunt of lawyers and doctors and other people with too much money, like auto mechanics. From what I'd heard, it specialized in overly rich sauces and undercooked steaks and ambience. Personally, I preferred the ambience of my own unpretentious kitchen. Now I had to go out and buy something suitable for Darrow's.

"That's it, then." Howard clapped his hands together, and Ken's chin snapped off his chest. "Let's get back to work, shall we? Paige, I want you to help me clear out Doug's office."

"I've got a lot to do," Paige said, which clearly meant she had a lot of lip pencils to count, since they were lined up on the table in front of her like crayons.

"I'll do it," Missy said instantly. She gave Ken a smile that would have melted his brain, if he'd been fifty years younger. "You don't mind, do you, Ken?"

He waved away the thought and pulled out his hankie to blot drool from his lower lip. "I should mention the barbecue will go forward as planned in two weeks. I hope you'll all see fit to attend. I think it's important to remain united right now."

"United. Yes." Howard nodded and looked pompous.

"Yes, indeed." Wally nodded and looked as pompous as a baby lawyer could look.

"I'll be upstairs," Missy said, shoving back her chair hard and stalking out of the conference room.

"I should get to work," Janice said, and stalked out of the room right behind her.

"I, um, need to, um," Donna said, and skittered out after both of them.

Ken turned and looked at me.

"You know," I said, shifting, "Donna does magnificent work."

Wally smirked. "How would you know?"

"Donna who?" Ken asked.

Hey, I tried.

CHAPTER SIXTEEN

——

At ten-thirty, I took my last pack of cupcakes into the kitchen for my morning break. Everyone seemed to be avoiding the kitchen; the orange juice and Danish were collecting dust in the conference room, and Howard had sent Paige for take-out coffee rather than brewing a fresh pot. Day-old dishes were sitting in the sink, and the cabinet where Dougie had kept his protein powder still stood open, the police having confiscated the can itself. It was too quiet and too full of Dougie at the same time. It wasn't long before the gruesome reel of Dougie's collapse began replaying in my mind. It was almost enough to kill my appetite.

By the time I'd finished the last cupcake, I'd decided I should try to put the kitchen right, so I rinsed and scrubbed and stacked and stored, and when I was through, it didn't remind me of Dougie quite so much anymore. It reminded me of my poor housekeeping skills.

I was replenishing the paper towels and exchanging used hand towels for fresh ones when the back door slammed open to frame Hilary Heath in black leather. Usually I can sense her impending arrival by the drop in room temperature, but this time she caught me by surprise, in more ways than one. Her gaze, usually direct and intense enough to cauterize, seemed distracted Her skin was pale and mottled, and it took me a second to realize it was because she wasn't wearing any makeup except crimson lipstick.

I felt a flash of sympathy for her that pretty much disappeared when she opened her mouth. "Go get Howard, and bring him to me."

The dirty towels fell out of my hands. "All of him or just his head?"

The distracted gaze sharpened nicely and sliced into me. "What did you say?" She went right on the attack, a panther in stiletto-heeled black boots, covering the floor in long strides, stopping only when she had me cornered against the counter. That sort of aggressiveness is probably what had attracted Dougie to her in the first place. Well, that and the size of her bra. "I know you and that dimwit Paige were here when my husband died," she said. I leaned back and trembled. "I know that Howard killed him. What I don't know is how."

"Howard didn't do anything," I said, inching down the counter. When I was out of her reach, I scrambled to put the table between us. She might not look like Hilary, but she scared the hell out of me like Hilary. "They were arguing is all, and Doug—"

"Ah ha!" She jabbed a blood red nail into the air. "So it was about money! I should have known. It's always about money with Howard."

Not true. Sometimes it was about Wally.

"I can't remember," I lied. "It might've been about the commercials."

She propped both hands on her hipbones. It was a wonder she didn't slice her silk sheets to ribbons with those hipbones. "I like those commercials."

"So did Howard," I lied again. "He was just suggesting a more..." Sophisticated? Ethical? "...subtle approach."

"Subtle, my ass," Hilary snapped. Perhaps the wrong choice of words, since her ass was anything but subtle, it being Pilatesized and liposucked to the size of a peach, and shrink-wrapped in very unsubtle black leather. "Howard hated those commercials. Howard hated the way Doug did business." She splayed her fingers to display her diamond rings. "You see these rings?"

I shielded my eyes from the flash.

"My husband bought me these rings," she said. "My husband was a successful man with a lot of money. But Howard still wanted to kick him out of the firm. That's what they were fighting about, isn't it?" She narrowed her eyes. I inched closer to the doorway.

"If you feel that way," I said, "why'd you ask Howard to speak at the funeral?"

She recoiled. "What?"

Uh-oh. "Oh, I..." I'd stepped in it, is what I'd done. "I thought—but I could be wrong—I thought he mentioned you asking him to say a few words at—"

"Where is that little worm?" she demanded. "He's not saying a word at the funeral. If he's smart, he won't even show up. Is he in his office? I'm damned well going to speak to him. Maybe *you're* afraid of him, but *I'm* certainly not." She stormed down the hall, and I could have sworn I heard secretaries diving for cover.

I kept my mouth shut and let her go, even though she had it all wrong. Truthfully, I was afraid of *her.* She had a way of sucking all the air out of a room, and I was feeling lightheaded and trembly. Probably I should step outside for a second to get some air.

I yanked open the back door and fled.

* * *

"Where've you been?" Paige asked an hour later, when serenity had been restored to the office. Since Hilary was still upstairs, that likely meant Howard had written her a nice fat calming check. "Wally's been looking for you."

Great. "I've been outside. I'm not feeling too well." I flipped through the paperwork Wally had left at my desk. Motions and Answers to Interrogatories, a few from Dougie's files. Of course. The lawyer dies, but the inanity lives on.

"Yeah, she has that effect on me, too." Which proved Paige wasn't as dumb as she looked. She ran a lipstick across her lower lip and gave me half a shimmering pink smile. "You missed a good show, though. She was really on a tear."

"Tell me about it." I began stacking the work in order of priority: things I'd do that afternoon and things I'd bribe Missy to do for me.

"She accused Howard of killing Dougie." Paige rooted in her handbag, pulled out a bottle, spritzed her neck, and inhaled deeply. "Ylang-ylang," she said with deep satisfaction.

Whatever that meant.

"You know what?" she said. "I think she might be right. Howard can be pretty scary. If he was yelling at me, I just might keel over, too." She dropped the bottle back in her bag. "If I ever listened to him."

I sighed. "Where's Missy?"

Paige's eyes rolled up toward the ceiling. "Howard's still got her upstairs working. He wants to get Dougie's office cleaned out before Monday." She wrinkled her nose. "Why do you think he's in such a rush? The poor guy just died."

"Wally probably wants to spread out a little," I said, which wasn't close to what I thought. From the morning meeting, it was clear Howard wanted to scrub every trace of Dougie from the building, and he wanted to do it immediately. Maybe he had a guilty conscience.

The front door opened and Curt came into the waiting area, looking sharp in black jeans and black shirt and scuffed black boots. To anyone who didn't know him, he must have looked dark and dangerous. To me, he was the Food Guy, provider of pizzas, procurer of Chinese food. "What are you doing here?" I asked him.

"Oh, look," Paige said, "it's the poor man's Johnny Cash."

Curt gave her a look. "You know that lipstick's the wrong color for you."

Paige's hand flew up to cover her mouth as she ducked behind her computer monitor. One hand reached out to snatch a tissue from the box on her desk.

Curt turned to me. "Let me talk to you for a second."

I glanced at Paige. She was in the middle of a frantic remediation job, with her makeup bag open and her various lip pencils scattered. That could go on for a while, so I motioned for Curt to follow me into the kitchen. There, I motioned for him to join me at the table. When I was done motioning, I said, "What's going on?"

He slung his right ankle over his left knee and reached into his shirt pocket for a notepad and a cheap-looking pen with *Fat Eddie's Pizza* written in script on the side. Then he let me wait while he made a few entries on his notepad. When I was tired of waiting, I said, "Why are you here?"

He tucked the notepad back into his pocket. The pen slid in beside the notepad. He let out a long breath. He ran his hand over his chin. He looked like the Greek god Hades, without the light-heartedness, and I almost looked around for a three-headed dog. When he looked at me, his expression gave away nothing, but told me everything. "I talked to my brother this morning. They're still waiting on the toxicology results—"

"Oh, God," I said.

"—but it looks like Doug Heath may have been murdered."

I don't remember what I said at that moment, but it must have ended in yelling, because the next thing I knew, Paige was grabbing my shoulder, and Curt was grabbing my hand, and I was looking around the kitchen a little wildly because I'd probably destroyed evidence, and why had I seen fit to clean someone else's kitchen in the first place when I hardly cleaned my own?

"If you don't shut up," Paige said in my ear, "you'll bring Hilary down here."

That did it. I clamped my lips shut like a dental drill was headed my way. It was hard enough processing Curt's news on my own; with Hilary at hand, it would be impossible.

Curt swung toward her. "Hilary Heath?"

Paige shrugged. "The human stiletto herself. She's upstairs with Howard."

"She hates Howard," I said, though I don't know why I said it.

"She loves his checkbook, though," Paige said with a smirk. So I wasn't the only one imagining a fat payoff to the grieving widow.

Curt touched my shoulder. "I've got to get back to work. You all right?"

I nodded. "No."

"Maybe I shouldn't have said anything," he said. "But I thought you should know." I nodded. Paige frowned at us, trying to put the puzzle together without all the pieces. "Let's wait for the official word, okay? Then you can decide what you want to do." I was in full bobblehead mode, incapable of speech. Curt squeezed my shoulder and stood.

Comprehension lit Paige's newly-painted face. She jabbed me with her elbow. "Are you pregnant?"

That did what talk of Dougie and autopsies couldn't: snapped me out of it. "*What?*"

Curt chuckled, which didn't confirm or deny. Typical man.

"It happens," Paige said. "Were you using protection?"

"Paige—"

"Doesn't matter if you were. These things fail. Trust me. You think you've got all the bases covered and *wham*, a two-run triple, right up the middle."

Someone was outright laughing. It wasn't me.

"Well, you are dating the nice man in black," Paige said. "Aren't you?"

"We are not dating." I was probably more forceful than I needed to be. Curt didn't seem offended. Too busy laughing. "He's my landlord."

"Sweet." Paige took a step back to appraise Curt from head to toe. "He's got good bones, but he could use a little fashion advice."

"Like never wear white Nikes after Labor Day?" Curt said.

"Be snide if you want," she said. "Seven dates a week can't be wrong."

I blinked. "*Seven* dates a week?" I couldn't manage seven dates a month. Even Dougie hadn't had a batting average that high. Before he was murdered. My stomach twisted at the remembered image of him collapsing onto the floor, dead.

Curt's eyebrows lifted. "That what you call the boys down at the Black Orchid? Dates?"

I pushed the gruesome images aside and asked, "What's the Black Orchid?" When he didn't answer me, I asked Paige. "What's the Black Orchid?"

"Ask your landlord," she snapped. "He seems to have all the answers."

"Haven't you heard?" Curt said. "It's the digital age. A camera in every cell phone. I wouldn't be surprised if the cops show up looking for you."

Paige smirked. "Let them come. I'm sure I'll break the case wide open for them."

"By the way," he said, "the guy in the feather boa was a little old for you, wasn't he?"

"That is a bad man," Paige snarled at me when Curt and his good bones had left. "I hope you don't intend to bring him back here again."

I didn't bother pointing out that I hadn't brought him in the first place. I followed Paige back to our desks, puzzled by her hostility toward him. Usually she saved it for her co-workers. For some reason, the mention of the Black Orchid had made her sprout fangs, and I intended to find out why when I talked to Curt later. The more I learned about Paige, the more layers she seemed to have. Seemed there was more to her than a rainbow of lip pencils.

Of course, "later" was hours away and I was the curious type, so I pulled out the phone book and flipped to the business pages. There was no listing for the Black Orchid. I checked the nightclub listings in the Yellow Pages and found nothing there, either. It was possible I was looking in the wrong phone book, but it was hard to be discreet with a dozen of them piled on my desk, and Paige sitting across the room, so I let it go for the moment.

For the next hour, no one came or went except for the mailman, who mumbled something sympathetic and fled, in case whatever had offed Dougie was contagious. Paige pouted at her desk, occasionally glancing at her watch but not saying anything and not going anywhere. My stomach began to growl after about forty-five minutes, so I headed to the kitchen for another snack. I didn't taste a bite of my Ho-Ho, but that didn't stop me from eating three of them, just for something to do. I really wanted to go home to bed, where it was safe and comfortable, and lawyers never got murdered. Even if killing Dougie had been something we'd all considered at one point or another, none of us was actually capable of it. We were just regular people, after all, with ill-fitting suits and unbalanced checkbooks and overdue dental appointments. Murderers were dark and menacing and full of malicious intent, like the silhouetted figure on those Neighborhood Watch signs. Except there was no one skulking around Parker, Dennis, and Heath fitting that description, and yet Dougie was dead.

Which gave me a rollicking case of the willies. To calm myself down, I slapped together a peanut butter and jelly sandwich, poured a glass of soda, and helped myself to a few cookies from Janice's private Oreo collection in the cupboard above the fridge. I had no fear of being discovered by Janice. Well, I had a little fear, but I hadn't seen her for a while, so I assumed Howard had her whitewashing the accounts to accommodate Hilary's payday, thus leaving me free to commit petty larceny.

But once I sat down to eat, even with Oreos and Ho-Hos, I found I couldn't stay there. Bad enough being in the room where one of my bosses had died; impossible, knowing he'd been murdered. In fact, I wasn't even comfortable in the building. I knew that Dougie excelled at pushing people's buttons and had instigated his share of fights in and outside the courtroom, but I couldn't imagine any of the people I worked with killing him. Firing him, yes. Quitting on him, sure. Divorcing him, of course. All those things were a long, long way from murder.

I stared into space, thinking. When I didn't come up with any answers, I got up to wrap my sandwich and put it in the fridge. Then I returned Janice's cookies to the secret stash and went back to my desk. I didn't have the stomach for work, but I had less of it for lunch. Things had changed around the office, and I was one of them.

CHAPTER SEVENTEEN

———

"Tell me about the people you work with," Curt said later that night, after we'd both changed into jeans and were in his Cherokee on our way to my parents' for dinner. Because he hadn't wanted to arrive empty-handed, we had a huge tray of cookies from Leonetti's on the back seat, wrapped in green plastic wrap with a big green bow. I sat angled in my seat like I was giving Curt my full attention—him being all shaved and after-shaved and everything—but those cookies were looking just a little better than he was. Probably because it was seven o'clock, and I hadn't eaten all day. I'd spent a lot of the afternoon thinking about what I'd seen, what I'd heard, and what I might have seen or heard that I didn't realize I had. By the time I was done thinking, I felt like the fossil on an archaeological dig, with its details being unearthed bit by excruciating bit.

He was waiting for an answer, so I said, "What do you want to know?" to the cookies.

"Whatever you think is worth telling." He put on his turn signal and swung a tight right onto Station Road. "Any of them ever fight with Heath?"

"All of them," I said. "But it wasn't their fault. Dougie had that effect on people."

"One more than others, it seems," Curt said. Which implied one of the office staff had killed Dougie. Which is what I'd been considering all afternoon. Which gave me the willies all over again. "What about you?" he asked.

That got my attention. "I got along with Dougie most of the time," I said. "The times I didn't, I stayed away from him."

"That couldn't have been easy in a small office." He hooked a left onto my parents' street. I pointed to the house up on the left, and he slowed and parked at the curb.

"What are you not saying?" I asked when he'd killed the engine. "You think I murdered Dougie? Let me save you some time. I didn't."

"I didn't think so," he said.

"Then why'd you ask?" I wasn't trying to be smart with him. I genuinely disliked being accused of something I didn't do.

"It's the way it works," he said. "I want to know something, I ask."

"Well, I'll give you five bucks to knock it off," I grumbled.

"If that's a bribe, you'd better up the stakes a little," he said.

I think he was kidding, but I was in the mood to pout, so I slouched down and stared at my parents' house. It was the house I'd grown up in, a white Cape Cod with blue shutters and a blue front door. My mother had planted impatiens and gladiolas and tulips along the front of the house and the walkway, and a series of small wooden cats all painted black scampered across the lawn toward the dogwood tree. They reminded me of the Neighborhood Watch silhouette, and that reminded me of Dougie, and that got me moving, out of the Jeep and up the walk before Curt had the cookie tray out of the back seat.

"You're late!" Sherri met me at the door with a hug. She was decked out for a night of lane swapping in skintight black jeans and a pink midriff T-shirt. I took a closer look and noticed the ring in her belly button. I pointed. "When'd you do that?"

"Better question is why." She winced. "Don't ever pierce body parts. It hurts like hell."

Not to worry. I fainted if you pinched me too hard.

She was staring over my shoulder. "I thought you were kidding about him."

"Don't worry. He's not going bowling with us."

Curt nudged me in the back with the tray. "Why not? I like bowling."

I took a step sideways. "Because Sherri's looking for a husband, and she doesn't need a man hanging around her."

"Gonna make it kind of hard," Curt said. "Maybe I should've brought handcuffs."

Sherri stared at me. I shrugged. "His brother's a cop. I guess men gossip."

"Good." Sherri yanked Curt inside by the forearm. "Then you can sit next to Frankie Ritter and gossip all you want."

"Oh, my God, he's here?" I said, and Sherri nodded and gave me an eye roll meant, I presume, to infer my mother's insanity.

"Who's Frankie Ritter?" Curt asked me.

"What's the Black Orchid?" I asked him.

"What do we have here?" my mother asked both of us. I bent to give her a kiss on the cheek. My mother got shorter and rounder and softer every year. "Curtis, how nice to see you again." She stretched up, and he bent down, and they met in the middle for a quick hug. "What did you bring me here?" Her cheeks flushed with pleasure. "Cookies? Aren't you a doll? Isn't he a doll, Jamie?"

"A doll," I said, craning to look for Frankie Ritter. I wanted to see for myself if he looked like Marilyn Manson.

"I hope you didn't make dessert," Curt said, handing the tray over.

"Certainly not," my mother said, although she didn't cook dinner without fixing three different desserts to go along with it. In about an hour her dining room would look like a bakery.

"Come with me." My mother passed the cookie tray to me and took Curt's hand. "I want you to meet our guest."

"He's not a guest, Mom," Sherri said. "It's Frankie Ritter."

"If he doesn't live here, then he's a guest," my mother said firmly. "You could be nicer to him, honey. He is an eligible bachelor, after all. I'm sure his sperm is perfectly fine."

Curt's jaw slackened, and he shot me a look. I mouthed, "Grandbabies," and he nodded and tightened his lips in a grim line. I knew how he felt.

"Mom!" Sherri flushed a rich burgundy. "We are not discussing Frankie Ritter's sperm over dinner!"

"Of course not, honey." My mother smiled over her shoulder at Curt. "It wouldn't be polite. I'm sure Curt's sperm is fine, too."

I ignored Curt's stare as we entered the dining room, where my father was sitting with Frankie Ritter. I put the cookie tray on the sideboard and focused on Frankie. He looked sort of like Marilyn Manson, if Marilyn Manson had weighed three hundred pounds and had blond tips. Other than that, Frankie looked pretty much the same. Tattoos, piercings, pathetically hopeful expression.

"You're looking good, Jamie," he told me, pulling out the chair beside him with a little eyebrow wiggle. I immediately sat down on the opposite side of the table. Sherri caught on fast and rushed to take the seat beside me, leaving Curt to buddy up to Frankie. He had it coming.

"So, Jamie." My father passed a glass of wine my way. He'd been passing wine my way for fifteen years now without noticing I never drank it. "How're things at the office?"

"Could be better." I pushed my wine glass subtly toward Curt. Curt subtly ignored it. Payback, I guess. "Dougie Heath was murdered on Tuesday."

My father set the wine bottle down heavily. My mother dropped her bowl of mashed potatoes on the table with a crash.

"Smooth," Curt said to me as he lifted the potato bowl off the breadbasket.

"Shut *up!*" Sherri said, slapping my arm.

"Cool." Frankie plastered a squashed dinner roll with butter. "What happened? He eat some lead?"

Curt gave him a sideways look.

"No, he didn't eat some lead," I said.

"Why didn't you tell me?" Sherri asked. "I called you just the other night, and you never even told me!"

"Well, you had your problems," I said. "What with the whole wardrobe thing and all."

"That poor man." My mother tsk-tsked her way through several slabs of meatloaf, plopping them on each of our plates in turn and adding a generous splat of mashed potatoes. "Take some vegetables," she admonished Curt, and he dipped into the green beans with a pained expression. "You're quitting that job," she told me. "I'm signing you up for cosmetology school tomorrow."

"I'm not going to cosmetology school," I said, looking to Curt for help. He was staring at the green beans on his plate. Fearless.

"So what happened?" my father asked.

I kicked Curt under the table. He jerked and said, "I hear he may have been poisoned, sir."

"Poisoned!" My mother dropped into her seat, fanning herself with her hand.

"I don't like the sound of that," my father said.

Neither did I. I did a quick mental inventory of the things I'd eaten at the office and decided they'd be the last things I'd eat at the office.

"Cool." Frankie nodded his approval. Bread crumbs tumbled off his lower lip onto his plate. "What, someone pass him some bogus narcotics?"

"You know," Curt said to him, "I know someone might want to have a talk with you."

Frankie blinked. "Why? He know where I can score some righteous narcotics?"

I could tell from my mother's expression that Frankie's sperm stock was plummeting fast. Sherri, on the other hand, looked interested for the first time.

"How…" My voice trailed off in a squeak. I cleared my throat and tried again. "How was he poisoned, exactly?"

Curt shrugged and forked a mound of mashed potatoes into his mouth. "My money's on that crap everyone says he was drinking when he collapsed." He glanced at my mother. "Sorry about the language, ma'am."

"It was coffee, wasn't it?" Sherri said. "I *told* you coffee's no good for you."

"Makes you impotent," Frankie agreed.

"It wasn't coffee," I said. "It was a protein shake. He had one every day."

"Which reminds me." Curt patted his lips with his napkin. "We still need to have that discussion."

My mother's ears perked up. "Discussion?"

"She don't know nothing," my father said at once. "And she's quitting that job tomorrow."

"By phone," my mother said, nodding.

"I can't quit my job," I said. "How will I pay the rent?"

My mother gestured with her fork toward Curt. "I'm sure Curtis will be perfectly happy to work something out."

"Then how will I pay my mortgage?" Curt asked.

"I'm sure the bank will be perfectly happy to work something out," my mother said.

Curt looked at her with wonderment.

"They have a point," Sherri said, less than helpfully. "You don't want to work with those awful people anymore, do you?"

"They're called lawyers," I said.

"Oh, hey, people," Frankie said, both arms up like an umpire calling time-out at the plate. "Let's not get all excited here. Just 'cause the dude was killed don't mean it ain't the place to be." He glanced at Curt. "You seem a little constipated over this, dude. Guy a friend of yours?"

"Curtis' brother is a policeman," my mother said, sitting straighter since she had at least one reputable dinner guest, even if he was standing firm on the rental negotiation policy.

"No shit." Frankie looked at Curt with renewed respect. Curt looked at Frankie with renewed suspicion. "Let me do you a solid," Frankie told him. "Check out the dude's secretary. Everyone knows you can't trust the secretary."

"*I* was one of his secretaries," I snapped.

"Huh." Frankie mulled this over while he chewed his meat loaf. "That's a bitch. Hope he signed the payroll before he checked out."

"Speaking of checking out." I slid back my chair and stood up. I was beginning to think I'd have been better off eating at the office. Off Dougie's plate. "Sherri and I have to leave."

"So soon?" My mother pointed to my plate. "But you didn't even finish your meal!"

"I lost my appetite."

"But you need protein," she protested. "At least eat your meatloaf."

"I don't think so."

"I'll fix you a doggy bag," she said, standing up.

"I'll help you," I said.

CHAPTER EIGHTEEN

———

"Well, that wasn't so bad," Curt said on the way home. Sherri was tucked in the back seat with the doggy bags, not saying much. I was pressed against the passenger door, saying less. I didn't know whether to be mortified or angry or resigned, which is how I usually felt after having dinner with my parents. "Your mom's a hell of a cook," he added.

"I'm surprised you could eat anything." I turned the air conditioning down.

"Why, because of Ritter?" Curt shrugged. "He's harmless. I think." He glanced in the rear view mirror at Sherri. "You're not dating him or anything, are you?"

Her shudder rocked the Jeep. "God forbid. I half expected his head to start spinning around. He looks awful."

"Looks." Curt nodded. "Good to know you have your priorities straight."

"Sherri likes blonds," I told him. "That's why we're going bowling, so she can find herself a blond."

"Jamie!" she squawked. "Don't tell him that!"

"Like I don't already know," Curt told her. He looked at me. "I want to talk to you. And I want to do it tonight. So where's this bowling alley?"

I shook my head. "You can't come. This is girls only. You'll crimp our style."

"So will getting arrested." He glanced in the mirror at Sherri. "Again."

Sherri kicked the back of my seat. "I didn't tell him!" I snapped.

"She didn't have to," Curt said. "That story traveled faster than the space shuttle. Next time stick to citrus fruit and leave the kumquats alone."

"It was a cucumber," I said helpfully. "One of the biggest cucumbers I've—"

"*Jamie!*" I could tell by Sherri's voice she was close to hyperventilating. "Please! Can't we get rid of Mr. Produce here?"

"Your gutter balls can wait," Curt said. "This can't. Jamie's got to get out from under this Heath mess. I'm trying to help her."

"How?" Sherri asked. "By embarrassing me until I confess?"

"It's a new tactic." He smiled at her in the rear-view mirror. When Curt smiled, women tended to forgive him on the spot.

Predictably, she kicked the back of my seat.

"Okay, how's this. If you're so determined to figure this out tonight, Sherri can get a lane and warm up while we talk." I glanced at her for approval. She nodded dubiously.

"It'll have to do," he said. The Cherokee slid to a stop at a red light. "And by the way, this isn't a date."

No kidding.

Once we started moving again, I said, "So, what did you think about Paige today?"

He glanced over. "Why? You think she did it?"

"*Paige* did it?" Sherri squealed.

"I don't know who did it," I said. "She just seems…irritated by the whole thing is all. As opposed to grief-stricken."

"Grief-stricken?" Curt shook his head as he swung out from behind a slow-moving Cadillac. "Honey, no one's grief-stricken about Doug Heath's passing. Including Mrs. Heath."

"I knew it," Sherri said, which was pretty much what I'd been thinking. A fat check from Howard had been all the sympathy Hilary needed. "She probably killed him for the insurance money."

When Sherri wasn't shopping for a husband, she was busy watching *Murder, She Wrote* reruns on TV Land.

"Hey, I know!" She was on a roll now. "How about that young guy, Waldo? Maybe he figured getting rid of Dougie would put him on the fast track to partner!"

I lifted my eyebrows at Curt. His mouth tightened, considering it. "Oh, come on," I said. "Wally didn't do it. He didn't have the time. Too busy sniffing after Howard."

"Then Howard did it," Sherri yelled. "Wally was paying too much attention to Dougie, and Howard got jealous."

I twisted in my seat. "Would you, please?"

"Let her go," Curt said. "At least she's entertaining."

"Maybe I should become a detective." Sherri looked pleased. "I've got a real knack for this stuff. Don't you think?"

"You're a natural," Curt told her. "Now where do I turn?"

* * *

A half hour later, I was finishing up my second root beer, and Curt was making his food shopping list while nursing a Pepsi and waiting for me to talk about something other than adding Ding-Dongs to the list. It was my feeble way of stalling, since I didn't want to talk about Dougie. I think Curt knew it, but since he liked Ding-Dongs, too, he played along. Sherri had snagged an open lane next to a gaggle of teenaged boys and was growing her confidence by the minute. "You know this is just between us," he told me for the third time.

"Good." I pushed back my chair. "Then just between us, we're done. Now I can go get a ball and some ugly shoes."

"Not so fast." He put a hand on my forearm that stopped me cold. "I want to talk to you."

Thing is, I didn't want to talk to him. I didn't want to talk to anybody. I'd already talked to the cops, and it hadn't helped me get my mind around any of this. Curt suspected it was Dougie's protein shake that had killed him. Missy routinely made Dougie's protein shakes. She'd had plenty of opportunity to mix poison into the can of powder. Missy had pilfered the mystery paper from Dougie's desk. It wasn't looking good for Missy, but I didn't want to be the one to cast suspicion on my friend. "Why?" I said. "This isn't even your brother's case."

"Jamie." The single word carried enough scorn to make me blush. "You're my tenant and my friend. You work in that place. The sooner we can figure out who killed Heath, the safer you'll be."

"I know. You're right."

"So talk to me," he said, and I did, giving him the redacted version. "So what do you think about Sherri's theory about Wally?" he asked when I was done.

"There's nothing to it. Wally's got a partnership. He wouldn't do anything that stupid."

"Like knocking off a partner?" Curt asked.

I couldn't think of anything to say to that, so I said nothing for a minute or two. Curt didn't press it. He'd made his point. Finally I tipped my head toward the snack bar. "Do I get a refill here?"

He headed off for another root beer while I sat there wondering why I was being so mulish, skirting around betraying a friend when she couldn't possibly have poisoned Dougie's protein shake in the first place. Probably it had something to do with dinner. My parents had struck a nerve in suggesting I should quit my job, even though it was an impossibility for me since I had no prospects and no savings to float me for even two weeks. Companies were stretching their personnel and trimming their payroll instead of hiring; I saw it on the news every night. On top of that, there was absolutely no way I was going to ask Curt to reduce my rent. I might have been late once or twice, but I'd never missed a month and never bounced a check.

"So who was in the office on Wednesday?" Curt asked me when he came back with my soda.

"Everyone, I think. But only Howard was in the kitchen with Dougie."

"And you and Paige."

I nodded.

"What about Wally?"

I gave it some thought. "He was upstairs, I guess. Ken was in deps in the conference room."

"What about that other girl, the paralegal?"

"Donna?" I shook my head. "Don't waste your time. She's Country Mouse with a law library. She can't even stand up for herself, let alone kill someone."

"It's always the quiet ones," he said. "What's Donna's last name?"

"Warren. You don't really think she—"

"I don't think anything," he said. "Cam can do that."

Cam was Curt's older brother, and he'd become a decorated member of the police force after some years as a Navy SEAL. He was a six-feet-four human monolith with only testosterone and adrenaline in his veins.

"This is strictly bonus footage," Curt said. "Two buddies chatting."

I wasn't buying it. Buddies chatted about sports and dating and movies, not murder investigations. But I was willing to be the helpful to a point, as long as the root beer kept flowing.

"Now, Janice." I took a drink. "She's got no assertiveness problems. I think she could go toe to toe with Hilary."

Curt stopped jotting notes and looked up at me. "Where was Janice on Wednesday?"

"I couldn't tell you," I said. "But I know we were all in the conference room after Dougie—afterwards. Ken said some things and went to call Hilary."

Curt nodded, thinking. "How long was he gone?"

"I don't know," I said. "I didn't really pay attention. We were all in shock. Why does that matter?"

Curt shrugged. "Probably doesn't. You told me before that everyone had fought with Heath at some time or other. About what?"

I considered. There had been so many reasons, some of them ludicrous, some of them legitimate. Howard once hadn't talked to Dougie for four days because Dougie had taken his parking spot. "You name it," I said finally. It was as good an answer as any. I didn't have a better one.

I turned to check on Sherri. She appeared happily in the midst of throwing serial gutter balls, and the teenagers beside her appeared happily in the midst of gawking at her. If I didn't get over there soon, she'd become someone's junior prom date.

Curt waved his pen in front of my face to get my attention. "*You* name it. You brought it up."

I sighed. "Dougie's commercials. His choice of cases. His behavior. His girlfriends." Like Missy?

Curt nodded and made some more notes. "Hilary know about the girlfriends?"

I thought again about Howard's payoff check. "Probably, but other things seemed more important to Hilary. Besides, she was nowhere around when it happened. She didn't come to the office until this morning."

"How's she get along with the other partners?"

"Hilary gets along with no one," I said. "Except possibly her plastic surgeon."

"Yeah, from what you've said, I kinda got that impression of her." He slapped his notepad shut.

"Then there's Adam Tiddle," I said. The notepad opened again. "He tried a gun, a knife——" I shuddered. "——and a can of Static Guard."

Curt blinked. "Static Guard?"

"He thought he could gas Dougie," I said. "He seemed determined to kill him. But he seemed so…inept about it, I doubt he could have pulled it off."

"You believe in coincidence?" Curt said.

"No, really," I said. "I mean, he cut off his own finger. He thought Static Guard was a lethal weapon."

"And if he'd had a single bullet," Curt said, and I looked at him. In a weird way, it was comforting to think Adam Tiddle might have actually killed Dougie. It would mean I didn't work with someone capable of murder, and I wouldn't have to go job hunting. But I'd seen Adam Tiddle in action. He was like the geeky kid who couldn't find a seat in the cafeteria at lunchtime. I doubt he'd had success in any aspect of his life, and that included attempted homicide.

But clearly we'd reached an impasse on Adam Tiddle, so I thought I'd try a different tack. "So what's the Black Orchid?" I asked, hoping to ambush him.

He didn't even blink. "Someplace a little flower like you should never go. Now go beat up some alleys. I'll see if I can pick up a game of eight ball."

"But Paige goes there," I said. "How bad could it be?"

He let out an exasperated sigh that reminded me of my father. The kind that said Jamie had just made yet another unwise life decision. "People aren't always what they seem to be," he told me, which even sounded like my father. I'd been getting that kind of sage advice all my life, and it didn't satisfy me now any more than it had before.

But it was all I was going to get. Curt pushed back his chair and got up, tucking his pad and pen away, and putting on the inscrutable cop face he'd learned from his brother.

"We'll probably be awhile," I warned him, even though I didn't really want to be awhile. It had been a long day, and I was tired. Plus I was getting hungry. Maybe I could go out to the Jeep and have a little dessert.

I took another look at Sherri. She was snuggled up to a reedy blond guy learning the finer points of ball handling, so I made a fast break for the exit as soon as Curt disappeared into the billiard room. He'd parked at the corner of the building in a row of impractically massive SUVs, and of course he'd locked the doors. I pressed my nose to the rear passenger window and stared at the bags in the back seat. Meatloaf in one, spice cake and Italian cookies and marble cupcakes in the other. The windows were cracked a minuscule amount in deference to the Northeastern summer weather; I took a deep breath and the faintest scent of inaccessible food taunted me. Not an infrequent occurrence in my life, metaphorically speaking.

It took everything I had to turn my back on it, but I managed to push myself away from the Jeep and head back inside to get my sister away from the children and keep her out of jail.

I was out of bail money.

CHAPTER NINETEEN

———

Usually I regarded weekends as a treasured break after five days of chaos and mayhem. I felt a little different on Saturday morning. The weekend stretched ahead of me, empty of everything but the opportunity to think some more. Problem was, I wasn't thinking; I was visualizing. Missy, making Dougie's daily protein shake. Donna, going out to buy protein powder. Dougie measuring the poisoned powder and pouring it into the blender, then taking a drink and collapsing. I didn't want these thoughts in my head, but I couldn't let them go.

I drifted aimlessly around my apartment for a few hours, listening to thunder rumble in the distance. Hopefully a thunderstorm would break the stifling grip of humidity. To snap my lethargy, I did a quick yoga session, which only increased my lethargy when I fell asleep during Shavasana. Then I took some time for less transcendent activities. I stripped the sheets off my sofa bed and changed them, scrubbed the bathroom down, and wiped the kitchen counters. Dust bunnies followed along beside me at baseboard level, and those I kicked beneath the microwave cart. There was a limit to my industry.

By lunchtime, I was tired of waiting for rain and cogent thought, so I grabbed my car keys and headed out to visit my sister.

Williams Bridal was a small salon nestled between big box stores, a throwback to the pre-bridal warehouse age. Sherri had been there through four years and two owners. Its delusional present owner considered the store exclusive enough for Rodeo Drive. She was right, if Rodeo Drive sold bridal gowns for $99 with free alterations. The store had a unique hub-and-spoke layout, with the selling floor as the hub and private fitting rooms as the spokes. It sounded posh, except Clark Kent would have had trouble changing in one of those rooms.

I found Sherri by a rear spoke holding an armful of wedding gowns and gnashing her teeth. "Wait'll you see this one," she hissed at me. "She's getting married at *twenty*. It ought to be illegal."

I took a few of the gowns off her hands and together we stood like servile mannequins, waiting for the twenty year old in the fitting room to issue orders.

"Do you have time for lunch?" I asked over a mound of seed pearls. "I need to talk."

"Twenty years old." Sherri craned her neck to look at the wristwatch buried beneath a cloud of tulle. "Not for half an hour. I mean, what does a twenty-year old know about marriage?"

No less than either of us did. "Listen," I said, "I need a dress I can wear to Darrow's."

Sherri brightened. "Hot date?"

I grimaced. "Funeral."

"Oh." She took a look around at acres of whites and pastels. "I'll have to lend you something. Is navy okay? Never been much of a fan of black."

"Navy's fine."

A perky brunette flounced out of the fitting room in a mile of white satin. "I need to see something else," she announced. "This makes me look old, like thirty or something. And it doesn't show off my chest."

"Her chest," Sherri muttered under her breath. "What does a twenty—?"

"Here you go." I stepped forward with my supply of gowns. "Maybe there's something here you'll like. And congratulations."

She cocked her head, appraising the dresses, then pointed. "I want to try that one."

That one was at the bottom of the pile, naturally. I juggled and shifted and with Sherri's help, pulled out the right dress, and the brunette disappeared back into the fitting room without a word.

"You see what I put up with?" Sherri asked, pulling a face in the brunette's direction.

"It doesn't show her chest. She wants to show her chest, she should get married in a bikini." She fell back against the wall with a sigh. "God, what a day. So what do you want to talk about? I didn't know that guy was only sixteen, I swear."

"It's not that," I said. Although it might be, later. "It's Dougie. I'm not dealing too well with his murder." I swallowed hard. "I think Missy might have had something to do with it."

Sherri's eyes widened. "You're kidding. Why?"

"I think they were having an affair." I shifted the bundle of dresses in my arms. "She took something out of his desk and wouldn't tell me what it was. Plus," I lowered my voice, "she always made his protein shakes. She could easily have put something in the can."

"Wow." Sherri stepped aside to let a matronly looking woman enter a fitting room with a peach satin dress featuring a large floppy bow in precisely the wrong place.

I shook my head sadly. "That's not going to work."

"Tell me about it." Sherri slung her armful of dresses over a rack, lifted mine from my arms, and piled them on top. The satin and tulle rustled gently. "So if she's having an affair, what's the point of killing him? He can't be that bad in bed."

I thought of his eleven fingers. Maybe he could. Then I thought about Missy's motive. "Maybe he refused to leave his wife."

Sherri snorted. "'So what? She could still get the bucks out of him without being saddled with his name."

Interesting logic for a woman desperate to marry. But it held some truth. "You've got a point," I said. "I don't know why she'd want to kill him." I had a sudden thought. "He did hit on a new client recently, right in front of her."

Sherri rolled her eyes. "Like that's never happened before."

"It's all I've got," I admitted.

"It's not enough," she said, and she was right. Unless I was missing something, Missy was lacking a motive to kill Dougie. I flashed back to all the late-night crime shows I'd watched. The experts claimed there were three main motives for murder: money, sex and... I was blanking on the last one. Probably because I didn't want Missy to be guilty. I didn't want

Dougie to be dead, either, which only proved sometimes you don't get what you want.

"And here's something else," Sherri said. "Is Missy the only one with access to the can of powder? Do you lock the kitchen cabinets?" I shook my head. She poked me in the shoulder triumphantly. "There you go. It could've been anyone. It could've been Howard."

I fished for a motive for Howard and found one without too much trouble. Howard hated Dougie's way of doing business. The commercials, the crassness, the spandex in a pinstripe office. If I remembered right, he'd mentioned buying out Dougie, which meant he wanted him gone. But how badly?

The brunette was back, plucking at her seed pearls with the exasperation of a bored little girl. "This doesn't show off my backside," she announced, spinning around so we could judge for ourselves.

Sherri let out a groan that sounded like metal twisting. "Here's a thought." She brushed the girl's hand aside and smoothed the folds of the gown. "Why don't you save us all some trouble and get married in the nude?" She grabbed my arm and tugged me in the opposite direction. "Come on, let's go eat."

CHAPTER TWENTY

———

Plenty of people showed up for Dougie's funeral on Tuesday, and not all of them came to mourn. Curt begged off at the last minute because he got tapped to drive to New York City on a delivery, so I sat alone in the back row in my borrowed navy dress, unnoticed by the movers and shakers, watching judges and lawyers and clients and the merely curious file past the deceased. Hilary stood among the explosion of flowers at the head of the casket accepting condolences and looking lethal in black Donna Karan. She eyeballed them all as if she were calculating their net worth. Maybe she was shopping for her next husband. Her twin daughters stood to either side of her like bony bookends, their vulpine faces expressionless. At eighteen, they were already chips off their mother's glacier.

Most of the purported mourners looped right out the door after paying their respects, eager to get back to their unopened mail and unreturned phone calls. A few past and present clients lingered, chatting with Ken and Howard and shaking their heads at the senselessness of premature death. If they only knew. I wondered what it had cost the firm to keep everyone from finding out Dougie had been murdered. I'm sure Janice was aware, but she wasn't talking. To anyone. She was off in a corner playing with her key ring and fidgeting. Donna was invisible, as usual. Wally was circulating, shaking hands and patting shoulders and swapping war stories with trial lawyers, although he was still in basic training while his audience was filled with five-star generals. It was sad and tedious and a little ugly, both there and at the cemetery, and I was relieved when the funeral director announced the luncheon at Darrow's to the leftover stragglers. A fraction of them made the trip, and we remained grouped more or less by socioeconomic status as we were seated, which meant I'd be sharing my chicken picante with the other secretaries. Janice had been cast off with us and didn't look any too pleased about it. Donna hid behind her water glass and speared me with dirty looks. It didn't take long to decide I'd have been better off making a wrong turn on the drive from the cemetery, and that feeling got stronger when Hilary Heath slithered up behind me and laid a bloodless hand on my shoulder. I had to bite my lip to keep from screaming.

"Can I talk to you for a moment?" she hissed in my ear.

Around the table, conversation ceased.

As soon as my chills had passed, I followed her into the ladies' room, which was a little too isolated for my taste, although it was a beauty of a room, with shiny marble and granite, and lots of benches with rose-colored upholstery so you could take a rest from the exhausting task of relieving yourself.

Hilary ignored the benches, and since I made it a practice never to look up to Hilary, I did the same. We stood in front of the sinks, Hilary primping in the mirror and me ignoring my reflection and both of us inching up to something big.

"The reason I wanted to talk to you," she said while she added another layer of paint, "is you're the only one at Parker, Dennis, and Heath I can trust."

"That's not true," I said instantly. "What about Ken?"

Her surgically petite nose wrinkled. "Ken would sleep through his own murder."

Interesting choice of words. "Howard, then."

Her eyebrows met in the middle of her forehead. "Howard can't see past his own ego."

"Wally?" I knew I was reaching, but I didn't want to be Hilary's confidante.

She stopped fussing and fixed my reflection with a glare. "I trust you."

That sounded like a threat. I swallowed hard and kept quiet.

"The police tell me my husband was murdered," she said after a frosty pause. "I want to know who did it. You're going to help me."

Oh, God. I was shaking my head before her mouth had closed. "You should let the police handle it," I said. "They know what they're doing."

"So they say." Hilary put away the makeup and brought out the comb and hairspray. I inched carefully to the right because I despised hair spray, and I wasn't too crazy about Hilary. Another two hundred inches or so, I'd be home free. "You, however, are an insider," she went on. "You see what goes on in that sorry little place day after day."

That sorry little place had bought her a Mercedes, but maybe it wasn't the right time to point that out.

"For the life of me, I don't know how you can work there." She picked and cajoled her hair back into a helmet. "Didn't you go to college?"

"Well," I began. "When I—"

She shook her head, picked up the hair spray, and engulfed both of us in a sticky cloud. I closed my mouth before my lungs took on a touchable but firm hold. "I mean, don't you have any marketable skills other than making coffee?"

Gee, she was a master motivator.

Mercifully, the fumigation stopped. Hilary shoved the comb and can back in her purse. When the mist had settled and she was as close to perfection as she could get, she moved in for the kill. "Tell me who you think did it."

"I think you should let the police do that."

It was the safe answer, but Hilary wasn't buying it. "Was it that bitchy Paige girl? Or that weird little quiet one, Darma?"

"Donna," I said.

"Or Melissa." Hilary tapped her front teeth, thinking. "She was his personal secretary, wasn't she?"

"Not really," I said. "We operate as a pool. Whoever's free—"

"Don't give me that crap," she snapped. "You think I don't know when it came right down to it, she was his favorite?"

The door opened, and an elderly white-haired woman shuffled past us into a stall while Hilary urged her along with an arctic glare. After an eternity, the lock slid into place, and Hilary turned back to me. "Don't try to deny it, Jamie. For God's sake, he asked me to pick up her Christmas gift last year."

That was a twist, the wife picking out gifts for the girlfriend. *If* Missy had been Dougie's girlfriend. And I didn't know that for sure, although it felt uncomfortable enough to be true.

"What'd you get her?" I asked, since I couldn't think of anything else to say.

"That," she said, "is not important. I want you to look through her desk, find anything incriminating that you can."

I pushed myself away from the counter in alarm. "I can't do that." Suppose I found something. Suppose Hilary had planted something for me to find. Suppose I got caught and fired or arrested for attempted theft. Visions of orange jumpsuits and cavity searches sprang to mind.

Something else sprang to mind. Hilary was crying, or at least she was trying to. Her eyes were glistening and she managed to squeeze out a single fat tear that sluiced through the layers of foundation and powder and blush on her cheek. Her mouth was twitching with the effort to control herself. Her hands were clenching and unclenching. It was painful to watch, and it hit me hard somewhere in the area of my heart. Here was a woman who had just lost her husband and was trying to struggle along as a newly-minted widow, and she was asking for my help. I supposed I'd done worse things in my life than snoop through someone's private papers. Really, it wasn't asking all that much. Five minutes, just long enough to assure her that Missy wasn't harboring anything incriminating, and I'd have Hilary as a friend for life. For all the good that would do me.

"All right," I said, "I'll do it. How will I contact you?"

The lone tear dropped off Hilary's jaw. Her hands relaxed, and her mouth resumed its normal hard line. Hilary the Bereaved Widow had morphed back into Hilary the Horrible. "I'll contact you," she said. "And you won't regret it," she added, but she was wrong. I regretted it already.

* * *

"Where've you been?" Missy demanded as soon as I got back to the table. "We were about to send out a search team."

"I was in the ladies' room." I slid into my seat.

She nodded. "I know what you mean. This food is terrible."

My lunch had been delivered in my absence, and someone had pilfered the side salad. I glanced around with narrowed eyes, noticing Janice's salad bowl was overflowing with baby carrots. The hell with it, she could have them. I was through wrangling with tough and scary women for the day.

The old woman from the restroom suddenly appeared in my peripheral vision, heading for our table. I'd forgotten all about her. When she got there, she put a gnarled hand on my shoulder and said, "Don't do it, honey. Pride is all we've got."

If pride was all I had, then I truly had nothing. I turned to thank her for the unsolicited advice but she was already on her way back to her own table. I could feel the eyes on me before I turned around. Just great. My first foray into espionage and I already had four witnesses.

"Don't do what?" Missy asked, suspicious now. "What did Hilary want?"

I shrugged and picked up my fork. Very casual. My hand was shaking. "She wanted to talk about Dougie, that's all."

"Uh-huh." I didn't like that look. She was watching me like a dog watches a porterhouse. "And instead of her own kids, she chose you to confide in."

"She claims she trusts me." I nibbled at a piece of chicken and forced myself to swallow. "Give her a break," I added, for effect. "She's a widow."

"She's a piranha," Missy said. "Never forget it. Look at her. The poor widow seems pretty dry-eyed to me."

Give her a second, I wanted to say, but of course I didn't. What I said was, "People express grief in different ways."

I actually felt a wave of heat coming off Missy. "What are you, the U.N.?"

Suddenly I was finding it easier to understand Hilary's request. There was no reason other than a guilty conscience for Missy to dislike her so intensely. Instinct told me she must be hiding something, and I meant to find out what it was.

CHAPTER TWENTY-ONE

―――――

The office was eerie at six-thirty in the morning. Lots of shadows and silence and plenty of room for the imagination. I knew I was alone, since mine was the only car in the parking lot, so I wasn't worried about being caught. Well, I was a little worried, but I planned to do my dirty work and be back home before the early risers showed up for the day. I would have been more worried about Adam Tiddle making an appearance, but Dougie's death had probably removed that possibility.

I sat in Missy's chair and opened her kneehole drawer. Pens, pencils, erasers, tape, spare change, her notary seal and stamp in their little black pouch. Nothing incriminating there. I moved to the first of the bigger drawers on the left. It was filled to near capacity with manila file folders. Missy had labeled some of them in obscure legalese like RFPs and Form C Rogs and Sub. D.T., and those I interpreted and passed over, concentrating instead on the blank tabs. One by one, I pulled those files out and flipped them open, finding only that Missy had surprisingly inadequate organizational skills.

The next drawer was half filled with office supply catalogs. That made sense, since she was more or less the office manager, so I closed that drawer and moved on. Computer manuals, a collection of software CDs and jumpdrives, a half dozen candy bars. Hilary was going to be sorely disappointed. As far as I could see, Missy wasn't hiding anything except a sweet tooth.

I closed the last drawer with a relieved sigh and stood up, and that's when I noticed the little photograph taped to the far side of her computer monitor. It showed a thirty-something man with a thatch of dark hair, wearing a white lab coat and a goofy grin. Must be Braxton Malloy, the pharmacist. Missy's standing

Monday night date and a man with access to and knowledge of any number of potential poisons.

Huh.

I stood there looking at the photo for a little while, alternately condemning Missy and exonerating her. She'd cared for Dougie and loathed Hilary, but then she'd worked with Dougie longer than any of us, and everyone loathed Hilary. It was only natural to develop affection for a person you worked with day after day, and to be upset if something should happen to him or her. I turned it every which way and it made no sense for Missy to have killed Dougie. Which made me wonder if she had.

Something did occur to me while I was studying Braxton Malloy's photo: I had the perfect opportunity to check out Dougie's office. I was up the steps and at his doorway in seconds. With traces of Dougie scrubbed away, the office looked and felt enough like Wally that I was reluctant to enter. Chances were good that Dougie's personal papers had been collected or shredded or removed by Hilary–or Missy—but I was there, so I began looking. Fifteen minutes later, I stopped looking. There was nothing but Wally's things there, and if he had secrets, I didn't want to know what they were.

I was on my way downstairs when good judgment failed me outside Donna's office. She'd been shooting me dirty looks for days now, and part of me wanted to snoop just to get even. The other part of me was simply nosy. I put the two together and stepped over the threshold.

Donna seemed to be starting her own law library. Books were stacked knee-high on the floor, with torn strips of yellow legal paper serving as bookmarks. Piles of paper smothered the blotter. Her laptop was sitting open on the L-shaped wing of the desk, a copy of the red hardbound Law Diary lying closed beside it. This was a place where important work got done. I felt like I was treading on sacred ground.

Then I noticed the receipt, a tiny white strip of paper floating on a sea of yellow papers. $26.99 plus tax to Health Concepts for a can of protein powder. Dougie's protein powder. Donna went to go buy the new can. And Dougie had asked Donna not to come back to the courtroom.

Another day, another suspect.

I headed back home with the feeling that things were about to get even more interesting at Parker, Dennis, and Heath.

* * *

I was back at the office shortly after nine o'clock, yawning and clutching a large hot chocolate. A furniture delivery truck was parked at the curb, and two men in dark blue uniforms were inching toward the front door with an oak-colored credenza. Wally's new furniture.

Missy was at her desk, tapping away at her keyboard, looking diligent. Maybe she was typing her letter of resignation. I put my hot chocolate down, powered up my own computer, and headed to the kitchen for a slice of toast. Paige was there, working over a bagel sandwich. She didn't look up when I came in, which was just as well, since I was focused on the cabinet over the sink. While my bread was toasting, I opened the cupboard door and found an empty space where Dougie's protein powder had been. The police had confiscated both cans. One of which had my fingerprints all over it. A chill shook me as I closed the door.

I was troweling butter onto my slice of toast when Missy's voice came over the intercom informing me of a phone call. I picked up the kitchen extension.

"What did you find?" Hilary. It was only nine-fifteen, and she sounded like she'd been skinning secretaries alive for hours already.

"Nothing," I said.

A moment of silence. "Did you look?"

"Yes." I could feel the weight of Paige's curiosity. Nothing I could do about that; I was trapped.

"Damn it," Hilary said, more to herself than to me. "She's smarter than she looks."

I wish I could've said the same for myself. Hard to believe I'd been suckered in because Hilary could cry on cue. But at least the deed was done. "Sorry things didn't turn out better," I said. "Wish I could've done more."

"You can," she said. My lips clamped shut. I had the feeling I was skidding off into a dark and dangerous place. "Come to my home at lunchtime, and we'll talk about it."

"I don't eat lunch," I said. I didn't have the stomach for breakfast either, at the moment. I put down my toast.

"Maybe you should start," Hilary said. "You could use a few pounds."

I gritted my teeth. "I only get a half hour for lunch."

"Not today," she said. "Howard can talk to me if he has a problem. I'll tell him you were bringing me some of Dougie's things. There must be some piece of crap lying around there that belonged to him."

Once I worked my way past her sentimentality, I thought of Dougie's vitamins but dismissed that idea almost immediately. They would mean nothing to Hilary and they certainly weren't reason enough to take an hour for lunch. That meant I'd have to ask Missy where she'd put Dougie's things, and that wasn't something I wanted to do. "Listen," I said, "I don't think I'm the right person for this."

"Make it around twelve-thirty," she said. "I'm in Kings Walk. Do you know it?"

Only by rumor. The Kings Walk development was an oasis surrounded on all sides by golf courses. Driving past, the only building you could catch a glimpse of was the clubhouse, and even then only if the cloud of exclusivity parted.

She gave me the street address. "Don't be late," she said. "I'll let the guardhouse know you're coming."

Oh, the guardhouse. Good. I hung up the phone feeling weak.

Paige was staring at me with toast crumbs on her lips. "What was that all about?"

I shook my head. "Nothing." I reached for my toast and it was gone. Just as well. I didn't think I could get it down anyway. I knew I wouldn't be able to eat any lunch. The way I was feeling, I might never eat again. Which was really the worst part of all this.

CHAPTER TWENTY-TWO

———

My first mistake had been falling for Hilary's crocodile tears. My second was assuming that an invitation to lunch included food. There wasn't so much as a piece of cheese laid out in her kitchen. I don't think a cockroach could have survived there. No crumbs, no dust, no smudges on the floor, white on white, with stainless steel appliances to complete the surgical suite look of it. I shivered passing through it.

I'd brought Dougie's trial bag with me, a battered black case with DJH engraved in gold lettering near the clasp, and she tossed it into the mudroom off the kitchen without looking at it. She didn't offer me anything to drink, either, which was somewhat more of a problem, since a barrel of wine might have taken the edge off. Of her. She seemed deeply agitated, and I wondered if it had something to do with me or with the stack of mail piled on the kitchen counter. I'd assumed money wasn't one of her problems, but you never knew.

The twins were nowhere in sight. Probably off sharpening their teeth on some innocent schoolboy.

Hilary got us settled in the family room, a room large enough to have end zones, and then she got to the point. "You have to get into Melissa's home. If there's nothing at the office, she's hiding it there." She narrowed her eyes at me. "Assuming you actually did look."

"Oh, I looked," I said. And I wasn't looking again. In Missy's desk, her home, or anywhere else. Hilary could hire people to do her dirty work from now on. "Has it occurred to you she didn't kill your husband?" I noticed a photo of Dougie in a silver frame on the mantle. He looked very young and very happy. I squinted at it. And very thin.

"No." Hilary snatched a pack of cigarettes off the side table, lit one with a silver lighter, and blew a stream of blue-gray smoke toward the ceiling. She watched it curl upward while I waited in the relentless trajectory of Dougie's smile. I'd never known him to be that thin; he'd been a gym rat when I'd started working for the firm. This was almost like seeing him in another life. A happier life. Bachelorhood.

Hilary noticed my distraction. "Isn't that a good picture of my Doug?" She unfolded herself and vamped over to the fireplace with the cigarette bobbing between two fingers. A second later she was pressing the photograph into my hands. "He was still in law school when this was taken. He never wanted to be a lawyer, you know."

I didn't know, but I couldn't see how it mattered anymore.

She sucked on the cigarette and turned her head to the side to blow out the smoke. "His mother never thought he was smart enough to be a lawyer. She wanted him to work in insurance." Her lip curled in disdain. "Imagine that. My Doug, selling insurance. It's a good thing for him he met me." Another suck, another blow before she lowered her eyes to the picture. "That was during spring break in Cancun. Have you ever been to Cancun?"

I shook my head. I'd never been to college, either. And I'd certainly never live in Kings Walk. As far as I could see, this visit was nothing more than a painful demonstration of my own failings.

"He proposed during that trip." Hilary wrenched the photo out of my hands, kissed the fingertips holding the cigarette, and pressed them gently to the glass. Ashes wafted onto Dougie's face. "Let me show you something," she said.

I didn't want to see anything Hilary had to show me. I didn't want to be sitting in her house, in Dougie's house, and I didn't want to feel like an accomplice in her vendetta against Missy. But she was coming at me with a photo album in her hands and a strange small smile on her face. "He loved his photographs," she said, running blood-red nails lightly across the gold-filigreed cover of the album. "He was quite sentimental. Did you know that about my Doug?"

I shook my head.

She thrust the album onto my lap. "Go on, open it."

God knows, I didn't want to open it, but I did it anyway. There was Dougie, standing outside the front gate of a small white Cape Cod, his smile wide and proud.

"Our first house," Hilary said. "Can you believe that?"

"It was cute," I said.

"It was a mouse hole," she said. "It was all we could afford." She crushed out her cigarette and pointed with her chin. "Go on."

I went on to see Dougie smiling from the driver's seat of a succession of cars: an old Nova, a Honda Accord, an Infiniti, a Mercedes; Dougie smiling from the front walk of a succession of houses: the Cape Cod, a Colonial, the current contemporary ice palace. Dougie on vacation, at the office, in the courtroom. Must have bribed a court officer for that one. Interestingly, there were no photos of Dougie in the gym.

By the time I got to the back cover, Hilary was sniffling. "It's hard to believe that's all gone now," she said, taking the album from me to drop it on the coffee table. "That he's gone." She tore a tissue from the box on the side table and blotted in the vicinity of her eyes without actually touching anything. "I feel so alone."

"I'm sure you've got plenty of friends," I said, although I wasn't sure at all. In fact, I suspected I was being recruited for the job. "And you've got your kids," I added.

"Did he ever tell you how we met?" she asked.

I glanced at my watch. "I, um, should really—"

"I was going to sue him." She lit up another cigarette but didn't smoke it. "I was shopping on Madison Way. Do you know it?"

Hardly. Madison Way was as tony as Kings Walk. Walmart was more my speed. On sale days.

She sniffed. "I suppose you don't, on your salary. Anyway, I was crossing the street carrying my shopping bags and my Gucci purse, and he bumped me with his car." She smiled faintly. Or maybe she grimaced. "He couldn't do enough for me after that. He proposed six months later. Against his mother's wishes, of course."

Dougie's mother must have had a crystal ball.

"He was such a romantic." She sighed and rolled her eyes up to the ceiling, remembering. "Flowers every week. On Sunday nights, he cooked me dinner. He bought me jewelry."

The practice probably came in handy when he began hitting on clients. I wondered when that had been. Hilary was painting a picture of wedded bliss unseen since Elizabeth Taylor and Richard Burton. And look how that had turned out.

"He was a scrawny child," she was saying. "The kind of boy who gets picked last in gym class. You know the type?"

Know it? I *was* the type. This was hitting below the belt. As if I wasn't feeling inadequate enough, now I was being forced to remember the inglorious days of my childhood. I took another look at my watch and uncrossed my legs. "Look, Hilary, I have to—"

"That's why he worked out so much," she said. "To compensate. To overcompensate, really. He didn't have a girlfriend all through high school, you know. Then he became a lawyer, and women threw themselves at him." She looked at the balled-up tissue in her hand with surprise, as if she hadn't known it was there. She put it down on top of the photo album on the coffee table. "And he caught them," she added with a touch of bitterness. "Every single one of them."

I was about to suggest that some women would throw themselves at a wallet lying on the street when I heard the distinct click of a door closing. I stiffened. "What's that?"

She blinked. "What's what?"

"That noise. I heard a noise." I turned to look at the French doors leading to the back deck. "Did someone come in?"

"I can't imagine," she said, although what she couldn't imagine, she didn't say.

Now I heard something else. The gentle creak of floorboards. The hairs on my neck began to prickle, and I stood up fast. "Thanks for the..." I was going to say food, or drink, but I'd had neither. "...memories," I finished lamely. "I have to get back to work now."

"If you must," she said. "You'll keep me posted, won't you?"

"I'm sure Howard or Ken will be in touch," I said, edging past her.

"That's not what I meant," she said, following me through the kitchen, close on my heels. "Don't you understand? I need to know who killed him."

"The police will tell you that." I reached the front door and yanked, but it refused to open. "After they investigate." I twisted and pulled. Nothing.

"The police are idiots," she snapped, stabbing her arms across her chest. "You think they care about one less lawyer in the world?"

"Maybe you should show them your photo album," I said. The deadbolt was engaged. I unlocked it and jerked the door open.

"I need you to under—"

"For Christ's sake, Hilary, let her go."

That was a man's voice, coming from the second floor landing, and it sounded irritated. At me. I didn't bother turning to see who it was. It was bizarre enough that the whole time Hilary had been romanticizing the state of her marriage, she'd had another man stashed away upstairs. An impatient man. Maybe a homicidal man.

My skin was prickling along with my hairs now. I bolted for my car and had myself locked inside before the front door closed behind me.

CHAPTER TWENTY-THREE

———

"People have affairs, Jamie." Curt brushed barbecue sauce across the chicken breasts and rolled the foil-wrapped potatoes over on the grill before picking up his bottle of beer and joining me on the deck. "If that's what it is."

"I know that." I tipped my head back to breathe in the smoky barbecue scent. It was an uncharacteristically cool night, with a northerly breeze and a cloudy sky. I had borrowed a zippered sweatshirt from Curt and had it zipped up to my throat. I couldn't shake my chill. I also couldn't shake my thoughts of Hilary and her mystery guest. "But don't you think the timing is awful?"

"The timing of what?" Curt studied my face in the gathering darkness. "So she has a male friend."

"Boyfriend," I corrected him.

"And how do we know that?"

I thought about it and admitted to myself that I didn't. The man hadn't used any terms of endearment. He could have been walking around in a towel or a priest's vestments; I hadn't taken the time to look. Hilary obviously had known he was there, and hadn't seemed in any particular hurry to get back to him, but she was the type of person that dealt with the world on her own schedule. "I don't," I admitted.

"Maybe he was her father," he said. "Or brother. Or insurance agent."

I gave him a look. "Don't you know love is a common motive for murder?"

"No," he said. "Do *you* know that?"

"I've read it." I sounded defensive.

"Well, if it's true," Curt said, "then Heath probably killed himself." He sat with his legs apart, forearms on his knees, picking at the label on his beer bottle. He seemed less engaged than the flies hovering nearby, waiting on the barbecue.

"Well, aren't you being pragmatic tonight." I came off as snippy, and I meant to. If I was George to his Nancy Drew, the least he could do was take me seriously.

He lifted his head, tuned in enough to recognize dripping sarcasm when he heard it. "What's the matter with you?"

I was scared, that's what. I had to find Sherri a husband before she wound up in jail, and Dougie's killer before Hilary strapped me to a fiery stake. I shook my head. "Nothing. I'm sorry I brought it up."

"Now tell me you're not going to ransack the office for clues. No matter how much your new best friend cries."

"I wouldn't know what to look for," I said. "It's in your hands. Well, your brother's hands."

He nodded, satisfied. "Good. We're not going to be stupid about this."

We sat in silence for a few minutes, then I said, "So what should I do"

He gazed off beyond the barbecue at something rustling in the bushes that I couldn't see. "Let's put it this way," he said finally. "I wouldn't eat anything from the office. Don't drink anything, either, that you haven't brought in yourself, that day."

Something prickled up my spine. "You're scaring me. What have you heard?"

He got up to turn the chicken. "Rumors."

"Was it the protein powder?" A plume of barbecue scented smoke drifted past me. All around me I heard the sound of flies licking their lips. "I mean, it was obviously the protein shake," I said. "Was it the powder?"

I didn't think he was going to answer. He began piling slightly blackened chicken on a plate with a pair of tongs. I joined him with a second plate, forked the potatoes over, and began tearing the foil from their skins. I didn't say anything. This must be why he seemed so disengaged; he was worried. Well, that made two of us. Hopefully while I kept on worrying, Curt could figure something out. I knew Curt well enough to know when he was thinking, and I didn't want to push him. I just wanted information. I split each unwrapped potato and knifed a pat of butter into the center of each of them.

"Ever hear of Spanish fly?" he asked finally.

"I don't know. I guess so."

"People used to consider it an aphrodisiac. Stupid people." His shoulders lifted and fell in another sigh. I didn't get the chance to say anything, because he put down the plate of chicken and went inside to get the corn on the cob he'd microwaved. I gathered salt and pepper, retrieved fresh beers, folded napkins and tucked them partly under both of our plates, and waited. When he came back, I said, "If it's an aphrodisiac, I'm not surprised that Dougie might try it. Too much of a good thing?" I didn't know if I was hoping or asking. Maybe both. Something that would suggest Dougie hadn't been murdered.

Curt put an ear of corn on my plate, and I sprinkled pepper down its length. "It's not a good thing," he said, sitting down across the table. "Spanish fly's not an aphrodisiac."

Now I was confused.

"Cam attended Heath's autopsy." Curt sliced into a chicken breast and forked a piece into his mouth. I put my ear of corn down and covered my mouth with a napkin. "He was telling me what Spanish fly does to a person. It's not pretty."

"I get it," I said. I pushed my plate away. I'm no doctor, but what he was saying, and not saying, sounded gruesome. Dougie hadn't deserved that kind of death.

Curt cut another piece of chicken. "And there's no antidote. Heath was dead as soon as he swallowed. Even if he didn't know it."

I thought about that as I studied the food spread out on the table, considered the groceries I bought occasionally, remembered the meals I'd ordered in restaurants. There was no way of knowing when or if something had been tampered with. Curt was making the simple act of eating or drinking sound like Russian roulette. Which triggered something in my memory. "Wait a minute," I said. "People have bought tainted food in supermarkets and—"

"Not this time," Curt said.

"—brought it home that way. Whoever did this might not work at the firm." I frowned as his words registered. "Why not?"

He ran a napkin across his lips and sat back. "Because I heard the can of powder was already nearly empty."

The can I'd handled. I rubbed my hands on my jeans as if I could rub off invisible residue. "But there was a newer can," I said. "A full can." I hesitated. "Donna bought it." Because Missy had sent her to buy it. Still, Donna was holding a king-sized grudge against Dougie for the courtroom eviction. It wasn't really a stretch to wonder if she'd added a special ingredient to the open can when she'd restocked the cabinet.

It was a quantum leap.

"It wasn't opened yet," Curt said. "At least that's what I heard. What killed Heath came out of the other can." He coated his ear of corn with butter. "Look, this is an ugly situation, but not a random one. Whoever offed Heath must have known no one else used that powder. They specifically wanted him dead."

That wasn't much, but it was something. It made me feel a little safer. And a little selfish for feeling that way, but I could live with that. As long as I could live.

Of course, only my co-workers knew that the protein powder was Dougie's alone

"I guess the cops will want to talk to Donna again anyway," I said.

"They'll do what needs to be done." His eyes met mine. "You ignore Hilary Heath and everything will be just fine."

I knew better. I'd stared evil in the face and that face belonged to Hilary Heath. I had the feeling if I ignored her, everything would be just fine except for me.

CHAPTER TWENTY-FOUR

———

"Howard said the police were here again last night," Missy said. "He said they took more things out of the kitchen. He said they kept him here until almost midnight."

Howard hadn't said that much to me in all the time I'd worked there. Interesting how Missy had become his new confidante. "What sort of things?" I asked, although I already knew. I'd checked the cabinet first thing that morning, and Dougie's vitamins were gone. So were Janice's Oreos, but maybe that was pure coincidence.

Missy shrugged. "He didn't say. He seemed pretty annoyed by the whole thing."

Annoyed. "They're investigating a *murder*," I said. "His partner's murder."

"Now you sound like Hilary." Missy narrowed her eyes at me. "What's going on with you two?"

I shrugged, hunting in my desk for nothing in particular. "She's lonely. She just needs a friend, I guess." Other than the man stashed on her second floor, that is.

"She's a viper," Missy said. "I wouldn't be at all surprised if she took out a nice fat life insurance policy on Doug a few months ago."

I blinked. "You think Hilary killed him?"

Missy shrugged. "Why not? Makes more sense than one of us doing it."

Paige wandered in from the kitchen to sit at her desk. She ignored us.

"The police might not agree with that," I said.

Missy's eyes widened. "Why? What do you know about it? Your landlord told you something, didn't he?"

That got Paige's attention.

"He hasn't told me anything," I said. "Except..." I debated and decided there was no harm in telling her about the protein powder. Seemed to me it wouldn't impact any investigation, and it might put her mind at ease about drinking the office water. "Dougie's protein powder was poisoned."

"Jesus." Missy drew in a sharp breath. Even Paige turned pale under her Golden Sun bronzer. No one said anything for a while, then Missy snapped her fingers. "I know. Donna."

"I know Donna, too," Paige said. "What's that got to do with anything?"

Missy rolled her eyes. "Donna bought Doug's new can of powder, remember? She went out alone. She came back alone. She had plenty of time to do something to it."

"But the can wasn't open yet," I said.

"Sure it is," Missy said.

"Let's go see," Paige said. "I could use a break."

"Wait," I said, and they both waited. "It's gone. Both cans are gone. The police confiscated them."

"I thought your landlord hadn't told you anything." Missy said. She slouched in her chair in full pout mode. "Hell, what's the difference? Doug's dead either way."

"The difference," I said, "is that you made most of Dougie's protein shakes. You're the one who handled the cans the most. You're the—"

"Prime suspect," Paige said with a sort of awe.

"I am not," Missy said, but she didn't sound convinced. She sounded worried. And if she knew she was in Hilary's crosshairs, she should look worried, too. "Now that I think about it," Missy said, "I'm sure it was open. Donna brought it back open."

Even if I doubted that, I couldn't doubt that Donna had motive to want Dougie gone. Her job was her life, and by banning her from the courtroom, Dougie had metaphorically ended her life. Okay, a little dramatic, but I knew I was on to something. I also knew what I had promised Curt, but I wasn't doing this for Hilary. What harm could it do taking a quick peek around Donna's office? Trouble was, she rarely left it.

"Do me a favor," I said to Missy. "Ask Donna out to lunch today."

Missy recoiled. "You've got to be kidding. What would we talk about? Tort reform?"

I looked at Paige, and Paige said, "Don't look at me."

"Listen," I said, "if you take her out to lunch, I'll have the chance to search her office."

"Okay," Missy said, "but why does it have to be lunch? Why can't I ask her to go buy toilet paper or something?"

I sighed. "Because she wouldn't be gone long enough."

"Okay," Missy said. "Toilet paper and trash bags."

So much for the spirit of cooperation. I was on my own.

* * *

Donna might not take lunch, but she did take plenty of time for the law library. As soon as I saw her creeping around with an armful of books and papers, I made up some pretense of going to ask Wally about something and bolted upstairs.

Donna's office was still a sparsely-decorated fire hazard. Like before, papers and legal pads and law books were stacked on her desk, the client chairs, the floor. Pens and markers were rubber-banded together in colorful clumps. Her computer was on, the monitor humming with a wildflower screen saver. I jostled the mouse, and the screen saver dissolved into a half-written Complaint left dangling at Count III.

For the first time, I noticed a tiny photograph tucked in the corner of her bookshelf and stepped closer to look at it. Donna, with an expression that could have been a smile, sitting next to a plain-looking redheaded man with wire-rimmed glasses. Their heads were inclined slightly toward each other, and their fingers were touching tentatively, at the tips. I looked at that picture for a long time, although I couldn't say why. Something about it touched me. Maybe it was making me feel guilty that I was up here trying to find evidence that Donna had spiked Dougie's protein powder, while the popular suspect sat downstairs refusing to help me. Or maybe it was the shock that Donna might actually have a boyfriend.

"What are you doing here?"

I jumped and jerked around. Donna was standing in the doorway, her arms still full of books and papers.

"I, um…" I glanced at the photograph and thought fast. "I didn't know you had a boyfriend."

"You never asked." She dropped her armload onto the desk. A small explosion of loose papers fluttered upward and settled down again. She snatched the photograph off the bookshelf, cradling it to her chest.

"I'm sorry about that," I said. "What's his name?"

"Why are you here?" she asked.

So much for distraction. "I wanted to tell you I planned to talk to Ken later," I said. "About you."

Her scowl lightened into a distrustful frown. "Really? Why?"

"Because I know you want to go back into the courtroom, and I think Ken will green-light it." I felt like a louse. I had no plans to talk to Ken. I didn't even know if Ken was in the office.

"That's great! Listen, it doesn't even matter if it's with Wally. I just want to be where the action is." She hugged the photo tighter. "Thank you so much, Jamie. I knew you wouldn't forget about me."

Especially not while Dougie's killer was on the loose.

She held out the photo. "This is Jacob. I met him at a Paralegal Association function. He works for Kimmel and Raystein in Philly."

I took another look at the red hair, the wire rims, the chaste hand-holding. "He's cute," I said, unconvincingly.

"You think so?" She yanked open a desk drawer and produced a rubber-banded stack of photos. "Wait'll you see these." She slid the rubber band off and spread the photos on top of the mess on her desk. One slid off the mound and floated to the floor unnoticed. By Donna. I watched it all the way and stepped closer to her, using my foot to slide a legal pad on top of it. "Everyone says we make a cute couple," she gushed. "See, here we are at a paralegals meeting. Here we are at a paralegals seminar. Here we are——"

I nodded and smiled and let her run through the stack while I thought about how I was going to retrieve the photo from the floor. My chance came when her phone rang, and she turned to grab it. I bent quickly, lifted the legal pad and scooped the photo up and into my pocket before she finished the call. "I'd better get back downstairs," I said when she turned around. "You should probably make plans for the courtroom."

She flung herself against me, arms cinching me like a vise. "Thank you, thank you, thank you."

"Oh, I almost forgot." I extracted myself from her grip and took a step back. A big step. "I'm supposed to ask everybody where they were the day Dougie died." Not exactly subtle, but my skin was starting to crawl with the need to get out of her office.

Her jubilant smile faltered. "Why?"

I shrugged. "Something I was asked to do. I'm a lackey, just like you."

"Asked by whom?"

"I was asked not to tell."

"Oh." She began gathering the photos. "I heard Howard and Wally talking, and they said Doug was murdered. Is that true?"

"That's the rumor," I said.

She shuffled the photos into a neat pile, slid the rubber band around them, and dropped the stack back into her drawer. "He wasn't a nice man," she said.

Hm. "So, where were you?" I caught her frown and held out my hands, imploring. "Look, don't take it personally. We're all in this together."

She thought that over. "I was at the law library," she said finally.

"Oh." I nodded as if that made perfect sense. At least it was easily verified.

"Or maybe I was in my car on the way back," she said. "I can't remember."

Damn.

"It doesn't matter, right? I'm not a suspect, right?"

"I think we're all suspects," I said, feeling a little sick.

"That's ridiculous," she said flatly. "Anyone can see Paige did it."

I blinked. "Paige? Why would you say that?"

She looked at me like I was incredibly stupid. "The Black Orchid? Hello?"

I was really going to have to bring myself up to speed. I was starting to feel like a prop plane living in a Lear jet world.

CHAPTER TWENTY-FIVE

———

When I'd first started at Parker, Dennis, and Heath, the law library had intimidated me far more than my bosses had. All those rows and shelves and carts full of books fat with obtuse Latin phrases. I'd thought lawyers were brilliant creatures who digested obscure citations the way dogs digested kibble. I knew better now, but I still found law libraries intimidating. Must be all that gold leaf.

Despite my lack of common sense and confidence, I decided to spend my lunch hour Thursday at the local law school library, but after tiptoeing over the threshold, I started having second thoughts. I stood fidgeting on the glossy marble floor watching law students and paralegals hunkered over their research, feeling like an outsider. No one noticed me, or if they did, no one cared that I was there. I slipped my right hand into my pocket, my fingers sliding across the smooth surface of the pilfered photo. I had no business doing this, whatever *this* was. Then I pulled the photo out of my pocket and looked at it and remembered I was here to prove Donna was guilty. Guess I wasn't a very good friend, either.

I waylaid a harried-looking clerk on his way past. "Do you have a few minutes?"

"What do you need?"

I got right to the point, thrusting the photo of Donna and Jacob in front of his eyes. "Do you recognize this woman?"

"I recognize him," he said. "Comes in once or twice a month. Jacob something or other. Not Jake, Jacob."

I nodded. I didn't really care about Not Jake, Jacob. "What about her?"

The clerk squinted at the photo, then took it from me and held it to the side, where the light fell differently on Donna's grimace-smile. "I don't know. Maybe."

"Do you or don't you?"

"What're you, the FBI?" He glared at me. "I said maybe. Why? What'd she do?"

I shook my head and reached for the photo. "Nothing." He handed it over with a shrug. "Is there anyone else I can talk to?" I said. "Someone who was working last Wednesday?"

"Wednesday. Wednesday." He looked up at the ceiling and tapped his toe, thinking. "That would be Scott. Ellerman. Over there." He gestured vaguely to his left.

"You've been very helpful," I said.

"I can't imagine how," he said and went on his way.

Scott Ellerman was working on a desktop on the far side of the room, and he was more than happy to be interrupted. He sat back, lifted his glasses to his forehead, and rubbed at his eyes with his thumb and forefinger before taking the photo I offered him and studying it. "Yeah." He nodded. "I've seen her. Don't know her name, though. She kind of keeps to herself. Must be studying for the bar exam."

"So you recognize her." He nodded again. "Was she here last Wednesday morning?" I asked.

He thought about it. "I'm not sure, but—"

"Be as sure as you can," I said. "It's kind of important."

He looked at me. "Does she say she was here then?"

"I want to know what you say," I told him. Too soon to know for sure, but I might've been getting good with this interrogation stuff.

"I say no," he said finally. "I don't remember seeing her then."

Eureka! Caught in the act, or at least in a lie.

"But she's the kind of girl who's easy to miss," he added.

Damn. I knew just what he meant. I slipped the photo back in my pocket. "Thanks, Scott."

"You're gonna be a good one," he said.

I blinked. "What?"

"Lawyer. You're gonna be a good one." He grinned, and a tongue stud flashed, taking me by surprise. He didn't look like the tongue stud type. "I can always tell by the cross."

I didn't have the heart to disabuse him of the notion. "Let's hope you're right," I said and left him to his work and his delusions.

CHAPTER TWENTY-SIX

———

Fortunately, the office was teeming with people when I got back. No one noticed or questioned my lateness. Everyone seemed to have a client or a deposition or an urgent project. My own project was urgent, too, but I wasn't making much progress. For a fleeting moment, I wondered how long it took to graduate cosmetology school.

Sherri called as soon as I settled at my desk. "Frankie Ritter bought me a ring."

I sucked in a breath. "What kind of ring?"

Paige's head lifted. She was hard-wired to react to references to jewelry or money.

"What do you mean—what kind of ring?" Sherri said. "A diamond ring. At least I think it's a diamond. Wait." I heard a faint screeching sound, like she was scraping it across a piece of glass, and then she said, "Yeah, it's a diamond, alright. It's so small, I couldn't be sure."

"And why are you wearing it, exactly?"

"I've never had anyone give me a diamond before," Sherri said. "It's kind of nice."

I closed my eyes. "Is it kind of an engagement ring?"

"It can't be. It's a friendship ring. I think."

"Sher? Are you engaged to Frankie Ritter?"

There was silence for a few seconds, then Sherri said, "I guess I should give it back, huh?"

"I guess so."

"I mean, who'd want to marry Frankie Ritter? You know what my friend Rea Khrys heard? She heard he pierced his casabas."

"His what?" I asked?

"You know." She lowered her voice to a whisper. "His testicles."

Oh, God.

"I'd kind of like to see that, actually," Sherri said. "I mean, it must hurt a lot, right? A man would have to be some kind of stud to withstand that sort of pain, right?"

I didn't want to know that kind of stud. I didn't even want to hear about him. I had enough on my hands trying to figure out whom I could safely turn my back on in the office.

"But I guess I'll give it back." She sighed. "You want to see it first? It's really pretty nice, for an ice chip. It's square."

He'd probably used his head as a mold.

"How about tonight," Sherri said. "I'll stop by around eight."

"You really don't have to," I said. "You can just take a picture and—"

"I don't mind," Sherri said, oblivious to the fact that I did. "I can pick up my dress, and we can plan our next step in Project Husband. Since it won't be Frankie Ritter, I mean."

"Tonight might not be the best..." I began, but she'd already hung up. Evidently Sherri got her phone manners from the soap operas, where love meant never having to say good-bye.

"Who's engaged?" Paige asked immediately.

"My sister." I pulled open the printer drawer to add paper. "She's not engaged. He just gave her a diamond ring."

"Sounds like engaged," she said. "How big is the diamond?"

"I'm not sure," I said, "but it sounds like you've flossed bigger pieces of food out of your teeth."

That killed her interest. She wrinkled her nose and went back to work. Missy gave me a knowing smile and bent her head back to her keyboard. It was nice to see Missy smile again. Despite Hilary's suspicions, I didn't believe Missy had anything to do with Dougie's death. Or I didn't want to believe it. Sometimes I get confused between the two.

Each of us was deep in the pretense of being productive when Adam Tiddle appeared. "I'm here to see Heath."

Now this was interesting. If Tiddle didn't know Dougie was dead, he obviously hadn't killed him. Unless his stupidity was so pure that he had killed him and forgotten all about it. Or was trying to throw everyone off his track.

On the other hand, the man had variously shown up with a gun, a knife, and malice aforethought. Hard to scratch him off the suspect list.

Because we knew he wasn't a threat to anyone but Dougie, and it was too late for that, none of us wanted to be the first to acknowledge him. Paige held out the longest, so Missy got up to find a free lawyer while I got up to get a head start before he pulled out his weapon *du jour.* "You're a little late," I told him. "Mr. Heath passed away last week."

"He what?" Tiddle's bloated jawline slackened. Anyone who could fake surprise that convincingly belonged in Hollywood.

"Died," Paige said without looking up. "Cashed it in. Bought the farm. Went to the big courtroom in the sky."

"That's enough," I said. She shrugged and shut up.

"That sonuvabitch," Tiddle said, which wasn't the reaction I was expecting. "I come all the way up here with this." He reached for his waistband and pulled out a hatchet big enough to scalp a bison. "And now you're tellin' me someone beat me to it?"

"Got any ideas?" Paige asked. I glowered at her, and she gave me a wide-eyed w*hat'd I say?* look.

The front door opened on a horse-faced woman in a badly fitting coatdress and cheap shoes. Clearly she was a lawyer. She saw Tiddle and his knife immediately, and her mouth fell open. She reached out and slammed the door shut in her own face.

Tiddle didn't notice. "Well, hell." He tucked the hatchet back in his belt. "Who else you got?"

I was about to tell him no one was in, but Wally came thumping down the stairs, and I decided to hell with it. Let the Boy Lawyer work his magic.

"Mr. Tiddle." Wally grabbed his hand and pumped it vigorously, a large and disingenuous smile on his lips. "It's a real pleasure to meet you." He was a good liar; I almost believed him. "Because of the unfortunate demise of my partner, I'll be handling your case from now on."

"Partner?" Missy said.

Tiddle looked at him with suspicion. "What's 'demise' mean?"

Wally stared at him for a moment, then put his free arm around Tiddle's back and guided him toward the stairs. "Why don't we go on up to my office, and I'll bring you up to speed."

I suspected Adam Tiddle only had one speed and it wouldn't take long to reach it, but he followed along without protest.

"Wally handled that well," I said when they were gone.

"He learned that from Doug," Missy said.

Paige smirked. "He learned how to play kissy-face with the clients?"

Sometimes life is all a matter of interpretation.

CHAPTER TWENTY-SEVEN

———

Curt was nowhere in sight when I got home, which meant I had nowhere to hide from Sherri. I didn't want to entertain, even if it was my sister. I wanted to put on ratty clothes and eat junk food and create a nice organized spreadsheet of suspects and motives. I might be taking the detecting thing a little too far, but Missy was my friend, and the office was my livelihood, and I really didn't want to move back with my parents and go to cosmetology school. I wasn't altogether sure how to create a spreadsheet, but some things were nagging at me, and I hoped if I approached them logically, it might help set them straight.

But there was no time for that now. I made a pot of coffee, laid out the box of Dunkin Donuts I'd picked up on my way home and sat down with the day's mail to wait for Sherri and her diamond ring.

Unfortunately, she didn't arrive alone. She showed up fifteen minutes later with Frankie Ritter draped over her shoulder like a scarf and breezed into the kitchen waving her left hand. "See? Isn't it beautiful?"

"Cost me a bundle," Frankie said, going straight for the doughnut box. "But she's worth it. Ain't you, babe?"

"I am," Sherri agreed. Her cheeks were flushed, like she'd been walking in the cold, and her eyes were a little too bright. She wasn't happy. And I wasn't happy, either, because Frankie Ritter was eating the cinnamon doughnuts, and they were my favorite.

I gave her ring the obligatory inspection. "Nice."

"Nice?" Frankie ran his forearm over his mouth. "That's real ice, honey."

"Oh," I said. "Then it's very nice."

Frankie made a face in the direction of my sister, meant, I presume, to convey my lack of intelligence, which gave me an idea. If I could irritate Frankie, I could get rid of the two of them and get on with that spreadsheet. I could deal with Sherri later, when she wasn't reprising the role of a Stepford Wife.

"Do I smell coffee?" Sherri took a seat. The one farthest away from Frankie.

I nodded. "I just made it. This morning." I shoved the doughnut box toward her. "Here. I got you chocolate glazed."

"Uh-oh." Frankie waggled his forefinger at her. "You don't wanna be eating too many of them, babe. You got enough merchandise in the ass department." He ate half a cinnamon in one bite. Things were getting urgent. I was already down to two.

Sherri looked wounded, but I pushed the box under her nose. "Don't listen to him. Winters women eat what they want to eat. Right?"

"Right," she said doubtfully. She took a doughnut and nibbled a dime-sized piece from it.

"How about that coffee, hon?" Frankie yanked his shirttail out of his waistband. I caught a brief and blinding glimpse of chubby white belly.

Sherri nibbled coins from her doughnut while I gathered cups and spoons and filled each to the brim. To Sherri's, I added a dollop of milk and two teaspoons of sugar. To Frankie's, I added twelve teaspoons of sugar. I slid each in front of its respective target with a cheery smile and took a seat with my own undoctored cup. "Drink up."

Frankie took a good long swig and set the cup down with a wet smack of his lips. "That's good stuff."

It was worse than I thought. I turned to Sherri. "Don't do this."

"Do what?" She'd gnawed at least two solid half-dollars from the doughnut in her hand and was already eyeballing a Boston crème. Good to see Frankie Ritter and his pinhead diamond ring had nothing on a heaping helping of fat and sugar.

"You're not ready for marriage," I told her. "You love chocolate glazed. You love blonds. You—"

"I used to be a blond," Frankie said. "It's overrated. Hey, got any coffee cake? Coffee cake would really hit the spot here."

In the first place, if I had any coffee cake, I wouldn't have any coffee cake, because I'd have eaten it in my car on the way home from the bakery. Which was a shame, really, since that would deprive me of the chance to cut Frankie a nice thick slab powdered with Ajax or rat poison or—

I fell back against the chair, stunned. What was I thinking? I didn't even kill bugs. Well, okay, spiders, maybe, but spiders didn't count. How could it even enter my mind to off Frankie Ritter like that? Maybe I was no better than Dougie's killer. Maybe that person had hatched his or her scheme over something as stupid as coffee cake. That tasty crumb topping could warp a person's mind. But I couldn't sink to those depths. There were worse things than running out of bakery goods.

Then Frankie reached for the last cinnamon doughnut, and I couldn't remember what they might be.

CHAPTER TWENTY-EIGHT

———

It occurred to me later, after four aspirin and eleven hours of sleep, that I should have asked Frankie about the Black Orchid. Too late now that I was back at work, waiting for my computer to boot up and my coffee to kick in. That gave me time to think, though, and what I thought was no harm in peeking in Paige's desk. No telling what I might find there, and it would get Donna's accusations off my mind. Suddenly Parker, Dennis, and Heath seemed more like Southfork than a law firm, with everyone accusing everyone else of murder. Scary thing was, someone had to be right.

Paige's desk was pretty much what I'd expected, full of little plastic makeup containers and cotton balls and hand cream and some medieval-looking silver gadget with handles like scissors. Just looking at all of it made me feel too girly, so I slammed the drawer shut. Enough of that.

Just to be thorough, I slid another drawer open just a bit. What scant amount of work Paige did, she kept there. It all seemed legitimate, so I closed that drawer, too. There was nothing here. Paige wasn't up to anything more nefarious than searching out the perfect lipstick. So much for Donna's theory. Maybe she'd made those accusations to throw me off her own trail. They say you have to look out for the quiet ones, and a mouse was raucous compared to Donna.

The phone rang. I hustled over to my desk to answer it. "Hey, Missy," a male voice said.

I shook my head. "No, I'm not—"

"You've got to let me know what to do with the stuff here," he said. "I don't want it in my place anymore."

Oh, my. I closed my mouth and made a sort of muttering sound that might be interpreted, by the hearing impaired, to sound like Missy.

"I mean, come on, you told me you wouldn't keep it here longer than a few days."

"Sorry," I grunted.

There was a momentary silence before he said, "You got a cold or something?"

"Cold," I agreed.

"I'll bring you something for that." So it was Braxton Malloy, the pharmacist. "You think about what you want to do, and let me know. I want the stuff gone by the weekend." And he hung up.

The stuff? What stuff? Did poison qualify as *stuff*? Was he looking to get rid of evidence stashed in his home by Missy? My head was buzzing as I rolled my chair up to my keyboard. I'd wanted to rule out Missy, but it looked like she'd just been ruled back in. I wondered what Donna's theory was on that. While I was wondering, I wondered what she might do if I failed again to talk to Ken. Definitely too much to think about.

As if on cue, Ken wandered in from the kitchen, looking preoccupied. He was dressed for court. Since he didn't seem to notice me, I stood up to get his attention. "Ken, do you have a minute?" He glanced at me and shook his head. I gave him an engaging smile. "A second?" He shook his head again. Guess I wasn't that engaging. He brushed past me, so I followed on his heels like a puppy. "I was just typing one of Donna's motions," I said, although I'd been doing no such thing. "Do you have any idea what an excellent paralegal she is?"

"No raises this year," he said.

I forced a laugh. "She's not looking for a raise, Ken. She wants to appear in court again, that's all."

He stopped midstep, and I stopped just short of an embarrassing collision. "Why? Does she have outstanding warrants?"

He must have missed his nap. "No, she doesn't have warrants; she's not a criminal. She's a paralegal. And a good one," I added, in case he hadn't heard me the first time.

"Oh." He shrugged. "Then there's no reason she can't go to court, is there?"

"No, there is not." I smiled. "Can she go with you this morning?"

"No," he said, and disappeared down the hall.

Well, it was a start, and a pretty good one at that. I headed for Donna's office to fill her in, full of pride and vindication, when I heard Janice in her office speaking to someone. Angrily. I stopped outside her door and bent down to adjust my stockings, even though I wasn't wearing any. The door was slightly ajar, giving me a clear view of her desk, where she sat clutching the telephone with white knuckles and glaring at the desk blotter. Her free hand was tapping a pen in a sharp staccato rhythm on her desk. "I already told you, I had to allocate funds for new computers," she was saying.

I really needed to shave my legs more often. They felt like I actually was wearing stockings.

"When we got new computers, we got new software," she said in a tight voice. "When we got new software, we got new training. These things cost money, Art."

I blinked and straightened. The last time Parker, Dennis, and Heath had sprung for new computers, George W. Bush had been in office. Our software capability was only a step above manual typewriting. And our training had consisted of Howard tossing the manual on Missy's desk and telling her to read it.

"I can't help it if the firm's bleeding money," she snapped. I took a step back, stunned. What with the lawyers' fancy cars and ritzy suits and pricey lunches, I'd assumed their no-raise policy was a matter of cheapness rather than necessity.

"I don't care what Douglas told you," she said. "He hadn't been generating significant revenue for several years. Yes, I know about Flannery. Did you know Flannery's held up on appeal?"

I'd heard enough. I had plenty of money issues of my own; I didn't care to learn I was working on the Titanic. Janice could lie all she wanted about her imaginary new computers. I hurried back downstairs so I could earn a paycheck while there was still one to earn.

* * *

I earned it for a good five hours or so, shuttling clients in and out, serving coffee and tea and the occasional bottle of water. Then I spent the rest of the day wondering about the Black Orchid and office equipment and other mysteries of Parker, Dennis, and Heath. It seemed like the pieces weren't fitting anywhere, with anyone. Dougie was dead, Janice was lying about computers, Paige was evading about the Black Orchid, Missy was stewing in post-Dougie anger, and Donna still wasn't back in court.

And then there was Hilary. By the time I'd driven home and trudged up the steps to my apartment, exhausted from all the confusion, I wasn't too surprised to find her waiting for me on the landing. She'd swapped the leather look for suburbanite wear: white slacks and a light pastel sweater. She still managed to look terrifying.

She glanced at her watch, a thin gold band with a Chiclet-sized black face, while I reached for my keys. "Do you always get home this late?"

"It's five-fifteen." I pushed the door open. "What are you doing here?" And where was Curt? There was never a delivery driver around when you needed one.

She followed me inside. "I want an update."

"Okay." I bent to gather my mail from the floor. "My feet are killing me. and I have a headache."

"That's not what I meant." She snatched the envelopes from me and flipped through them casually. I don't know what she'd been expecting, but she didn't find it, because she gave the pile back to me with a little shrug and sauntered into the living room. Where my sofa bed lay open and unmade, as usual. "What a charming apartment." She ran a finger across the top of my television. Visions of Mommie Dearest danced through my head

I dropped the mail and followed her. "You can't just waltz in here like this. I want you to leave."

"Did you get into Melissa's home yet?" She paused at the bathroom door, assessing my linen choices. Her nose crinkled, but her Botoxed forehead remained glassily smooth.

"No, I haven't." I reached past her to slam the door shut. "And it might interest you to know that some people think Paige killed your husband."

"Some people." She turned her cobra-like stare on me. "Who?"

"I'd prefer not to say."

She snorted. "Melissa." She crossed to a window and pushed the curtain aside. Probably checking to make sure her Mercedes was still there. "I don't know why you insist on defending that little tramp," she said, still considering the view.

"It's that innocent till proven guilty thing," I said. "Why are you so sure it's not Paige?" Not that I thought it was Paige. I just didn't think it was Missy. At least I hadn't, until Braxton Malloy's phone call. Then there was Janice with her fictional computers, which made no sense. Now all I was sure of was a growing headache and the need to get Hilary out of my apartment.

She was ignoring me. Ordinarily, it wouldn't have bothered me to be ignored by Hilary, but I'd prefer she did it somewhere else. Like...

"Have you ever heard of the Black Orchid?" I asked.

Her hand faltered on the curtain. "I'm not sure." Her voice was not half as smooth as her smile when she turned around. "Why do you ask?"

So we were going to play dirty. I shrugged. "I heard Missy mention it before."

Hilary's smile collapsed and fell off her lips. "Get dressed."

I blinked. "I am dressed."

She looked me up and down. "Don't you have anything better to wear than that?"

I was wearing my best suit, minus the stockings, which I'd jabbed a hole in while getting dressed and hadn't replaced, and substituting a skirt for the slacks, which I'd spilled chocolate ice cream on, but still, I thought I was put together pretty niftily.

Hilary sighed as she broke into motion. "Come on."

"I'm not going anywhere with you," I said, following her only so I could nail the door shut behind her and hang a crucifix on it.

"I'm going home to put on something more appropriate," she said.

"Me, too," I said. "I'm putting on a pair of pajamas."

"Don't you want to know about the Black Orchid?"

I did, but I wasn't that easy.

She paused with her hand on the doorknob and turned, looking at me with knowing eyes and a hard little smile. "If you want me out of your life, you'll—"

"Give me five minutes," I said.

CHAPTER TWENTY-NINE

The first thing I noticed was the music. Throbbing, pulsing, with a stifling bass line that hammered at my skull from the inside out. The second thing I noticed was the semi-nude people. You might think I had my priorities screwed up, but the place was as dark as a cave and smelled like burning leaves, and it took a second for my eyes to adjust and the decadence to register.

I turned to Hilary. "I'm not dressed for this."

She shrugged. "I tried to tell you." She'd gone back to Dominatrix Hilary. Her heels were high, her vinyl was shiny, and her lipstick was scarlet red. I, on the other hand, looked like June Cleaver in a bad place.

A tall blond man-child strutted past, wearing nothing more than a metal-studded leather thong and nipple rings and a headful of Sun-In. Following closely behind, by virtue of a leash and a collar, was a stringy man wearing nothing but a piece of black macramé and a leather hood with cutouts in the places appropriate to sustain life. Which was ironic, because if I were ever seen in that getup, I'd certainly want to die.

"Hil!" The blond swooped in and gave Hilary a wet kiss on each cheek while Dog Boy instantly dropped to all fours beside him. "What brings you here tonight?"

"We're playing Nancy Drew." Hilary grimaced in my direction. "This is George." She tweaked one of his nipple rings. "I'm looking for someone. Melissa…" Her eyes cut back to me, searching for a last name.

"Clark," I said, trying not to look at anyone or anything.

"Melissa Clark. Sounds dreadfully dull. I don't think I know her, but you should ask Roddy." He cocked his head.

"How you doing, Hil? We all miss Douglas dreadfully. You hanging in?"

She shrugged. "What else can I do?"

It was all very touching. But in the midst of the sentimentality, it didn't escape me that Dougie had been to this place, was familiar to these people. I closed my eyes against the image of him in a thong and nipple rings or worse, on the wrong end of a leash. I sneaked a peek at Dog Boy, who was sitting on his haunches wide-eyed, looking like he'd just messed on the new family carpet. It was enough to make me give up sex. If I ever had sex.

The blond tipped his head toward me. "You breaking in a newbie, Hil?"

"Hardly." Hilary sniffed. "Look at her."

They chuckled together while my eyes trailed down the leash again. I figured I was doing all right; I might be dull by their standards, but at least there were no leather hoods in my closet. Dog Boy fixed his big brown eyes on me, and I think I saw sympathy in them. Or maybe he just wanted a bone. Anyway, he inched toward me on his shins with an expression that made me wish for a rolled-up newspaper. That kind of sex, I didn't need.

"You could use a makeover, hon," the blond told me. "Dreadfully. Let me take you to the dungeon and—"

I didn't hear what awaited me in the dungeon, because I was distracted by a familiar face off to my right. Paige, strapped into a black vinyl jumpsuit gleaming with buckles and dotted with strategically placed cutouts, taking a stroll in five-inch heels on a fat man's back. She looked like a sadistic Catwoman, and if those cutouts revealed the real thing, I could see why Batman had always had the hots for her.

"Oh. My. God." I closed my eyes and opened them again, and Paige was still ankle-deep in pasty rolls of fat.

"Honey, everyone says that at first," the blond said. "But it's not so bad. I'm telling you—"

He wasn't telling me anything I wanted to hear, even if I'd been listening. I was too busy connecting the dots between Paige and Dougie and the Black Orchid, and while I was at it, Hilary, too. Clearly she was no stranger to this world. All her silk blouses and designer bags couldn't compensate for the depravity on parade here. So that explained the second story man at Hilary's house. Maybe the grieving widow was really the black widow.

"Jamie." Hilary's elbow dug into my ribs. "Sanderson's talking to you."

Paige noticed me then, her eyes widening and her black-rimmed mouth puckering into a little "O". At the same moment, Dog Boy scooted closer and attached himself to my leg and began humping wildly.

"Teamu!" Sanderson yanked on the leash, and Teamu yelped and leaped back where he belonged. Now I knew why he was kept on a leash.

"Jamie!" Hilary's nails attached to my forearm, and the pain spun me around. "What's wrong with you?"

I clamped a hand over her fake tips. "Look over there."

She frowned. "What? Where?"

"We'll use the padded handcuffs," Sanderson was saying, like that was some good deal. I stared at him, and he stared back at me, clueless.

"Paige Ford is over there." I pried her fingers off and rubbed my arm. "Looks like you two have something in common, after all." Maybe more than she'd thought. Maybe her husband.

Hilary zeroed in on Paige, and her face melted into something I haven't seen since the movie *Alien* was released. "Let's go," she hissed, grabbing my arm again.

"I don't think I should—" I began, but then Sanderson made a move toward me, and I gave Hilary a good hard shove in the back to get her moving toward Paige and her date *du jour*.

* * *

"I don't have a lot of time here," Paige said. We were behind the club in a narrow alley clogged with trash cans and fire escapes. The pungent smell of garbage ricocheted between the buildings on the breeze. Paige was chain smoking, flicking ashes and black lipstick-rimmed butts onto the ground. She'd put a raincoat on over her jumpsuit and was cinching it at the neck with one hand. She looked embarrassed and awkward, or maybe it was me that looked that way. I know I felt that way.

To Hilary, she must have looked like dinner, because I could practically hear her sharpening her knives. She wasted no time. "What do you know about my Doug?"

Paige glanced at me and looked away with a shrug. "I know he came here. A lot."

My brain went into instant sensory overload. Dougie in spandex had been one thing. Dougie in rubber and vinyl and chains nearly made my head explode. As did the sight of Paige, here and now. "What are you doing here?" I blurted out. I couldn't help it. My situational context for Paige was behind a computer, playing with makeup, not in a place like this, in an outfit like that. I caught a peek of ridiculously toned thigh and thought well, okay, maybe in an outfit like that. Maybe she could give me some exercise tips.

"I'll handle this," Hilary snapped, although I couldn't see Paige being handled by anyone. Looking at her, I finally understood what girl power was all about. To Paige, she said, "Does your little friend Melissa come here, too?"

Paige's eyes narrowed against the column of smoke twisting upward from her cigarette. "Missy? Hell, no. She doesn't belong in a place like this." She shifted and the raincoat parted and I thought *I want those legs.* Without the heels. I could never walk in five-inch heels. I doubted I could even sit in them.

"I heard she came here," Hilary said.

"You heard wrong." Paige blew a stream of smoke straight into Hilary's face, and Hilary didn't flinch. It was a game of chicken. She propped both hands on her bony hips. "Have you been with my Doug?"

Paige glanced up at the sky. It was a very dark night, and not especially starry. A summer storm was probably moving in. "My client list is confidential," she said finally, very softly. "You should know that."

How would Hilary know that? Did she have a client list of her own? Clients who might want to dispose of her husband? And what exactly did Paige do for her clients? Paige had clients?

"Does this pay well?" I asked. I couldn't help myself. If Paige got legs like that from walking on fat men's backs, it could open up a whole new exercise craze. Maybe I could be open-minded for tighter thighs.

"You have." Hilary's voice was too quiet. I glanced up from my thighs in alarm. The skin on her face was stretched taut. Her lips had thinned to a crimson slash. Apparently the thought of her husband with Paige was more than she could take. I know it was more than I could take. Was there anyone in the office other than me who hadn't slept with Dougie? Or had Paige only tattooed his back with those stilettos? Either way, the visual rattled my brain.

"So what do you average?" I broke in, hoping Hilary's eyeballs would recede back into their sockets. "A hundred a night?"

"I can't disclose my client list," Paige told Hilary with a smirk. She was goading Hilary, and I had no idea why. I didn't think it was a good move, though. Hilary's heels looked like they could be lethal.

"You little bitch." Hilary stepped closer to her, close enough for the toes of their boots to touch. "Did you kill my husband?"

Whoa. It was a big leap from sex to murder, and I didn't think Hilary should be making it. "Hilary," I cut in, "maybe we should just—"

"That's rude," Paige said, her expression unchanging. I don't know how she stayed so calm.

"Did. You. Kill. My. Husband?" Like a snake poised to strike, Hilary went absolutely still and stared at Paige. Paige exhaled a slow, steady stream of smoke and stared back with languid eyes.

I stuffed my hands in my pockets to hide the trembling. "I'm sure she has no idea who—"

"Did you?" Hilary screeched suddenly, startling me into tachycardia and having no visible effect on Paige other than provoking another eerily calm smile. This was a Paige I had never seen before and didn't like very much. I'd never look at her the same way again. Maybe I'd look at her in an orange prison jumpsuit.

"If you killed my Doug," Hilary said, her quiet tone matching Paige's calm smile, "I will slit your throat. Do you understand me?"

My hands clenched themselves into fists while my stomach clenched itself into the size of a golf ball. This game of chicken was rising to a new terrifying level, and I wanted no part of it. I'd known Paige and Hilary didn't like each other, but now it struck me the basis of their dislike was competition, and neither one wanted to play fair. Suddenly it put a whole new spin on Paige's relationship with Dougie.

And maybe on her relationship to Dougie's death.

CHAPTER THIRTY

———

"Where've you been?" Sherri whined in my ear. "I've been trying to reach you for hours."

"You don't want to know." I dropped naked into a kitchen chair, holding the phone with two fingers. The Black Orchid experience had left me feeling filthy, and I'd shed my clothes onto the floor the second I'd walked through the door. Tomorrow I planned to burn them. "Hilary Heath took—"

"I saw Frankie Ritter with a redhead on Monmouth Road."

I closed my eyes at her statement, seeing Paige and Hilary instead facing off in my mind, and opened them again. I had to keep moving. I hunted down some comfort food, a single-serving box of Frosted Flakes, which I tore open and poured straight into my mouth while standing at the counter. "So what?" I said finally.

"Are you eating?"

I crunched a mouthful and swallowed. "No."

"You are so eating. I hear you. God." I could practically see her eyes rolling. "Thanks for caring."

"Well, it's not like you two are engaged or anything."

"Jamie. I'm wearing his *diamond ring*."

"Okay," I said. "A friendship ring. He's not being much of a friend. You'll give it back tomorrow." I upended the tiny box and scarfed down the second half. Not enough. I dropped it in the trash and rooted around for more fats and sugars.

"Maybe she was his sister," Sherri said.

"He doesn't have a sister." Frankie had been enough to handle on his own, even for Mrs. Ritter.

"His cousin, then." She was getting defensive.

"Fine. She was his cousin. Feel better now?" Ah, cheese crackers, leftovers of a care package from my mother. I used my teeth to rip the cellophane open.

"I must say, you don't seem very concerned about this. I thought you would *care* that Frankie Ritter's cheating on me."

"Oh, God." I froze in mid-bite. "You are not sleeping with Frankie Ritter."

"Certainly not," Sherri said. "He wants to, you know, but I told him not until he lets his hair grow out blond again. I have my standards, you know."

"Obviously." I turned with the crackers in hand and caught a glimpse of myself in the kitchen window that startled me into dropping the package. I was still too thin, but now I had flabby thighs and a little potbelly. "Oh, God," I said to myself.

And Sherri said, "Well, who are you to judge? You haven't had sex since Obama took office!"

Nice that she was keeping track. "I have to go," I said, closing my eyes against the reflection.

"What do you have to do that's so important?" she demanded.

"Find a tranquilizer," I said, and hung up.

* * *

Chemically speaking, my options were few. I couldn't find even a sleeping pill in my medicine chest, and I didn't like taking pills, anyway, so I gave yoga a shot. Five minutes in Shavasana only left me more out of sorts. I didn't need relaxation; I needed exercise. Sweaty, demanding exercise. The sort of exercise that would obliterate that appalling reflection of my naked body in the kitchen window.

But first I needed junk food.

I searched through every drawer in the apartment and couldn't find anything to blunt the edge. I didn't want to go to bed with images of Hilary and Paige facing off or of Sherri sleeping with Frankie Ritter, so I called Curt to see if I could borrow a bottle of wine. I intended to get dressed and go downstairs to get it, maybe even share it and my troubles with him on the deck, but he was knocking on the door before I had the chance. I darted into the bathroom to grab an oversized towel to wrap around my skinny, saggy, poochy self before I went to let him in.

"Found a bottle of Korbel instead," he said, offering it for inspection. His eyes widened at the towel. "Nice outfit."

I kicked my dirty clothes aside. "It's a long story. I'm not much of a champagne drinker."

"Perfect." He went into the kitchen. "Go take your shower. I won't start drinking without you."

"I'm not showering, I'm changing," I said. "And stop looking at me like that."

"Hey, I'm a card-carrying heterosexual." He fished two glasses from the cabinet, held them up to the light, then turned on the tap and held them under the faucet. "It's only your knobby knees keeping me at bay."

"My knees are not knobby." I leaned forward to check them out. They were knobby, all right. They were also fuzzy. So that was two things I wasn't very good at. I was beginning to understand why I hadn't had sex for more than five years. "My body is a mess," I muttered. Or maybe I whined.

"I doubt that." Curt dried the glasses with a paper towel. "But show it to me, and I'll let you know for sure."

"I am not showing you my body," I said, cinching the towel even tighter. It was already so tight I was starting to get lightheaded.

"Okay." He handed me a glass of champagne. "Now I know what we're not drinking to. So what's the occasion?"

"Let me put some clothes on," I said, "and I'll tell you."

I left him in front of the television while I found shorts and a T-shirt and ran a quick razor across my kneecaps. It was oppressively hot, and he'd already nearly emptied his first glass when I got back, so I figured I'd better talk fast.

"I'm confused," I said. I dropped onto the sofa bed, crossing my legs to sit Indian style. "Hilary Heath is convinced Missy killed Dougie, but Paige works at the Black Orchid, and she and Dougie were playmates, and Paige and Hilary hate each other, and now I think Paige might have had something to do with it and Janice—"

"Hold it." He held up a hand. "Now *I'm* confused. What are you still doing with Hilary Heath, and why are you doing it at the Black Orchid? Don't you know what that place is?"

"I do now." I took a gulp of champagne to dull that knowledge. "How did you know Paige works there?"

He twisted his glass slowly between both palms, as if embarrassed. "She was the featured entertainment at a bachelor party there."

I blinked. "You've been there?"

"Once." He shuddered. "Took me a week to wash it off."

"I know what you mean." I took a sip of champagne. It bubbled its way down my throat, leaving an unpleasant aftertaste. I didn't much like champagne. "Did she do her stilettos-on-the-back thing?"

He smirked. "No, her whip-on-the-ass thing."

"God," I said, "I'd be mortified."

"So would I, if it had been my ass."

I considered that while I drank more champagne. The unpleasant aftertaste was becoming a bit more pleasant, and the bubbles were stinging a bit less. Maybe I did like champagne. "So where does that leave Missy?"

"Right where she was before, still a suspect."

That's what I was afraid of. "I hate this," I said.

"Be worried if you didn't," he said.

I poured myself another glass of champagne. "As bad as Paige is," I said, "Hilary's worse. She's definitely on the warpath." I hesitated. "And Donna was pretty upset with Dougie. She even said she wished he'd fall down the courthouse steps."

"I doubt she was the only person who ever said that."

"And maybe Janice," I went on. "I heard her telling someone we bought new computers and software."

"So?"

"We didn't buy new computers and software," I said. "Not since I've been there. So what'd she spend the money on?"

Curt shrugged. "Maybe she bought herself a personality."

That wasn't a matter of "maybe." She hadn't.

He shifted his glass back to one hand and stood up. "Ready for more?"

I shook my head. "We're not so good at this crime solving stuff, are we? It looks so easy on TV."

"I know what'll help." He disappeared into the kitchen. I heard him rustling around, probably looking for some food to blunt the effects of the champagne. Not that I was feeling effects from two glasses of champagne.

"Food's not gonna help," I yelled. "I'm not drunk."

He popped into the doorway. "What are you yelling for? Haven't you got any whole grains in this place?"

"Have a bowl of Cheerios," I said. "What about Wally? Wally took over Dougie's office before Dougie was even in the ground. That's motive, isn't it?"

"A new office?" He chuckled. "Hot damn, I think you just broke the case. Heath was killed over a hundred square feet of Berber."

I bristled. "For your information, wars have started for less. Have you got a better idea?"

"Not yet. But it's percolating." He sat down with the pack of cheese crackers I'd been working on when I'd seen my reflection in the window. "Here."

"I don't want it." I took it anyway. Turned out I really did want it. Before I knew it, the pack was empty. "I've got some good stuff," I said. "You have to admit that."

"What you've got is an office full of kooks and perverts," he said.

"Yes," I said, "but those kooks and perverts have reasons to want Dougie gone. Not to mention opportunity. Take Missy, for example. I took a phone call from the pharmacist she's dating, and he said he wants her stuff gone. A *pharmacist.* Dougie was poisoned, right? What do you think that means?"

He came over to the sofa bed and took the glass from my hands. "It means we don't know anything, except that you have to watch your back. Which is what we knew before. Come on." He pulled me to my feet. "Time for bed." He left me standing there while he folded the covers back and fluffed up my pillow. He found the remote and laid it on top of the blanket. "You can even watch TV, if you promise not to watch any detective shows."

"You're being very condescending." I glowered at him as I climbed into bed, even though I kind of liked being tucked in. I was ready for some sleep, anyway, and I wasn't getting anywhere with the conversation. That was the problem with Curt. Too much taking, not enough giving. That kind of man was just no good for a woman like me.

He pulled the blankets up to my armpits, and I decided he wasn't so bad after all. "Remember," he warned me. "Only sitcoms and game shows."

I nodded, already fuzzy-headed from the warmth and the champagne. "Did I tell you my sister slept with Frankie Ritter?"

He reached over to switch off the table lamp. "Want me to kill him for you?"

"Nah." My eyes drifted shut. "One murder's all I can handle."

"I was hoping you'd say that." He pressed a chaste kiss on my forehead. "Good-night."

I didn't have the nerve to open my eyes until I heard the door close, and then I didn't shut them again for a very long time.

CHAPTER THIRTY-ONE

———

I finally fell asleep around two-thirty and woke up at five-fifteen with a hornet's nest of thoughts buzzing through my head. It was already hot and humid. My T-shirt glued itself to my back as I kicked off the covers and padded into the bathroom to splash my face with cold water. I left the light off because some things were better left unseen. I'd read once that some people functioned just fine on three hours of sleep a night. I wasn't one of them.

Since I was out of bed and marginally awake, I powered up my ancient laptop. Time for the spreadsheet I'd been putting off. Maybe laying everything out on paper would give it coherence.

First I typed the name of each person who worked at Parker, Dennis, and Heath, in descending order of importance. Ken and Howard at the top, Wally next, Janice and Donna, then finally the three secretaries. As an afterthought, I added Hilary's name at the bottom. Next to each name, I typed Dougie's respective relationships to them, or what I perceived their relationships to be. Partner. Partner. Boss. Husband.

Hilary. She had an assortment of classic motives: jealousy, an ongoing affair of her own (the mystery man upstairs), years of humiliation thanks to Dougie's own serial affairs. Not much in the way of opportunity, but I wasn't ready to cross her off just yet.

As for Ken and Howard, nothing there, unless you considered their shared distaste for Dougie's method of doing business. They'd been vocal enough about it that I was willing to consider it. As far as motives went, it was flimsy, especially since embarrassment hadn't hurt their bottom line, but it was all I had for the moment.

I moved down to Wally and typed a question mark. Curt was right: killing over office space was unlikely. On the other hand, where Howard went, Wally followed, so I couldn't rule him out completely. It was possible he'd acted on Howard's say-so.

For a refreshing change of pace, Janice had no sexual connection to Dougie, but she did have two very nice cars and access to the firm's finances. The ultimate fiduciary responsibility belonged to Arthur Fiore, the firm's off-site CPA, but still, Janice had the opportunity to cover her own tracks. I remembered her defense of the fictional computer expenditure. Obviously some money had gone somewhere. I wondered if that somewhere was Janice's pocket. Maybe Dougie had found out and threatened to report her to the police. That spelled motive for Janice.

Which brought me to Donna. There was plenty to think about there, so I sat back and thought about it. No one knew very much about her. She was an excellent paralegal, a model employee, a forgettable face and a complete mystery. She had a boyfriend and a grudge against Dougie. Plus she'd already made comments about wishing Dougie dead that had seemed offhanded at the time, but now rang sinister. I was willing to bet the wound from being excluded from the courtroom ran even deeper than she'd let on.

Ordinarily I would have glossed right over the secretaries. I worked with these women every day. I knew about their romantic histories, their food allergies, their taste in movies and music and cosmetics. After the past two weeks, though, I knew much more. I knew Paige worked at the Black Orchid and had had some sort of sexual contact with Dougie there. Or maybe she just wanted Hilary to think she had. I knew Missy was making her pharmacist boyfriend, Braxton Malloy, very uncomfortable by keeping something at his house. I knew she'd taken a mystery paper from Dougie's desk. Maybe a love letter, incriminating in the wrong hands.

I closed my eyes briefly. It was all too confusing. Look deep enough and it could be argued that even I had motive to kill Dougie. Curt was right. I was over my head trying to solve a murder. I knew nothing about police procedures, about whom to talk to, and what to read, and where to start. I only knew one thing, and that was I had nothing to do with Dougie's death. Not enough.

I powered down the laptop and got up to shower and dress for work. It wasn't until I was standing under the steaming spray that I realized I knew one other thing: I knew what had killed Dougie.

It wasn't much, but it was a place to start.

CHAPTER THIRTY-TWO

———

I'd only been at work five minutes on Monday when a voice said, "Excuse me."

I looked up to find Martha Mintzer hovering at my desk. Martha was a client of Dougie's and not his typical showgirl client. Martha was soft and round everywhere except for her mouth. She was flapping a half-sheet of paper at me that I recognized as the firm's stock memorandum form. We used it for quick, informal reminders to clients of appointments.

"You people scheduled an appointment for me to see a Doctor..." she glanced at the form, "...Finster."

I knew the name, from other cases.

"We didn't schedule it," I said. "It's a routine defense exam. They're entitled to have you examined by their doctor. "

She glared down at me. "Well, no one asked me. I can't possibly keep this appointment. I have a job, you know."

"I know it's an inconvenience," I said patiently. "But when you file a lawsuit—"

"Don't you lecture me," she said. "I have bunions that are older than you."

Lovely. "I don't mean to lecture," I said. "But you should be aware it's standard procedure."

"Missing a day of work to sit in some quack's office?" She shook her head. "This Dr. Finster isn't my doctor. My doctor would see me at night. I'm sorry, I can't do this." She dropped the crumpled memo on my desk. I glanced to Missy for help, but she'd slipped out at the first sign of trouble. Guess she had enough of her own. "Maybe you'd like to speak with Wally." I picked up the phone.

"Wally," she grunted. "I have hemorrhoids older than *him*,"

Good thing Dougie was already dead because I'd have killed him for signing a client like this. I buzzed Wally and thirty seconds later delivered Martha and her infirmities safely to his door. It wasn't until I got back downstairs that I realized I no longer thought of that office as Dougie's. Sad, how quickly that adjustment could be made. In fact, everyone seemed to be rebounding from Dougie's death. The phones were ringing, and the fax line was buzzing, and clients were coming and going. Victoria Plackett made a surprising reappearance for an appointment with Ken. Howard was out of the office at an arbitration.

Paige had called in sick, leaving a message on the voice mail system, but her empty chair glowered at me on her behalf. I glowered right back. My plans for Paige had to wait. Missy returned to her desk, but seemed sullen and angrier than usual. Between her attitude and Martha's, my stomach was in a twist. It was the new normal at Parker, Dennis, and Heath.

"Can I talk to you?" Missy asked a few minutes later, after the mailman had delivered a rubber-banded stack of mail to her desk and vanished. She began slashing envelopes open.

I kept one eye on the lethal looking letter opener and nodded.

"It's Braxton." Her shoulders lifted and fell in a huge sigh while she pulled mail out of the envelopes, tossing the empties and stacking the unfolded letters into three piles on her blotter for Ken, Howard, and Wally. I noticed a smaller fourth pile to her left. Dougie's.

I had a feeling it might be. "Trouble?" I asked.

"It's getting weird," she said, without specifying what *it* was. "He stopped by my place last night with a box of cold medicine. Said I'd asked him to do it. I haven't even talked to him lately." Her cheeks flushed slightly. "We're not getting along all that well."

Probably because she was stashing poison at his place.

"That is strange." I buried my face in Wally's latest opus.

"I think he wants to break up with me." She shoved the wastebasket back beneath her desk with her foot. "And right before Ken's barbecue, too. He asked me to clear my things out of his apartment."

Her things? I lifted my head. "I didn't know you'd moved in together."

"We didn't. You know how it is with a guy." Actually, I didn't. Curt was the only guy I had a relationship with, and that was strictly food-based. "At first you take all of your stuff home with you, then gradually things begin staying behind. Sweaters. A pair of shoes. Tampons." I cocked my head, thinking that sounded kind of nice. "I think he's seeing someone else," she said. "I mean, he must be if he wants my stuff gone, right?"

"It doesn't sound good," I admitted. Actually, it sounded great. The truth behind Braxton's call wasn't sinister after all. Suddenly I was more confident than ever of Missy's innocence.

"Yeah." She shuffled the piles of mail into neat square corners. "Hey, would you take the mail upstairs? I want to give him a call and get this straightened out."

Now that I had an explanation for her mood and knowledge that the "stuff" she'd stashed at Braxton Malloy's apartment wasn't deadly to anything but their relationship, I would have agreed to anything. Now I could focus on Paige. And Janice. And Hilary. And if I could redirect Hilary's attention to Paige, the two of them could slash each other to ribbons, and I'd be out of it. No more surprise visits or phone calls or trips to the Black Orchid. I could go back to the normal chores of life, like breaking up my sister's relationship with Frankie Ritter.

With a skip in my step, I began making the rounds. A stack of bills to Janice, two of the envelopes stamped Past Due. She didn't even look at me. A half dozen letters for Ken, all printed on thick, expensive stationery with fancy letterheads. A mixture of both for Howard, with an envelope on top that caught my attention. Missy had slit it open but hadn't removed the contents. She didn't have to. The envelope was custom printed with the return address of Howard Dennis, Sr., M.D. in the upper left corner.

Howard's father was a doctor. Doctors knew even more than pharmacists about poisons. Howard had despised his own partner, would have bought him out of the firm if Dougie had survived. Motive and opportunity, all in one family. My fingers lingered on the raised lettering as I put the mail on Howard's desk. Was it possible?

By the time I stopped debating and got around to Wally, he was nowhere in sight. Maybe Martha had eaten him. I dropped his mail on the desk and turned to leave when my eye was caught by his new artwork: his college and law school diplomas, matted and framed, hanging neatly on the wall behind his desk.

I stepped closer, admiring the gold seals and fancy lettering. He'd attended Villanova Law School with an undergrad degree from Rutgers. In chemistry. I blinked and looked again. In chemistry.

A shiver ran down my spine. It was quiet in this office, too quiet. Where before I hadn't felt Dougie's presence, he now seemed to be tapping me on the shoulder. Wally had repainted and refurnished, but it still held traces of Dougie. Accusing traces. Who better to understand and concoct poisons than someone with a chemistry degree? Especially when that someone was a lowly associate aspiring to the fast partnership track?

"Just when I think I'm getting a handle on things," I muttered. Suddenly I had two new entries for my spreadsheet. Looked like Frankie Ritter had gotten a reprieve.

* * *

Ken and Howard called an office meeting for the end of the day, so everyone gathered in the conference room at five o'clock with varying degrees of irritation. An hours-old pot of coffee sat on the sideboard next to a tray of Danish left over from the last office meeting. No one seemed in the mood to eat anyway. Well, I could have used a bite, but my life philosophy was one of conformance, so I stayed in my seat and dreamed of dinner instead. The atmosphere was tense and expectant, especially when Howard stepped to the head of the table. I couldn't look at him quite the same way. I couldn't look at anyone quite the same way.

"This won't take long," he said, skewering us in turn with nasty eyes that made me wonder what kind of impression he left on jurors. "First I'd like to commend everyone on the smooth transition since Douglas's passing. Now, there will be one more change I'd like to announce. Effective immediately, this firm will be known simply as Parker, Dennis." He paused, and I shot a glance at Wally. Thin lips, red cheeks, slitted eyes. I didn't think this particular transition was what he'd had in mind.

"Also," Howard went on, "out of respect for Douglas, Ken and I have decided to postpone the barbecue to next weekend. I'd like to see everyone there."

There was a spike in the irritation level in the room. Guess I wasn't the only one hoping the barbecue would be canceled outright.

Ken seemed oblivious to the hostility. "If you need directions, Missy was kind enough to print out a set." He smiled in Missy's direction, and all eyes temporarily shifted to her.

Howard cleared his throat. "Finally, I want to assure all of you that the harassment of this firm by the police is over. I believe we've been more than cooperative in providing information and permitting physical searches of the premises. I've informed the chief of police that any further invasion of our privacy will take place only with a court order."

That seemed a bit harsh, given that it was a murder investigation. Besides, I knew from Curt that police officers had no interest in harassing lawyers. Arresting, yes. Harassing, no. I wondered what Howard had to hide.

"If any of you are contacted by the police," Howard was saying, "it's up to you, of course, whether you'll cooperate with them." His eyes slid my way. "Should any of you have any…close relationships with an officer, I trust you will keep in mind the confidentiality of the firm's business."

That did it. "You're telling us to obstruct an investigation," I said. I'd heard that term on television. It had sounded good then, and it sounded pretty good now.

Wally smirked. "Some investigation. How hard could it be to find out which secretary had it in for her boss?"

That more than did it. I wasn't about to sit there and be insulted by the Boy Lawyer. Not when I was tired and hungry and marinating in suspicion of everyone in the room. I was used to having no answers come my way, but I wasn't used to accusations. I needed out. Maybe for good.

"You know, Wally," I said, "there are grudges, and there are grudges with chemistry degrees and a goal to become full partner." I pushed back my chair and stood while Wally sat and gaped. For me, the meeting was over.

CHAPTER THIRTY-THREE

———

"I broke up with him." Sherri ripped open a butter packet and snatched a roll from the breadbasket. "I confronted him about the redhead, and he said men have needs. Needs." She savaged the roll into halves and slapped butter on one half. "Don't talk to me about needs. I went back on the Pill this month because of my needs."

I stabbed a fork into my salad with a sigh. I didn't really want to hear about someone else's needs. I had needs, too. I might need a job. Rent money. A psychological evaluation. What had I been thinking, mouthing off to Howard (and Wally) and running out of an office meeting (I'd actually walked with alacrity)? Of course, I'd gone back, and, of course, Wally had played on my guilt to wheedle an hour of overtime out of me. So now, at seven-thirty at night, I was feeling both guilt and self-loathing for being so easily manipulated. I was also feeling some pride for mouthing off and running out.

"I don't know what I was doing with him anyway." Sherri sighed around her mouthful of roll. "I'm just so lonely. And he was there. But that's not enough, is it? I mean, I'm not even physically attracted to him. And he's sort of weird, don't you think?"

I'd been easily manipulated because I needed the money and the job. I had two hundred fifty dollars in my checking account and no prospects for a quick inheritance. I'd lose my apartment. I'd have to move in with my parents. Eat meatloaf every Friday for the rest of my life. Well, okay, the meatloaf I could take. But there was no way I was eating pork chops every Wednesday.

"He wasn't even good in bed," Sherri whined. "It was all about *him*. When is it ever going to be about me?"

I gave her a look. She didn't notice.

"I kept the ring, though." She waved her bare ring finger. "I mean, I can do that, right? It was a gift, right?"

"Well—" I began.

And she plowed right over me. "It's not like I asked for that ring. I don't even think it's a real diamond. It's probably cubic zirconium. When am I going to meet a guy who'll buy me real diamonds? It's never gonna happen for me, Jamie. I just don't feel it."

Maybe she didn't, but I did: A surge of anger and impatience and annoyance washing over me like a black tide. All of a sudden I'd had enough of the Hilarys and Howards and even Sherris of the world. I didn't care about Frankie Ritter. I didn't care about Hilary's grudge match with Missy or her vendetta against Paige. I didn't even care about Sherri and her diamond lust. I'd had enough of it all.

"Look." I leaned forward far enough to dip my collar into my soup. "I don't want to hear about your problems with men. Do you know how pathetic you sound? Who do you think's going to be attracted to desperation?" Her face slackened and went pale, but I was on a roll. "You've dragged me to singles bowling and singles shopping, and you've brought Frankie Ritter to my apartment. After you slept with him." I let my disgust seep into my voice. She deserved it. "You want some real problems, come work at Parker, Dennis. I work with a murderer, Sher. I don't have the luxury of spending nineteen hours a day trying to catch a husband. I'm too busy worrying about turning my back on the wrong person."

I blotted my neckline dry, crumpled the napkin, and threw it back on the table while Sherri stared at me, open-mouthed. Finally, she said, "Bad day at work?"

"You have no idea."

She buttered another roll and handed it to me. "Tell me all about it."

That was more like it. "I have to go to Ken's barbecue weekend after next. I don't want to be near these people. Any one of them could have killed Dougie. I don't know who to trust." I took a breath. "And honestly, I don't even like them."

"So don't go."

"I have to go." I chewed morosely.

"Okay." Sherri thought about it. "So consider it a chance to do some investigating of your own."

"Right." I sneered. "Look how far that's gotten me."

"That's because you're going about it the wrong way." She pushed her salad aside. "You need to be sneakier. Ask the right questions. Pretend you're interested in these people on a personal level, and then use the information they give you to crush them."

I stopped chewing. "You think that'll work?"

She smiled serenely. "It's worked with men for years. They never know what hit them."

"But you're better at that sort of thing than I am. I don't lie very well."

Sherri smothered her laughter behind a napkin. "Sure you do. You pretended it was okay for me to date Frankie Ritter."

"That was never okay," I said.

She rolled her eyes. "There's still time. Why don't you tell me about these people, and I'll help you figure out what to ask them. People love to talk about themselves. It's their greatest weakness."

I blinked. "You'd do that for me?"

"You bet." She sat back as the waitress approached with our dinners. "And after that, you can help me figure out how to snag someone better than Frankie Ritter."

With Sherri, the window of opportunity never stayed open for long.

* * *

An hour later, we were in my kitchen studying the spreadsheet. "Here's what I've done so far," I said. "I've laid out everyone in the office along with possible motives." I jotted down "B.S. in Chemistry" in Wally's column, "Dr. Dennis" in Howard's, and pushed it toward her. While she looked it over, I filled two mugs with water, put them in the microwave for two minutes, and gathered a jar of instant coffee, sugar, and creamer.

"You've been busy." Her face creased into a frown. "Looks like any one of them could have done it."

"Exactly. But does anyone jump out at you?"

She nodded. "When in doubt, go right to the top."

"Ken?" I shook my head. "It can't be Ken. He's just an old sweet man waiting to retire."

"Uh-huh. Didn't I read something in the paper about that old sweet man taking Community Hospital for five million dollars?"

"He didn't 'take' them," I said, offended. "He won a jury verdict. That's what lawyers do."

"And you know what money does," Sherri said. "It corrupts people. Oh, and look, you have right here, 'disgrace.' If that isn't motive enough—"

"Move on," I said, taking the cups from the microwave. I spooned instant coffee into them.

She took another look at the page. "Or it could be Wally. This chemistry degree is interesting."

"And he did take over Dougie's office," I said, handing her a cup.

"Yeah." Her lip curled. "That's a motive."

I narrowed my eyes at her. "It could happen. Maybe he's thinking first Dougie's office, then his partnership."

"Or," Sherri said, "maybe he's thinking he just likes the paint color."

"If you're not going to help—" I began.

And she said, "Or it could be Janice. Everyone knows you can't trust those shifty bookkeepers. You watch, one day she won't show up for work because she'll be lying on a beach in the Cayman Islands letting Parker, Dennis, and Heath buy her a real life."

I couldn't argue with that. Throw in a couple frozen daiquiris, and it sounded too much like a good idea. Besides, it was a realistic scenario under the present circumstances.

"Or," she said, "it could be Donna. I know *I'd* kill anyone who made me stay out of the courthouse."

I ignored the sarcasm. "She's a paralegal. She wants to go to the courthouse."

"So she's insane." Sherri handed back the spreadsheet, shaking her head. "You work with some real losers, you know that?"

"At least I don't get engaged to them," I said.

She screwed up her nose at me. "That was unnecessary. Just for that, I vote for old sweet Ken."

"It's not Ken," I said. "I just don't see it."

"Then what's he doing on your list?"

I creased the page in half and stuffed it in my handbag. "Do I look like I have all the answers?"

Sherri shook her head. "You don't even look like you have all the questions."

CHAPTER THIRTY-FOUR

———

I got to work early on Tuesday with a purpose. The purpose walked in five minutes later and poured herself a glass of orange juice. I joined her at the kitchen table, and she said immediately, "I don't want to talk about it."

"Neither do I," I told her. "I don't even want to know about it."

She shrugged. "It's a job."

So was cleaning toilets. "Paige." I leaned forward. "Tell me about Spanish fly."

Her eyes widened. "What?"

"Look, I don't care about the Black Orchid." Little white lie. Actually, I had all sorts of questions about the Black Orchid, but they'd have to wait. I wasn't sure I was old enough to hear the answers. "I'm sure you know people who've used it, and I need to find out what you know."

"I'm not naming names," she said.

"I don't want names, I want symptoms."

"Oh." She nodded. "That's easy. It makes you horny. That means—"

"I know what it means." I remembered the feeling, vaguely. "But I heard that wasn't true. I heard it can be very dangerous."

"I don't know who you're hearing from," Paige said. "But Hilary's wrong."

Hm. "It wasn't Hilary," I said.

"Missy, then."

"It wasn't Missy, either." She opened her mouth, and I said, "I'm not naming names."

A hint of a smile flickered across her face. "So you have some bitch in you after all."

"When necessary," I said. Truthfully, I didn't have much. Or maybe I did, but it never had the strength to get out before. Whichever the case, it felt pretty good now.

Paige got up to put her glass in the sink. "What are you, writing a medical textbook or something?"

"Or something."

She turned on the faucet. "Sorry. That's all I know. You'll have to do your Sherlock Holmes bit somewhere else."

The catch being, there was nowhere else. The murder had happened at the office, and the answer had to be at the office. Fortunately, a good-sized library was also at the office, and I planned to make use of it before the day started.

* * *

My mother used to say that a little knowledge was a dangerous thing, and after twenty minutes in the library, I knew just what she meant, because I'd learned little and felt dangerously incompetent because of it.

Because of his medical malpractice caseload, Ken had an impressive array of medical reference books, and I had several of them stacked on the table in front of me. I knew next to nothing about Spanish fly and nothing at all about how it could have ended up in Dougie's protein powder. According to the reference books, Spanish fly was not a fly at all, but a species of beetle which fed on flowering plants like alfalfa. It had once been used to formulate something called cantharidin, a blister-inducing agent used for medicinal purposes. Surely Dr. Dennis or the pharmacist Braxton Malloy, or possibly even Wally with his chemistry degree, would be aware of its medical applications. Deadly in small doses even to creatures as large as horses, it sounded as though a mere mortal like Dougie hadn't had a chance. Like Curt had said, he was dead when he swallowed. Sounded gruesome, except each book was careful to say that while it had been widely used in the past, it wasn't used at all in modern medicine. There was also some mention of its once-rumored benefits as an aphrodisiac, which brought me right back to the Black Orchid. Basically, back to the starting point.

I slid the books back onto the shelves. I wasn't much of a researcher. I hadn't learned anything I couldn't have found out by asking any hippie from the '60s. I certainly hadn't learned anything I could take back to Curt. I hadn't uncovered any new additions to my spreadsheet. It wasn't even nine o'clock, and I was already counting the day as a total failure.

Until I remembered Frankie Ritter.

CHAPTER THIRTY-FIVE

If the booth had been any farther from the entrance, I'd have needed a road map to find it. The hostess led me part of the way, thrust a menu into my hands, and pointed, and I understood why. Frankie Ritter was waiting, sprawled across the bench like a stain, wearing faded denim shorts and a white T-shirt with dark spots blooming in both armpits. I wasn't surprised he'd beaten me there; he didn't look like he'd ever turned down a free meal. I slid into the opposite side of the booth, pretending not to notice the sympathetic glances from the other diners.

"Thanks for the invite, babe." He gave me an oily smile. "I was just gonna have some Trix for lunch, you know what I mean? This is top frigging notch."

"The only five-star diner in the country," I said, but his slightly psychotic expression didn't waver. "I'll have a Scotch and soda," I called to the waitress hovering at the safety perimeter. I needed the reinforcement. The idea of drilling Frankie for information had lost some of its panache on the way from the office. For one thing, I'd seen Frankie eat. For another, there was the broken so-called engagement to my sister. The timing could have been better, but I had a murder investigation to bungle, and I figured even Frankie Ritter couldn't be classless enough to bring up the subject of Sherri.

"You know your sister's whacked," he said.

Wrong again.

"I mean, what's she lookin' for, anyway? I gave her a diamond ring, for Chrissake. Hey." He dropped his arms onto the table hard enough to make the salt and pepper shakers jump and drawing frowns from nearby booths. "You're a legal babe. She don't wanna give me the ring back. Don't she have to give it back? She broke her promise, right? I know about this shit." He bobbed his head up and down. "I seen it on Jerry Springer."

"I'll look into it," I said. What was keeping the waitress, anyway? I could fix the drink faster myself. I knew how to make a Scotch and soda. Hell, I didn't even need the glass. Or the soda.

He sat back, satisfied. "She say anything to you? She tell you why she broke it off?"

I shook my head. "Listen, the reason I wanted—"

"It ain't like I'm a stiff in the sack," he said. "I don't need none of that Viagra shit. I'm a plank, babe."

In more ways than one. I began shredding a napkin into rice-sized pieces. "Speaking of that," I said, "what do you know about Spanish fly?"

If he was shocked by the question, he didn't show it. His blowfish cheeks flattened out, and he leaned forward again, steepling his fingers like a professor. "Spanish fly," he said. "Comes from nasty little suckers called blister beetles. They travel in swarms, like killer bees, mate in the summer, and sometimes they get crushed when alfalfa hay gets harvested. Hay gets fed to some poor freakin' horses and punches their clocks for 'em in like two seconds. Nice life, huh?" I looked at him, and he shrugged. "I know a little about it. Why?"

"Do you know where I could get some?"

He blinked at me. "Babe, I had no idea you were so—"

"I'm not. I don't actually want any."

The waitress reappeared with my drink, slapped it down in front of me, and vaporized. I pushed the napkin bits aside.

"I don't get it." Frankie eyed my glass. Or maybe he was trying to look through it, to my chest. "Why do you wanna know where to get it if you don't want it?"

"I'm the curious type." I took a good long drink of watered-down Scotch. If that was the best they could do, I'd have to order by the pitcher.

"I think I dated the wrong sister," he said. "Tell you what, you help me get my ring back and it's yours."

"I don't want it," I said. "All I want is information. Where could a ridiculously low-paid secretary buy Spanish fly?"

"You mean someone like you."

"Okay," I said, and took another drink. I wasn't about to share my suspicions with Frankie Ritter. Even though his little lecture had given me more of them.

The waitress swooped in on us, pad and pen in hand. From one look at her, I could tell she was holding her breath. I ordered a cup of soup. I was pretty sure I could hold that down. Frankie ordered the roast chicken breast with mashed potatoes and mixed vegetables and a serving of cornbread on the side.

When the waitress had exhaled and left with our order, Frankie said, "Will you marry me?"

"Absolutely not," I said. "And I'm not paying for lunch if you don't help me out here."

"Christ. Women." He steepled his pudgy little fingers again. "Spanish fly, huh?"

I nodded. "How easy is it to get?"

"A whole lot easier thirty years ago. Before the brainiacs found out how it can make you dead quick."

"But nothing's *hard* to get if you know where to look, right?" Or so I'd heard. On TV, from the safety of my living room. Living dangerously is a relative thing.

He thought some more. "I know a place you might be able to score some, called the Black Orchid. Pretty scary place, you ask me. Babe like you might not want to go there alone."

"Been there," I said. And I didn't want to go back. But he'd just told me what I'd wanted to know. If Spanish fly could be had at the Black Orchid, then either Paige or Hilary could get it. Anyway, I now had ammunition to use at Ken's barbecue next weekend, which was worth the price of lunch.

His eyebrows lifted. "Wild. About that wedding thing—"

"No."

"Okay." He swung his massive head to the side, looking for the waitress. "But if you should get a little horny from this Spanish fly, you know who to call, right?"

"Absolutely," I said, and I meant it. I'd be on the phone to a therapist immediately.

CHAPTER THIRTY-SIX

"Here's the thing," Curt said. We were sitting side by side on his sofa watching the Phillies trounce the Pirates in a gentle rain. A bag of tortilla chips and a jar of salsa sat on the coffee table, and in keeping with the evening's theme, we each had a bottle of Corona. The front door was open, and I could hear the rain sluicing down the window and hissing off the front steps. Very cozy. If this was what marriage felt like, I could understand Sherri's lust for matrimony. "You have to stop playing with Hilary Heath," Curt told me. "Your little road trip to the Black Orchid wasn't all that very helpful and was, in fact, stupid. You don't want to play with those people."

I reached over to drag a chip through the salsa. "Why not?"

He took it from me and popped it in his mouth. "For one thing, you got Paige's antenna up."

"Hilary did that." I took another chip. "She accused her of murdering Dougie."

"See, now, that's what I mean." He frowned at me. "Did that seem like a good idea at the time?"

I slapped a hand to my chest. "Don't blame me. The two of them almost got into a brawl. I've never seen Paige like that."

"Maybe there's a reason for that."

"I know. People show you what they want you to see." I'd heard this lecture before. I glanced at the television, where Jimmy Rollins had just launched a fastball into the right field stands. Not all that impressive, since Citizens Bank Park was the size of a shoebox. "It was just so out of context to find her there. And by the way, she didn't deny it." I hesitated. "Did you know they walk people around on leashes in that place?"

He dipped another chip, laughing. A teardrop of salsa splattered onto the coffee table. "That sophistication's what I love about you."

Blood rushed to my face. "Don't make fun of me. I suppose you see that sort of thing all the time, but it's kind of rare in a law office."

Curt grinned. "You mean to tell me Heath never went to a sex club?"

"Not only did he go," I said, "he slept with Paige while he was there." Or maybe she tap-danced on his back in those heels, for all I knew. In truth, I still wasn't sure what went on in the Black Orchid. I knew it involved dungeons and leashes and leather, but I didn't know if it involved actual sex. These were the suburbs, after all. "The point is," I added, "they were together at the Black Orchid. I can't see Hilary green-lighting that."

Curt put down his beer bottle. "Maybe they had an open marriage. After all, they were both on a first-name basis at the Black Orchid."

He had a point. We were hardly talking about the Huxtables here. "Then there's Howard," I said. "His father is a doctor. And Wally has a degree in chemistry." I chewed a chip, thinking. "Oh, and Janice is probably embezzling from the firm. I heard her lying about—"

"New computers," he said. "You already told me."

I sat back, deflated. "You don't care."

"It's not that I don't care," he said. "It's that the more you learn, the less you know."

"And you have a short attention span," I said.

He grinned. "That, too. Look, why don't you just leave that place? You don't seem to have much in common with your co-workers."

"Is that a job requirement?" I snapped. Another addition to my pet peeves list: being told what to do. "What about your co-workers? The ones with wives and families? You don't seem to have much in common with them."

"Hey," he said, alarmed. "Don't take it so personally. I just don't want you to—"

"Have a brain of my own? Sorry to disappoint you."

"Get yourself killed," he said. "Is what I was going to say. Murder isn't a game, Jamie. The bad guys don't want to get caught. Usually they'll do what it takes to avoid it."

My lips snapped shut. I might be testy but I wasn't stupid. I glanced at the TV, where the Phils fans were standing for the seventh inning stretch, happy with a 7-2 lead and bellies full of overpriced beer.

"And here you are," Curt said, "holding hands with Hilary Heath—very publicly, I might add—with no thought to the position you might be putting yourself in. Not to mention, last time I looked, your resume said 'legal secretary,' not 'homicide detective.'"

That showed how much he knew. I didn't even have a resume. I shoved a tortilla chip in my mouth, chewed violently, and didn't bother to swallow before I asked, "Are you done?"

"Just one more thing." He ignored my admittedly juvenile display. "Don't make me say this again."

I accidentally knocked the bag of chips on the rug when I jumped up and stormed out of there, spilling salt and spiky shards of tortilla everywhere. Served him right. He had a boatload of nerve for someone not even involved in the investigation himself. I knew the Black Orchid was a bad idea. I knew Hilary Heath was bad news. I knew you didn't pull a tiger's tail. But no one seemed to understand the suffocating daily stress of looking into co-workers' eyes knowing one of them was capable of murder. Of all people, I'd have expected Curt to understand how that felt.

I stomped up the stairs and slammed into my apartment, reeling with anger. If that was what marriage felt like, then Sherri could have it.

* * *

By the time I'd showered and changed into dry clothes, I was marginally calmer. At least I was able to consider that Curt's motives might be pure; he didn't want to see a friend get hurt. A small, mean part of me also thought he didn't want to lose his rent stream. I clung to that part a little longer. I'm the stubborn type.

The phone rang while I was towel-drying my hair. "Jamie." It was my mother. "I just wanted to let you know, they're taking applications at Bertelli's Beauty School, over on Station Road. My friend Gladys told me her daughter graduated from there and is making six figures now."

I was making six figures, too, if you counted the ones that came after the decimal point.

"Of course, Estelle works in New York," my mother was saying. "I don't expect you to work in New York. They're crazies up there. But there are some perfectly good salons closer to home."

"I don't want to cut hair, Mom." I tossed the damp towel on the recliner.

"You don't have to cut hair. You could do nails."

That was worse than cutting hair.

"Or be a colorist," she said. "Those Hollywood colorists make all kinds of money."

From New York to Hollywood in five seconds. "I have to go," I said. "Tell Dad I said hi."

"Oh, your father." She sucked in a breath. "I almost forgot to tell you, he had a little stomach trouble today. We had to go to see Dr. Hurley."

I blinked. "Is he alright?"

"Oh, he's fine. The doctor said it's acid. He gave him some pills to keep it under control, but you know your father. He acts like it'd kill him to take an aspirin for a migraine. Men just don't believe in doctoring, do they?"

I hung up the phone with my mind spinning in a new direction. Suddenly I knew where to go next. My father might not believe in doctoring, but I knew another man who did.

CHAPTER THIRTY-SEVEN

I went home for lunch on Wednesday, mainly because I wanted some privacy. Since Dougie's death, it seemed like the office had a turnstile instead of a door. Dougie's latest commercial was still running and was bringing in both legitimate cases and nut jobs who'd heard of his passing and wanted to see the scene of the crime.

Howard was taking the opposite approach. His eagerness to erase every trace of Dougie from the office, including the firm name, gnawed at me. It almost seemed like guilt was provoking his overreaction.

I scrounged together a BLT without the bacon and ate it while I flipped through the Yellowbook. Howard Dennis, M.D. was listed under Psychiatrists, which surprised me a little. I'd expected Howard's father to be a neurosurgeon or a cardiologist, something more in keeping with the Dennis ego. I dialed the listed number and took a deep breath.

It was answered on the third ring by a crisply efficient woman. "Dr. Dennis's office."

"Yes, hello." My eyes shifted to the window. "My name is Sandy Kershaw, and I'd like to make an appointment with the doctor for sometime this week, if possible." I'd scripted this as carefully as possible. Sandy Kershaw was a hapless wretch of a woman, on her own from a young age, living on the streets, and using recreational drugs like Spanish fly to escape her miserable existence whenever money and opportunity allowed. I'd watched *Diary of a Teenaged Prostitute* twice to prepare. The thought of actually meeting Howard's father terrified me, but I didn't see any other way to explore the possibility that he'd inadvertently given Howard access to Spanish fly. His response to Sandy

Kershaw, if I played my role convincingly, should tell me what I needed to know.

Clearly I was fresh out of good ideas. Not that this was a good one. I'd have to pay for this burst of brilliance.

"I'm sorry, Dr. Dennis is not holding office hours at present," the woman said. "The practice is closed indefinitely."

I blinked. "Oh, I'm sorry. I've heard so many good things about him. Was he in some sort of accident?"

There was a moment of silence. "What is your name again?"

Outside, the buzz of a lawn mower suddenly broke the neighborhood silence. "Sandy," I said. "Sandy Kershaw."

"Dr. Dennis had a stroke six months ago, Miss Kershaw. We're not sure when he'll be able to resume his practice."

Six months, and he was still unable to resume working. So it wasn't possible that Dr. Dennis had aided and abetted in Dougie's death. My relief was tempered by sympathy for the man. I might be mildly dishonest but I wasn't heartless. "Please tell him I wish him a full recovery," I told her.

"Thank you. I'd be happy to refer you to a colleague of his if—"

"No, thank you. I've changed my mind." I hung up before I could change it again. Stupidity had been averted, at least for now.

* * *

It was a day of surprises. There were no clients waiting when I returned from lunch, but there were boxes. Lots of them. Big ones, small ones, stacked two high, stretching across the floor and blocking access to the desks. Janice was there, flushed and pleased. So were Paige and Missy, looking less pleased.

I inched as far as I could into the room. "What's all this?

Janice beamed at me. "New computers!"

"Can you believe it," Paige said dryly.

Janice ignored her. "Yours is over there, Jamie. I'll help you set it up." She climbed over a medium-sized box, as close to bubbly as I'd ever seen her. I stared after her in disbelief. There was a new computer system. Janice hadn't been lying. She hadn't been embezzling. Dougie couldn't have threatened to expose her.

Janice was in the clear.

"They're coming in to train us on the new software," Janice said over her shoulder. "So we have to get these things set up. We'd have had more time, but they couldn't get them built when I wanted them."

That explained a lot, including her conversation with Art.

"Not my job description." Paige stretched across some boxes to snatch her purse off her desk. "I'm going to lunch. I'll probably be late. I have an audition."

Janice whipped around to glare at her. "You'll be docked."

Paige shrugged. "Whatever. I don't plan to be here much longer anyway."

"Suit yourself." Janice turned back to the boxes. "There's 24 inch monitors!" she yelled after her, but Paige was gone.

Missy rolled her eyes. "Don't mind her. She's hot on this career change of hers."

Visions of the Black Orchid came immediately to mind, followed by visions of an office without Paige's surliness. Nice. I turned to Missy. "Audition?"

She shook her head. "Our Paige is going Hollywood. She thinks she wants to become an actress."

Janice snorted. "Yeah. That'll work."

I was thinking it might. Paige had played the role of inept secretary well enough to fool everyone at Parker, Dennis, and Heath. If I hadn't seen her in action at the Black Orchid, I'd be one of the people believing her biggest aspiration was to own the latest lipstick shades.

"Come on, guys." Janice was struggling with a block of packing Styrofoam. "Help me set up Jamie's new computer. We can worry about Paige later."

Not me. I'd be too busy worrying about my shrinking list of suspects.

CHAPTER THIRTY-EIGHT

———

A soft rain started falling late in the afternoon, and by dinnertime, thunder was rattling the windows, and the soft rain had become a downpour. I heated a can of soup for dinner and ate it in front of the news, not paying much attention to the stream of daily mayhem. A long empty night stretched ahead of me, and it didn't seem like a good idea to be alone with my mind. On the one hand, I was relieved that Janice's computers had arrived and thrilled that Paige might be leaving. On the other, every suspect crossed off my spreadsheet only managed to cause more confusion. Probably I should follow Paige's example and look for other work and forget about Parker, Dennis.

Except I thought someone should care enough about Dougie to find out who had prematurely retired him. Someone who knew and cared about him. Or at least knew him.

I rinsed out my dishes, stacked them on the sideboard, dried my hands, and decided I'd had enough solitude. Twenty minutes later, I pulled into my parents' driveway and shut off the engine. Sherri's car was gone, which was no surprise. Unfortunately, it was Sherri I'd hoped to see. Ken's barbecue was edging closer, and I had no idea how to strike up a real conversation with the lawyers, outside of the context of work. I was relying on my sister to lay out a strategy for me.

My mother was waiting at the door. She reached for my umbrella before I had both feet inside. "Here, give me this. You're soaking wet. Have you eaten dinner?"

"I had soup," I said while she hustled off to deposit my umbrella in the bathtub. She came back shaking her head. "Soup's not dinner. You need some real food. Come with me."

I followed her to the kitchen and sat at the table, watching her gather dishes from the cabinet and plastic-wrapped bowls from the refrigerator and utensils from the drawer. After a little chopping and slicing and microwaving, she was sliding a steaming plateful of roast chicken in front of me. "Eat."

I didn't think I was all that hungry, but before I knew it, my pile of corn niblets had disappeared along with my dinner roll and half my baked potato.

"So." She leaned forward on her forearms. "Gladys picked up an application for you from Bertelli's."

I would have protested, but my mouth was full of baked potato.

"I tore it up and threw it in the trash."

I stopped chewing.

She shrugged. "Estelle's only getting herself into trouble up in New York, and Hollywood is no place for a young woman on her own."

I wondered who had gotten to her. It certainly hadn't been me.

"You'll get yourself another job," she said, managing not to sound too fatalistic about it. "When you're good and ready."

She reached for my bread plate. I put my hand over hers and looked at her hard. "Thank you."

She flushed and nodded. I let it go at that. I cut into the chicken breast. "So where's Dad?"

My mother tipped her chin upward. "Upstairs, trying on some old clothes. I told him he should buy a new wardrobe, but he claims the one he has is perfectly serviceable, and he means to prove it." She snorted softly. "You should see the socks I have to darn. Serviceable." I grinned. "At least he wears clean underwear," she said.

I stopped grinning. Too much information.

Footsteps pounded through the living room, and my father burst into the kitchen wearing a navy pinstriped suit of indeterminate vintage. "Have a look at this, Muth." He stopped cold when he saw me, his face reddening. "Oh, honey. I didn't know you were here. Glass of wine?"

"No thanks," I said automatically. I nodded at the suit. "Sharp," I said, and it would have been, thirty years ago. Now, the seat of the pants was shiny. The waistband was hidden beneath the swell of his belly, and his wrist bones jutted from the sleeves of the jacket. He looked pathetic and endearing at the same time, and seeing my mother's expression made me wish I had a man just like him.

Her fingers drifted down his lapels and lifted his tie, a broad swath of blinding yellow and black checkerboard. "It looks ridiculous, Al," she said fondly. "And what's this?" Her hand stopped at mid-tie, and my father wrapped his fingers around hers on his chest. "It's the tie tack you gave me on our first anniversary. Don't you remember?"

"That ugly thing," my mother said, flushing. "I can't believe you still have that. It's so out of style." She glanced my way. "He uses an old earring back to hold it together, you know. The original clasp fell apart a month after I gave it to him."

"I think it's great you still have it," I said, thinking Sherri knew what she was doing when she left and wondering if I should follow suit. The thunder had slackened but the rain was still falling, and the soothing sound together with the scent of good food made the house a cozy love shack.

"You look like an old gangster in that getup," my mother told him. "Go take it off."

"I could use some help," my father said, leering at her, and that brought me to my feet. "I should be going. I'll just, uh, leave Sherri a note..." I fumbled in my handbag for a pen and scrap of paper, scribbled something, and slammed the pepper shaker on top of it to hold it in place. "Thanks for dinner," I called over my shoulder, but I don't think either one of them heard me. They were too busy playing with my father's tie tack.

On the drive home, I didn't know whether to laugh or cry.

* * *

Curt still wasn't home, which made me wonder if he'd had an out-of-state delivery. I parked at the head of the driveway, leaving plenty of room for his Cherokee, and took the stairs to my apartment two at a time, feeling curiously light despite my full belly. I spent fifteen minutes straightening up and another ten flicking through game shows and cable news channels and year-old movies before I gave up and decided to unwind with some yoga.

I was barefoot and curled into child's pose when someone knocked on my door. Pulling myself upright, I brushed the hair from my face with a frown. Since Curt wasn't home and Sherri didn't seem to be working too hard on my barbecue cheat sheet, my roster of potential visitors was limited.

But not limited enough. It was Hilary Heath dripping on my landing in a classic Burberry raincoat, flat shoes, and Gucci handbag.

"I, um..." I meant to say. "I'm on my way out," but I was standing there barefoot and probably couldn't have pulled that off.

"I'm not happy about this, either." She followed me into the kitchen. I was determined not to let her near my bed; last time that had happened, I hadn't been able to sleep right for two nights. "I'll make it quick."

"A phone call would've been quick," I said.

She dropped her handbag on my stack of mail and a dark stain blossomed on my phone bill. "Forget about Paige."

"Done," I said, handing her purse to her. "Good-night."

"I'm serious." She took it and set it down on my newspaper. "I know Paige didn't kill my Doug."

That got my attention. "You do."

She nodded. "So I'm sorry for the misdirection. Innocent mistake." She cocked her head, looking at me. "You look different tonight."

"So do you," I said nastily.

"Oh. That." She didn't bother to look embarrassed. "I wouldn't expect you to understand a place like the Black Orchid. People like you aren't meant for that world."

People like me. I took her by the elbow. "I think you should be going. I'm in the middle of something."

"I didn't mean it as an insult," she said.

"Sure you did." I opened the door for her. "Good-night."

She turned and looked at me with her strange viper eyes. "So this means you're going to reconsider Missy, right?"

I blinked. "Missy?"

"Don't you see? If it wasn't Paige, it had to be Missy."

"What about Howard?"

She waved an impatient hand. "I know the lineup. It wasn't any of those people. It was Missy. You'll see." She stepped out onto the landing. I noticed the rain had stopped. It was probably afraid to fall on her. "We'll talk later," she said. "I think I'll have an offer for you that you won't want to refuse."

What she lacked in originality, she made up for in shock value. I couldn't imagine what that offer might be, but I had no intention of accepting it.

CHAPTER THIRTY-NINE

———

I reconsidered that intention around ten-thirty the next morning when I was confronted by Theodore Faulk, the new client most likely to become the next Adam Tiddle. I was trying to clear a week of Wally's calendar due to an impending trial when a sheaf of papers dropped onto my desk. "These are all wrong." Theodore was standing in front of me with his lips pursed and his face pinched. He looked like a drawstring bag with the string pulled too tight. "Wally told me you typed these. You made a lot of mistakes. I don't appreciate that."

Suppressing a sigh, I flipped through the pages. "But you came in last week to meet with Wally to answer these." No typos that I could see. "If the answers are incorrect, you should take it up with Wally."

He snorted. "You legal people, you're all alike. Always passing the buck."

"I don't amend the content, sir," I said. "I only type what you and Wally have written."

"But I didn't write this." He jammed his hands in his pockets. "I said I didn't see the stop sign. You people said I saw it but my brakes failed. That's not true."

Oh.

"The lawyer said something about suing my mechanic." His shoulders lifted and fell. "I don't want to sue my mechanic. He didn't do anything wrong. My brakes were fine. I just didn't see the stop sign." His cheeks reddened. "I was looking at a girl on the sidewalk."

Geez. This guy had come to the wrong law firm. Parker, Dennis never expected their clients to be completely truthful, and they were rarely disappointed.

"Mr. Faulk." Missy appeared at his elbow. "Tell you what, let's go see if Wally's free right now. I'm sure he'd like to know about this." Her eyes slid to mine as she guided him into a turn toward the stairs. I mouthed, "Thank you," and headed into the kitchen for my midmorning sugar reinforcement.

What I got was a shock. My sister and Ken Parker were cozied up together at the kitchen table, her hand resting on his forearm, her brown head close to his white one as if she'd been whispering in his ear. Maybe she had; he was blushing like a frat boy. Both were ignoring their cups of coffee and the open box of doughnuts on the table. I hadn't even known she was there, and she'd managed to hone in on the senior partner. Maybe she did have a working plan after all. Still, the entire scene was so surreal it knocked me into autopilot, heading straight to the doughnuts. I nodded at Ken, but I don't think he noticed. "When did you get here?" I asked Sherri through a chocolate glazed.

She shrugged and gave me a tight little smile "A few minutes ago. I thought I'd stop by since I missed you last night. I went to the movies." She looked at Ken. "Do you like the movies, Kenny?"

Ken nodded mutely, watching her like a dog watches a T-bone.

"Shouldn't you be at the store?" I asked. I didn't like what I was seeing. Actually, I wasn't *sure* what I was seeing. But I was sure I didn't like it. I reached for the doughnut box. Something flickered across Ken's face, and I pulled my hand back. Guess Sherri's misbehavior was the only thing he was willing to overlook.

"I took the day off." She winked at Ken. "Do you ever feel like taking the day off and just staying in bed, Kenny?"

Ken's head bobbed up and down. I tried to block the image of him in bed all day, with my sister or anyone else. It was like picturing Santa Claus in his birthday suit. "I need to talk to you," I said to her. "There've been some developments."

She squeezed Ken's arm. "You don't mind, do you, Kenny? I'm sure a man like you understands about important business."

He kept on smiling while I dragged my sister into the hall. It was a little scary. She'd rendered one of the most eloquen trial lawyers in the county speechless. "What the hell do you think you're doing?" I hissed. "He's married." I glanced over my shoulder, lowering my voice. "And sixty-eight."

She sighed. "You don't get it, do you? I'm practicing what I preach."

I blinked. "Huh?"

"You're a woman, Jamie. Don't you know how much power you have? An arm pat here, a whisper there, and before you know it they're handing over the keys to their vacation house." She shook her head. "Men are so easy."

"I will not flirt with my boss," I said. "There must be a better way."

"If there is, I haven't found it." She patted my shoulder. "I was trying to lead by example, but I can see I'm wasting my time. And after I went and typed everything out for you." She pulled a sheet of paper from her handbag and thrust it into my hands. I unfolded it and stared at the single word typed dead center in boldface 24 point print: FLIRT.

"No way." I crumpled it and shoved it in my pocket. "If that's the best you've got—"

"It's not the best," she said. "But it's damned good. It got me invited to the barbecue."

That stopped me in mid-rant. "You did not." She only smiled serenely, and I gave her arm a smack. "You can't go! Everyone will want to know what you're doing there. Including his wife."

"Relax." She rubbed her arm. "I have no intention of going. These people are too weird for me. I just want you to realize what you can do with a little—"

"Fondling?"

"Okay." She frowned. "Make fun of me, but it's the right formula. You'll see."

Maybe I would, and maybe I wouldn't, but I didn't have time to debate it. My break was almost over, and the phones were ringing. "Let me tell you." I pulled her to the end of the hallway as Paige walked past. She looked Sherri over, assessing the threat level, and evidently saw none, because she veered left into the kitchen. "Janice's computers came," I told her, speaking low and fast.

Her eyes lit up. She got it. "Microsoft 7?"

Maybe she didn't get it. "Not the point. The point is—"

"I was just wondering," Sherri said. "Might as well get the best, right? So she did buy them after all. How do you like that?"

"That's not all," I said. "Howard's father is a doctor. A psychiatrist. I tried to get an appointment with him—"

"Mom would be proud," she said.

I ignored that. "But he's recovering from a stroke, and the office is closed for now."

"Meaning it wasn't Janice, and it probably wasn't Howard." Sherri tapped her front teeth, thinking. "What about Wally?"

"I haven't ruled him out."

"No, I mean what about Wally? Is he free or is he dating someone?"

I rolled my eyes. "You are not dating Wally Randall. He's only a step above Frankie."

"Say what you want about Frankie," she said, "but he never killed anyone." She glanced at her watch. "Look, I can't hang around here all day. I've got things to do."

"Shopping?"

She flashed a smile. "Of course. Need anything?"

"A bathing suit for the barbecue." I didn't have the stomach to step into a fitting room while my body resembled a tube of Play-Doh.

Sherri was unfazed. "You got it. Hot pink thong?"

"One piece, black."

She sighed. "You really need some drama in your life."

"Are you kidding?" I said. "I've got all the drama I can handle. Look where I work."

* * *

Sherri stopped over later that night with a Macy's bag. "Size six," she said, tossing it to me.

"Did you get anything for yourself?" I peeked into the bag. Plain black and yes, one piece, proving that Sherri did occasionally pay attention when I opened my mouth.

"Yes. A new outlook." She followed me into the living room, grimacing at the Phillies game on TV. "Maybe I'll go to the barbecue after all."

I hit Mute. "Ken's married."

"I know." She grinned. "But Wally's not."

"Sher—"

"I'm keeping Frankie's ring. Just so you know."

"Okay," I said.

Her shoulders lifted and fell. "It's just that sometimes I think it'll never happen for me. I want it to happen for me."

Touched, I put my hand on her forearm.

"I mean, Wally's got to have decent sperm, right?"

I pulled my hand back. "Please," I said. "Please." I hardly knew where to go from there. Please don't go to the barbecue? Please don't take up with the Boy Lawyer? Please don't put pictures in my head that only Valium can remove?

"I don't know." She sighed hugely. "Maybe I'll just go home and watch Lifetime."

"Better idea," I said.

"Mention me to Wally," she said. "Tell him all about me. Will you tell him all about me?"

"Down to your bra size," I assured her.

"Okay." She smiled, pleased. "You're a good sister, Jamie. You know you'll be my maid of honor when it finally happens for me."

"I'm busy that day," I said.

CHAPTER FORTY

On Friday morning, I was sitting bleary-eyed in my car jabbing my key at the ignition when Curt knocked on the roof and leaned into the open window. "Got a minute?"

Clearly he'd just gotten back from his run. He was wearing a T-shirt and shorts with a towel slung around his neck. He looked like every item on the dessert menu wrapped in black cotton. I had more than a minute for a man who looked like that. I had a lifetime.

He opened the door and slid into the passenger seat on a faint musky breeze. His eyes seemed dull and tired, and tiny lines stitched his lips tighter than normal. "Found out a little something about your friend Hilary."

I lifted my gaze from his shorts and opened my mouth to say "She's not my friend" but something stopped me. Probably the gravity of his expression. In an instant I could tell he'd talked to his brother. In all the years I'd known him, Curt had never discussed Cam's work with me. Our relationship had always been easy and our conversations light. That seemed about to change.

"She's got herself a new career," he said. I switched on the air and rolled the windows up, although I already had a chill. "She's making movies. The kind you don't show the kiddies on rainy days."

I stared at him. "Porn?" He nodded. "Hilary Heath is making porn movies," I repeated, in case I'd heard him wrong, o he'd said it wrong, or the earth had skidded off its axis when I wasn't paying attention. "That makes no sense."

"Turns out Heath didn't leave her with a whole hell of a lot in the way of financial security."

I thought instantly of Janice and her claim that Dougie had lost his last few trials.

"But porn," I said. "I just can't see Hilary Heath in an X-rated movie."

"You won't." He ran the towel over his chest. A rush of heat hit me. I ratcheted the air up a little higher. "She's playing director. And producer. And she's recruiting, so you're not allowed to play in her sandbox anymore."

"Recruiting."

"Shopping for talent. Such as it is."

I couldn't help but wonder how much talent Curt possessed. I sat up straighter, wondering what was wrong with me. Two minutes ago I'd been in a fog from the July heat. Now I was wide-awake and just plain hot. "Wait a minute," I said. "Paige left early two days ago for an audition. You don't think—"

"Sure I do," he said. "Those Black Orchid girls aren't exactly known for their shyness."

The thought of Paige and Hilary as a team was more shocking than the thought of Sherri and Ken as a couple. But in a twisted way, it made sense. Both moved in the same world. They had a common denominator in Dougie. They hated each other but loved money. It was inevitable that sex would bring them together.

Curt reached for the door handle. "I'm gonna go shower up. You'd better get to work."

I'd have rather watched him shower up, but I settled for watching him cross in front of the car and let himself into the house.

Suddenly I no longer felt up to facing the parade of demanding clients at the office, let alone the people who worked there. It seemed I didn't really know anyone. Not that I'd held an angelic image of Hilary Heath, but her descent into porn was still surprising. Paige's participation was less shocking. For her, it probably represented a lateral promotion.

I backed down the driveway, my mind buzzing. Now the man on the second floor of Hilary's house made even more sense. He was probably an actor, auditioning for one of her films. Did she use her own house as her studio, her own bedroom as her sound stage? And who operated the camera? I eased the car to a stop at a red light as another thought struck me. Hilary had said she had an offer for me. What was it Curt had told me? She was *recruiting.* Maybe I was being recruited. But for what? I wasn't much of an actress. I didn't have the memory for dialogue and I didn't have the body for porn.

My thoughts shifted to Dougie and I wondered if he'd known of his wife's aspirations. Maybe she hadn't even known of them when he was alive. Need, financial or otherwise, often drove people to do desperate things. I hoped she at least got her daughters out of the house before the camera rolled. They'd already lost their father; they deserved better from their mother.

Playing hooky hadn't been on my conscious agenda, but before I knew it, my car turned away from Parker, Dennis and stopped in front of Leonetti's Bakery, where I bought a bag of sesame bagels and a tub of strawberry cream cheese before heading for Voyager Park. I had some thinking to do. If it got me fired, I didn't think I'd be worse off for it.

I found an empty bench under some maple trees near the children's playground and spent the next hour eating bagels with cream cheese and watching children play. Tomorrow was Ken's barbecue. I had the bathing suit and Sherri's dubious directive for extracting information from the lawyers and absolutely no desire to attend. But as long as I was part of the office, there was no graceful way out of it. I'd just have to consider it a favor to Ken; I still adored him, even if he'd let my sister run roughshod over his dignity.

Thinking about all of it made my head hurt. I spread cream cheese on the last bagel, took a bite, and let my mind shift to Curt. That made me a lot happier. The man was something of a mystery to me, and I'd always liked a good mystery. Especially when it came wrapped in black running shorts with legs like his. Before that good-night kiss, I hadn't realized Curt *had* legs. Since then, my gears hadn't been meshing quite right when it came to him. This morning I'd realized it was because they needed a good oiling.

The bagel bag was empty. I crumpled it into a ball and gathered up my plastic knife and tub of cream cheese and deposited all of it into a nearby waste can. I hadn't done much thinking, and I'd found no answers, but I finally felt strong enough to go to work.

CHAPTER FORTY-ONE

————

Ken's estate took up almost five acres of prime landfill-free real estate that might otherwise have been developed into yet another Jersey strip mall. He'd managed to build it miles away from civilization as I knew it. Without traffic lights and stop signs to guide me, I took three wrong turns before finding the access road that served as his driveway. There, a brook babbled along beside me for a distance before veering off to chase shadows into the woods. That struck me as a better use of the day than attending the barbecue, but I kept driving anyway. Eventually the driveway curled into a giant U shape in front of the house, which was huge and white and columned, squatting on a gentle grassy slope. Climbing out of my car, I could see red painted stables behind the house. The faint smell of horses and freshly cut grass and old money wafted toward me on the summer breeze. Nice place to come home to.

Six other cars were parked at various points along the U in apparent order of worth. The lawyers' BMWs were closest to the house. I indulged myself in a quick peek as I passed by. A tennis racquet and tennis balls and black trial bag in Wally's back seat. Bottled water in Howard's cup holder, a few unopened envelopes on the passenger seat. Like their owners, there was nothing interesting there.

Behind the house, a lush green backyard stretched the length of a football field, interrupted at roughly the thirty-yard line by an enormous in-ground pool. Janice and Donna were huddled together under a giant striped umbrella at a poolside table. Missy was sunning herself in a hot pink bikini on a bilious green float. In accordance with the office hierarchy, the lawyers were keeping their own exclusive company on the overstuffed patio furniture, close to the food and drink.

The grill was already smoking, and Wally was at the helm with a giant spatula in one hand, a bottle of barbecue sauce in the other. He didn't look too happy to be there. The apron clashed with his J. Crew ensemble, and his perfectly arranged hair had been steamed into flatness, making him look about fifteen. All he needed was the acne.

Which was where Paige came in. More accurately, Paige's chin zit, which entered my line of sight a few seconds before the rest of her. She'd dabbed and painted and powdered, but not even Maybelline could conceal Mt. Everest. She was slouched miserably on a lounger off to the side, tilting her unsmiling face up toward the sun, but it was going to take more than some UV rays to solve her problems. It was probably the stress from her new profession. Served her right.

"Jamie." Ken bent to kiss my cheek. He looked wonderful in white slacks and a navy shirt and loafers. "Thank you for coming. Did you have any trouble finding the place?"

I shook my head. "You're very lucky to have this much property. It's beautiful."

"Eleanor needed it for her horses. Do you ride?"

"Once," I said. "When I was twelve. I fell off."

He smiled, showing chemically whitened teeth. "Well, if you want to get back on the horse, my groom will be happy to saddle up Silver Coin for you. Until then, there's plenty to eat." He gestured to the buffet table set up just outside a beautiful set of French doors. "Help yourself."

Wedding receptions had nothing on Ken's buffet table. Cakes, cookies, and condiments of all sorts rubbed elbows with pasta salad, potato salad, fruit salad, and plain old garden salad. Wine, soda, beer, and bottled water sat on a smaller table to the side. I could eat for a month from the buffet table alone, and better than I normally did left to my own devices.

Wally came over to retrieve the barbecue sauce. "I'll take a breast," I told him.

"You could use it," he muttered, proving that team spirit was a myth.

So much for my new eighty-dollar bathing suit making an appearance. I bypassed the low-cal fruit salad and loaded a plate with pepperoni slices and cheese squares and potato salad instead.

"So I had to tell her we couldn't handle her case," Howard was telling Ken when I rejoined them. "It's a pity. What a beautiful woman."

They must be talking about Victoria Plackett, Dougie's pet client. I perched on the edge of a lounger, the plate on my lap, to nibble and eavesdrop.

"That's just one example," Ken said. "He also brought in Angelo Fasini, remember?"

Howard snorted. "His only million dollar verdict. Fasini was a daisy growing in a field of crap."

This was beginning to sound like Dougie bashing, and I didn't like it. At least Ken seemed to be standing up for his dearly departed partner. "The truth is," he said, "I owe a few of my golden years to Douglas. The wife and I will retire very comfortably thanks to him."

"You've got to be kidding." Howard wiped barbecue sauce off his fingers onto a wad of napkins. "He accepted a broken shoe case."

"Don't forget that Tiddle creep." Wally waved a plate loaded with barbecued chicken breasts in front of them. "He belonged to Doug, too. I'm still trying to figure out how to deal with him."

"Try being honest," I said. Wally gave me a look that said no chicken would be coming my way for a very long time. Gee, I'd been lucky to win him in the secretarial lottery.

"Nonetheless," Ken said, unruffled. "When I leave the practice on January first, it will be with fond memories of Douglas." His smile wobbled. "Mostly."

I sat up straighter, blinking. "Leave the practice?"

Ken nodded. "I'm sixty-seven years old. The law practice is for younger men."

Wally thrust out his chest and preened.

"It's also for gentlemen," I said, ignoring the Boy Lawyer's evil stare. "The office won't be the same without you."

He patted my hand. "That's kind of you to say."

It was more than kind; it was true. I wasn't sure I could work at Parker, Dennis without Ken Parker. His leaving could only mean Wally was ripe for partnership. The very notion of Dennis and Randall was repulsive enough to make me start compiling my resume.

Janice stormed over to grab a piece of chicken before plundering the buffet table. Donna followed in her wake, letting Wally pawn off the smallest piece. Missy climbed out of the pool, dried herself with exhibitionistic slowness, wrung out her hair, and joined the circle, which by now included everyone but Paige, who hadn't moved. I was beginning to think she was unconscious.

"How'd Doug get a law degree anyway?" Wally apparently had no compunction against speaking ill of the dead.

"I heard it was mail order," Howard said with a snicker. Emily Post wouldn't have been too proud of him, either.

"What made you want to become an attorney?" Ken asked Wally. "Too much jury duty?"

Wally chuckled politely. "I wanted to have a positive impact on peoples' lives." He sounded like he was reading off a Teleprompter. "I wanted to help the aggrieved find justice." He glanced at Howard, who tipped his head meaningfully toward Ken, and Wally said dutifully, "How about you, Ken?"

"I wanted to make a lot of money," Ken said.

"I wanted to become a lawyer." Donna's voice was almost lost in the laughter. "I've always loved the law. My father was a police officer. I—"

"You don't have enough charisma," Wally told her. "You'd never keep a jury's attention."

Donna sat back, red-faced.

Maybe it was the wanton denial of the chicken or his general pomposity, but I couldn't stand for that. "Hey," I began.

And Janice went on the attack, beating me to it. "That's a hell of a thing to say to her. Who do you think you are?"

Wally flushed. His Adam's apple jumped. Sweat would have beaded on his upper lip if he'd had one. It was all I could do not to cheer. Even Paige turned her head and opened one eye.

"If she wants to be a lawyer," Janice said, snapping off each word, "she should be a lawyer."

"Agreed. Agreed." Wally held both hands up in surrender. "Donna's a bright kid. She should go to law school if she wants to."

"Damn right she should," Janice snapped. "She'd be a hell of a lawyer."

"I'm sure she would," Wally said, eager to placate.

I grinned, happy now that I had a blueprint for dealing with Wally: unrestrained aggression.

"How about you?" I asked her, to diffuse the situation. "Did you always want to be a bookkeeper?"

"Hell, no." She took a long drink of lemonade. "Who in their right mind would want to crunch numbers all day long?"

"She wanted to be a veterinarian," Ken said. Janice glanced at him with open surprise. "You said so in your interview," he told her. "In fact, didn't you go to vet school for six months?"

When I got home, I had to cross Ken off my list of suspects. He really was just an old sweet man. With a frighteningly good memory.

"I did." Janice sounded almost wondering. "But I decided medicine's not for me."

Instantly it occurred to me that maybe medicine wasn't, but poison was. Six months of vet school could have given her enough knowledge to use Spanish fly as a method of murder. I'd never known about Janice's first career choice, and it surprised me. She didn't seem warm enough to work with animals. She hardly seemed warm enough to work with ledger sheets. I'd never felt completely comfortable with Janice. Of course, she'd been telling the truth about the computers, and I didn't feel comfortable around most people.

"The first time I witnessed a euthanasia," Janice was saying, "I cried for three weeks. I decided right then and there I didn't have the stomach for that line of work."

Huh. Cried for three weeks and changed her chosen profession. That didn't sound much like a murderer.

"How about you, Howard?" Wally asked. "I'm surprised you didn't go into practice with your father."

Howard shook his head. "He got my brother Frank. That was good enough for him."

"You're still in one of the big three professions," Missy assured him with a smile and a strategic slip of the towel. I blinked. Was Missy hitting on Howard?

"What about you?" he asked her, smiling right back while he ogled. Sap. "I imagine you probably wanted to be a singer or dancer, something like that."

"Not me," she said, and his smile faltered. "I always wanted to meet a rich man and be a kept woman."

The group fell into stunned silence until Missy giggled. I wasn't convinced she'd been kidding, but I laughed along anyway. Paige had turned her face back to the sky, and Howard's cheeks were pale. But officially, camaraderie had been restored.

"To tell you the truth," Wally said to no one in particular, "my family tried to push me into engineering. You know my brother's a chemical engineer." I nodded along with everyone else, although I hadn't known Wally even had a brother. "That's why I majored in chemistry. But the thought of doing that kind of work for the rest of my life..." He shuddered. I almost felt sorry for him. "So I became a lawyer instead," he finished.

"And your parents disowned you," Ken said with a small smile.

Wally shook his head. "Let's just say they hold a dim view of attorneys in general."

And him in particular was the unspoken completion of that sentence. Now I officially felt sorry for him. Sitting there in his sauce-smeared apron, he looked like a little boy anxious for his parents' approval. Maybe Wally's obnoxiousness was the byproduct of years spent trying to impress his family with his success.

"I'm going to need you for a few hours Monday night," he told me. "I've got to get some things together for the Barrett trial."

"Well, this isn't Monday." Missy reached for my hand. "It's Saturday, and Jamie and I are going swimming." She smiled down at me. "Aren't we?"

"There's no way—" I began, because I'd already planned to bury my swimsuit in Curt's backyard when I got home.

Kelly Rey | 206

"Oh, I almost forgot." Wally pulled something out of his pocket. "I found this under the kitchen table last week. You're always so well dressed—I knew it must be yours."

Ken shook his head. "I don't think so. Perhaps it belongs to Howard."

"It's not mine," Howard said, slipping an uncertain glance toward Missy, who'd already given up on swimming, covered back up, and was munching on a slice of watermelon.

I craned my neck to see. It was a beautiful mother-of-pearl tie tack, the sort of accessory a lawyer would wear to impress a client or a jury or a mistress. Ken wore them all the time. Howard and Wally never did; they relied on their purported dazzling legal minds and their BMWs to impress the masses. Apparently tie tacks were becoming yet another symbol of the death of gentility. The thought gave me a twinge of nostalgic sadness, thinking of my father in his worn-out suit, showing such pride in the tie tack my mother had given him years ago. But it wasn't just the tie tacks. It was Dougie's death, Ken's retirement, Paige and Hilary's new hobby, Sherri's futile husband search, my own unrequited lust for Curt's legs.

I cracked open a beer. If I was having any more fun, I'd have to start taking antidepressants.

CHAPTER FORTY-TWO

———

"It was death," I told Curt on Sunday night. We were sitting on his deck watching fireflies play hide and seek in the yard. Rain was in the forecast, and the air was heavy with humidity. Curt was milking a bottle of beer. I was ignoring a Coke. Ken's barbecue was a day behind me, and my depression was still rampant, weighing down every cell in my body. Guess I wasn't adapting well to all the changes taking place. I was confused and angered by my inability to win the shell game my colleagues were playing. It was starting to feel like even I'd had motive to kill Dougie. He was certainly demanding more of my attention in death than he ever had in life.

I took a sip of Coke. It scraped down my throat while I stared gloomily into the darkness. "Did I tell you Ken's retiring?"

"Three times."

"The place won't be the same without him."

"Right," he said. "When he goes, that'll leave only the wackos. Present company excluded." He frowned. "I think."

If he was looking for a fight, he'd have to work harder than that. "They're not all wackos," I said. "Missy is—"

"Shopping for a guy who's loaded." Curt looked at me. "Sure you don't want to quit that place?"

I shook my head. "Not unless you're giving me a pass on the rent."

He grinned. "We could work it out in other ways."

Whoa. That kind of thinking was what had kept me up all night. It was a tempting idea, but I didn't think it was a good one. I might not respect myself in the morning.

"You know, there are other jobs out there," he said, talking more to his beer than to me. I watched him, noticing the slump of his shoulders, the hang of his head. It was clear something was bothering him. Maybe the same thing that was bothering me. After four years of regarding Curt as a brother, I was suddenly seeing him as a man with great legs attached to a better body. I didn't have great legs, and no one had ever told me I had a great body, but I was the only female living under his roof and maybe that counted for something.

I shook my bottle of Coke a little to watch it fizz. "I'll leave soon," I said. "I'm just not ready yet."

"When will you be ready?"

I glanced at him. "What is this?"

A firefly lit up beside his head. He swatted it away. "I'm worried about you. I don't want you there until the cops can nail this down. It's hard to believe you're safe."

"Wait a minute." I tried to ignore the shiver than ran through me. "You told me it wasn't random. You said because it was the protein powder—"

"That Dougie was the target." He nodded. "He was. That time. What about next time? What if this is some kind of vendetta against Parker, Dennis, and Heath?"

"If that was the case, I'd have started with Wally." He wasn't smiling. "Come on." I nudged his knee. "You don't really believe someone's out to get the entire office. We've made some people a lot of money over the years."

"And cost some people a lot of money."

"That could be said of any law firm." It was my turn to smirk. "Or brokerage house, for that matter."

"But it's not any law firm we're talking about." He tossed his empty bottle into the recyclables can on the edge of the deck. "It's yours."

I'd thought I was too frustrated to be scared, but that wasn't the case. Thanks to Curt, I had a hefty case of the creeps. It was hard to believe everyone in the office might be targeted, but it was harder to discount the idea when it came from someone like him.

Suddenly I thought of something. "Yesterday, Wally showed everyone a tie tack he had found in the kitchen, and no one knew who it belonged to. But now I have an idea." I shifted to the edge of the chair. "Before he died, Dougie met with a new client named Victoria Plackett. She had a lousy case, but he took it anyway and managed to hit on her at the same time. Her husband found out and threatened to sue the firm."

"I'm listening."

"Howard handled it," I said. "At least he said he did. But diplomacy isn't Howard's strong point, and maybe he didn't handle it as well as he thinks he did." The more I talked, the better it sounded. "I'll bet the tie tack was the husband's. I'll bet he sneaked into the office through the back door, put the poison in Dougie's powder, and was gone without anyone knowing he'd been there. Except he lost his tie tack in the process." I snapped my fingers. "Ronald is his name. Ronald Plackett."

"I'll pass it on to Cam," he said. "But don't get your hopes up. People lose jewelry all the time. Hell, I lost my brother's wedding rings on the way to the church."

"You hate marriage that much, huh?" He stared at me. I put my hands up in surrender. "Kidding. What's going on with you tonight, anyway?"

"Nothing." He straightened then arched his back slightly, stretching. "I've got to work some things out."

I wondered if one of those things was me. He didn't seem as comfortable as usual, and the female in me wanted to take credit for that. The chicken in me said I had nothing to do with his mood. Even if I did, there were still plenty of obstacles. He was a confirmed bachelor. We might not be as compatible in other rooms as we were in the kitchen. Then the relationship would be ruined and I'd have to move, and I didn't want to lose my apartment. It was small, but it was in a safe neighborhood, and it was cheap. I also didn't want to lose our deck time. It was the best relationship I'd had with a man for two years.

Speaking of which. "Sherri broke it off with Frankie Ritter," I told him. Maybe that would cheer him up. I knew it cheered me up.

"Ritter's not so bad," he said, proving that his world was definitely off its axis. He put his beer bottle down and stood up. I had to move fast. I smiled up at him. "How about a tradeoff? Dinner tomorrow night for Ronald Plackett."

He lifted one eyebrow. "What if Plackett's in the clear?"

I grinned. "Then I'll pay."

He scratched his arm, considering. "This kind of offer doesn't come around too often."

"That's how sure I am."

"That's how cheap you are," he said, and grinned.

I grinned back. Suddenly life was good. "There's just one caveat. You'll have to pick me up at the office. Wally's got me working late tomorrow."

"Tomorrow might not be good," he said. "I've got a run to—"

"We'll only be a half hour," I cut in. His eyebrows shot up. "An hour, tops. You've got to eat. Plus you get bragging rights if it turns out that I'm right." And I was pretty sure I was. Either way, at this point, if he'd agree to pick me up at Parker, Dennis, I'd have agreed to tap dance naked on the planks of the deck. In the dead of night, of course. Under a thick cloud cover. "Which I am," I added. "Right, that is."

He shook his head but I saw the glimmer of a smile. "Pretty sure of yourself, Winters."

Regarding Ronald Plackett, I was. When it came to Curt I didn't know what the hell I was doing. I just didn't want him to look that way anymore. Already he seemed more like the Curt I knew. And the Curt I wanted to know better.

"Okay," he said, somehow unaware that I'd just forced my heart out of my throat. "I guess I could handle a taco or two."

"Tacos, hell," I said. "We're going to do it up right. Lincoln Diner or bust." I looked down at my feet. "I'm sure I can borrow the money from someone."

"Christ." He slid his arm around my neck, came in low and fast, and planted a kiss on my mouth that left me tingling all over. "It's a good thing you're cute," he whispered into my hair.

It was also a good thing I was sitting down. Ten minutes after he'd gone inside, I was still staring at the house in weak-kneed shock.

CHAPTER FORTY-THREE

———

I was a bundle of nerves on Monday, and it showed. I broke a coffee mug in the kitchen, dropped an expandable file, put outgoing mail in the wrong envelopes, and punched the wrong telephone buttons cutting off several clients and interrupting others in mid-conversation with the lawyers. By quarter to five, I was disgusted with myself for acting like I'd never had a date before. Not that my dinner with Curt was a real date, more like the payoff on a bet. I'd only worn a new pair of pantyhose in case I had an accident. And my shoes had needed polishing, anyway. My hair needed cutting, too, but I didn't have time for miracles.

I hadn't heard from Curt whether Ronald Plackett had been investigated, but the more I thought about it, the more convinced I was I'd fingered the right man. Thanks to Wally and his tie tack, of course, since my so-called investigation hadn't resolved a thing. But I wasn't letting that ruin my mood. Not when my nerves could do it much more effectively.

"Jamie." Missy punched the *hold* button on her phone and slid the receiver down to rest at her collarbone. "Can you run upstairs and pry Wally and Howard apart? I've got Ronald Plackett on line two, and he's not in a good mood."

"Plackett?" That couldn't be coincidence. Maybe Cam had gotten to him. Maybe he was looking for a criminal defense attorney.

"The ethics complaint," Paige said, evidently thinking I'd forgotten the name.

I started to get up then hesitated. "How can Plackett file an ethics complaint when Dougie's dead?"

"Against the firm," Missy said. "And Ken doesn't need that."

He didn't deserve it, either. "On my way," I said. As I headed upstairs, I thought it very odd that every client of the firm seemed to be dissatisfied with one thing or another. They wanted their lawsuits filed or withdrawn or expedited. They wanted their cases settled or tried or arbitrated immediately. They had no time to appear for deposition or arbitration or independent medical exams, or they demanded that those things be scheduled at once. Plus, Wally was making noise about upgrading his baby Beamer now that he was a tort away from making partner, and he naturally wanted Howard's blessing at the contract signing.

And now Ronald Plackett was on line two.

I knocked on Howard's doorframe and poked my head inside. "Ronald Plackett, line two."

He glared over the top of his half glasses. "You couldn't buzz me?"

Wally popped out from behind the door. "You couldn't buzz him?"

I resisted the urge to flash an obscene sign and thought some obscene thoughts instead. Wasn't quite the same.

"Don't make plans for tonight," Wally added. "Remember I need you to type up some things for me."

"I can stay until seven," I told him. "I have a date tonight."

"That's funny," he said. "That sense of humor will come in handy in life."

Especially working for him. I retreated to my desk and got to work churning out pages for his use at trial. As time wore on, people started leaving for the day, and as the office grew quieter, my nerves grew louder. I'd have to call off dinner. There was no way I was keeping food down when even my hands on the keyboard were shaking.

Finally just Wally and I were the sole survivors, and he'd burrowed into his office with his file while I finished up the typing. I still had a half hour to go before Curt was due to pick me up, and I was right on schedule. Plenty of time to get in my car and flee the scene.

The front door opened, and my fingers froze on the keys. Curt couldn't be early. He was never early for anything. I ran a hand over my hair, huffed into my palm a few times, and sat up straighter, but it wasn't Curt who came into the office. It was Mack Ramsey, immaculate as usual in a gray three-piece suit that was a little too heavy for the season. His hair was slicked neatly against his skull and his wingtips were scuff-free. He looked better than I did, and I was the one dressed for a date.

Not a real date, of course.

"Mr. Ramsey!" I stood and offered him my hand. His skin felt thin and dry and cool. "How are you feeling?"

"Feeling?" His bushy eyebrows drew together in puzzlement, but his eyes remained huge behind his glasses.

"Last time I saw you, you were a little under the weather," I said. "You had to sit down in the kitchen for awhile, remember?"

"Ah, of course, I remember." He gave me a strange smile, as if his upper plate didn't fit quite right. "I'm feeling much better now, thank you."

I nodded. "Good."

He pressed his palms together in prayer fashion. "I wonder if I might speak to Mr. Randall."

"Just a second, I'll buzz him." I thought Howard had taken over Dougie's clients, but it was entirely possible Mr. Ramsey had been pawned off on Wally. Secretaries tended to be either the very first or the very last in the loop. I buzzed Wally's office. While I waited for him to pick up, I said, "Is there something I can help you with?"

"In due time," he said, reaching for the corner of Paige's desk to steady himself.

Wally wasn't picking up. Maybe he was in the bathroom. Or maybe he was busy worshipping at the altar of Howard. I punched a few buttons just for the sake of appearances then gave up. "I'll have to go get him. He isn't in his office." I stood up and came around my desk. "Can I get you something, Mr. Ramsey?"

That strange little smile again. "A protein milkshake would be lovely."

I froze in midstep. "I'm sorry?"

"I believe you heard me."

I believed I had, too, but I wanted desperately to be wrong.

"Mayhaps you should stay right here with me," he said, his giant eyes fixed and steady on my face. "I'm an old man, after all. I might find the need to rest a bit. Mayhaps in the kitchen. I do believe the kitchen's my favorite room in the house. Don't you think so?"

What I thought was almost unthinkable. The kitchen. Mack Ramsey had been in the kitchen just before Dougie had died. Alone. With access to everything in the refrigerator and the cabinets. I tried to remember how long he'd been there, but suddenly I couldn't think straight. It didn't matter, anyway. It would only take a few seconds to poison the powder and beat a fast exit out the back door. I'd been wrong in thinking the killer had sneaked in and out unnoticed. The killer had been a sad old man who'd gone unnoticed right in front of us. Mack Ramsey, the model of sartorial splendor, who always wore and evidently sometimes lost tie tacks, was on some sort of vendetta against the lawyers who had failed him.

"But I thought you wanted to talk to Wally," I said, taking another step toward the doorway. Buying time always seemed so easy on television; in real life, it was the hardest thing I'd ever tried to do. I didn't know what to say. I didn't know how to say it.

"Why don't you go back behind your desk," he said, his tone almost pleasant. "I'd like you to type a letter for me."

I wasn't sure I could find the keyboard at the moment, let alone use it. And I certainly wasn't taking dictation. *It's a suicide note,* a nasty little voice whispered in my ear as I fell into my chair with nerveless legs.

"What would you like to say?" I hoped my voice wasn't shaking along with the rest of me. It couldn't be Mack Ramsey when it was Ronald Plackett. Plackett had been furious with Dougie. He'd sneaked into the kitchen and done his dirty work, losing his tie tack in the process, then added insult to murder by filing his ethics complaint anyway.

Except, unless Ronald Plackett was psychotic, the punishment seemed somewhat of an overreaction to the offense. Mack Ramsey, on the other hand, had lost his wife to medical negligence and had come to Dougie to help put it right. And Dougie had failed him.

Ramsey was watching me, his eyes steady and unblinking, like a snake's. Maybe he was the psychotic one. "I'd like you to say you're sorry."

"I'm sorry."

"Not to me." He pointed. "In the letter. Say you're sorry, and you couldn't live with your mistake."

My mistake? How had I gotten pushed to the head of the line?

"Look, I know what we'll do." I spun the chair to find a notepad. "You can leave a note for Wally, and I'll be sure he gets it in—"

I heard a rustling and turned back to see Mack Ramsey holding a gun level with my chest. "Is he here now?"

I went limp with fear and despair. "Mr. Ramsey, please. No one suspects—"

"Of course they do." He didn't seem particularly anxious about the matter. "The officers who visited my house yesterday weren't selling tickets to the policemen's ball."

I blinked. "Officers?" The detectives must have gathered names of clients who'd had office appointments. Curt hadn't mentioned they were doing that.

Curt. Now I was praying he'd show up on time. Of course, on time might be too late for me.

Ramsey waved the gun, as if dismissing the whole train of thought. "It doesn't matter, you know. I'll be with Constance soon."

"The blown statute." Personal injury or wrongful death cases had a two-year statute of limitations, the window within which a lawsuit must be filed. Missing that window, when it was spoken of at all, was referred to in horrified whispers as blowing the statute. Dougie had not only blown Mack Ramsey's statute, he'd failed to even open a real file and pursue any investigation into Constance Ramsey's death. I could hardly blame Mr. Ramsey for feeling that his lawyer had let him down; he had. But his lawyer's secretary hadn't, although that didn't seem to matter to him.

I hadn't realized I'd said anything out loud, but Ramsey was nodding.

"All I wanted," he said, "was for you people to get justice for me. Those doctors killed my Connie, and you didn't even care enough to file a lawsuit."

"That's not true," I said. I had to believe that much. "Doug cared about his clients. It was a clerical mistake, really. The case slipped through the cracks. There are so many files..." I let my voice trail off when I realized I wasn't helping my own cause. Ramsey wasn't listening anyway. He was craning his neck to look around the corner, toward the stairs. He must have heard Wally moving around up there. My eyes flitted to the telephone. I wondered if I should punch the intercom button to yell for Wally. Of course, once he got wind of what was going on, he probably wouldn't come. He'd shimmy down the elm tree outside his window and be gone before Curt found my dead body.

I closed my eyes, wishing I'd gone to beauty school like Estelle What's-Her-Name. New York couldn't be more dangerous than Parker, Dennis at this moment. If I survived this, I'd enroll within twenty-four hours. I'd even learn to do nails. And I'd dress better. Pantyhose without holes. Underwear with fresh elastic. And I'd throw myself at Curt and drag him off to my bed once and for all. Enough with ogling his legs from afar. A girl could be assertive after she'd had a gun pointed at her.

"She's gone," Ramsey was saying, talking more to himself than to me. "She's gone, and I'm alone, and you didn't care. No one here cared."

"I care," I said. It sounded like a sappy greeting card, but it was the best I could manage. "The lawyers might not, but we secretaries do. And we can only do what we're told, after all."

He pursed his lips as if trying to decide whether to believe me.

"There's a procedure to follow." I went on. I didn't know if he was buying it or not, but talking made me feel like I might have some control over the situation. "The lawyers send out certain letters, ask for certain documents. If they don't tell us what to ask for, we can't do our jobs." With every ounce of strength I had, I was passing the buck to Howard and Wally and Ken.

"You could ask them," he said.

"Ask them?" I tried to smirk. "You can't ask lawyers anything. They don't answer questions."

He made a face that might have said he agreed with me.

"Let me ask you something," I said, sensing a warming trend. "Dougie mentioned that you were a farmer. Is that where you got the Spanish fly? From your farm?"

"Of course not." He shrugged. "I got it at the Black Orchid."

Of course.

He jiggled the gun at my computer. "The letter?"

That letter felt like the only thing keeping me bullet-free. There was no way I was typing so much as my name. "Wouldn't you rather speak to Wally?" I asked hopefully. "I'm sure he can explain to you what happened."

"I know what happened." He glanced at the wall clock. "You forgot about me. Now society will forget about you."

"No one forgot about your wife," I said. "Tell me about her." I edged my chair closer to the desk where my letter opener lay waiting possibly to save my life. "Do you have any photos of her?"

"You know, you're a dreadful secretary," he said. "You can't stay on the subject, and you talk too much."

"It might have something to do with the gun," I said. I wondered if letter openers could be thrown like knives. I couldn't see why not. But there was never a knife thrower around when you needed one.

"This?" He looked down at his gun with mild surprise. "This needn't make you nervous. Not yet, anyway."

Great.

"You know," he added, "I think I would rather speak to Wallace first after all. You've made some fine points in your own defense."

It was a start. "Howard will be in in twelve hours," I said. "Maybe you'll want to talk to him, too. There's no rush, right?"

He ignored that. "Try him again," he told me. "If he won't answer the phone, I'll go up and get him if I have to." He looked at the stairs doubtfully, and I realized he probably had bad hips or bad knees or both. No man his age could be sturdy and strong on his feet. That presented a new opportunity I hadn't considered: an old-fashioned football tackle. It would probably fracture his hip, but that was no more unkind than him shooting an air vent into my chest. Of course, I was on the wrong side of the desk for that, and something less than athletic, but I was willing to give it a try.

"I'd love to see Mrs. Ramsey's picture," I said again, since that was the best chance I had to gain a more strategic position.

"I know what you're doing," he said.

I glanced at the clock. Curt still had ten minutes to go. For once in his miserable life, Wally wasn't up and down the stairs annoying me. I was on my own. This was it.

No more overtime for me.

"I'm not doing anything," I said, trying to be soothing. "I understand how upset you are. I'd be upset, too. I'm sure you were married for a long time—"

"Fifty-seven years," he said. "And you have no idea how upset I am."

I took a deep breath. "Actually, I do, Mr. Ramsey. My mother died from a hospital's negligence eight years ago. Only a jury didn't see it that way. They didn't think the hospital did anything wrong." I crossed myself mentally and promised to throw a week's salary into the collection basket if I pulled this off. Plus, I'd apologize to my parents for everything I'd ever done. Including the twenty-two hours of labor I'd put my mother through.

The gun wavered slightly. "They did?"

I nodded, keeping my expression grave. Which wasn't hard. "That's the trouble with juries, Mr. Ramsey. You never know what they're going to do. They might have decided your wife wasn't the victim of negligence, either. And you'd still be alone." I swallowed hard. "Like my father."

"But she was the victim of negligence." He sounded confused.

"You're on the inside looking out," I said. "Juries are on the outside looking in. The view is never the same."

"I suppose it isn't," he said, but he didn't lower the gun.

The front door opened again, and I heard heels clopping into the entry hall. A second later, Sherri burst into the office wearing a sundress that made sitting an adventure in exhibitionism. "Hey, kiddo, I saw your car, and I thought I'd see how the barbecue went." She froze when Ramsey turned the gun on her. "What's this?"

"This is Mack Ramsey," I told her.

She nodded at him. "Why is he holding a gun?"

"He wants to kill Wally," I said.

"I want to kill all of you," Ramsey said.

"Right." I tried to swallow. "He wants to kill all of us."

"Why?" Sherri demanded. "What'd you do?" She scowled at Ramsey. "What'd my sister ever do to you?"

"Your sister?" His eyes grew even larger as he looked her up and down. "You look nothing alike."

He probably meant with the heels and the makeup and the teased hair, but Sherri took it slightly differently. "She's always had a little problem with her wardrobe. Between you and me, she's a mess." She edged closer to him, keeping her expression non-threatening and leading with her chest. And Ramsey was taking notice. He might have been eighty, but he was a man, after all. "Look at you," Sherri said to him, gesturing to his suit. "You're a very smart dresser, Mack. May I call you Mack?"

"No," he said.

Surprise flickered across her face and was gone. "I wish you'd let me call you Mack. It's a very…manly name. Virile."

"Call me Mack," he said, standing absolutely motionless while she moved in. I considered grabbing some paper and taking notes.

"Mack." She said it like she was tasting something sweet. "I can see you're a man with exquisite taste, Mack. That suit is lovely." She reached for his hand and lifted it, twirling slowly beneath it like she was dancing. "Do you like my outfit, Mack?"

"What there is of it," he said, but his tone was mild, and she noticed. She waggled a finger at him, scolding. "You don't fool me. You mature gentlemen like a nice turn of ankle as much as the younger guys." She stuck out her leg and pulled up her hem until the color of her panties was the only mystery left. At least I hoped she was wearing panties. "What do you think, Mack? Would you like to take me dancing?"

His jaw slackened a little and so did mine. I knew precisely what she was up to, but I didn't know how far she'd take it. It was like watching a brilliant trial lawyer playing cat-and-mouse with a witness on the stand. Mack Ramsey was the only one who didn't know where this was going.

"I used to dance with my Connie," he said, so wistfully that something tightened in my chest. Despite everything, he was a lonely old man. A lonely old homicidal man.

Sherri seemed unmoved. "Dance with me now," she said, taking his hand again. I noticed she ignored the one holding the gun. She was manipulative, but she wasn't stupid.

"I don't know," he said, letting her lead him to the center of the room, where she laid her cheek against his and conformed herself to his thin body, still holding fast to his free hand. He put his gun hand around the small of her back so the gun was nestled in the hollow there. Over his shoulder, she gave me a look that I recognized instantly as: *Do not screw this up.* I gave a slight nod. I had no intention of screwing it up.

As she hummed softly in his ear, she slowly maneuvered him until his back was to me. As soon as I saw his bald spot, I launched myself onto my desk and leaped onto his back, wrapping both arms around his shoulders and both legs around his waist, pulling and pushing and twisting all at the same time. He made a sharp "Awwk!" sound and pushed Sherri away, but it was too late. I'd startled him enough that he'd dropped the gun. I hit the floor and fired into the opposite wall, sending a little puff of plaster wafting out. Ramsey stumbled forward, off balance, and fell onto his knees, and Sherri scrambled out of his way, looking relieved and horrified and proud all at the same time.

Footsteps pounded on the stairs, and Wally burst into the room, his tie loose and his top two buttons unbuttoned over a hairless chest. "What the hell?" He immediately saw Ramsey kneeling on all fours, grimacing in pain. Then he saw the gun and the hole in the wall, and then he saw Sherri, and his eyes widened.

"This man murdered Mr. Heath," Sherri told him, giving her dress a few tugs to straighten it across her breasts. "And he made me rip my dress," she added, fingering a spaghetti strap.

"You poor thing," Wally told her, stepping over Ramsey to go to her side. "Let's sue the bastard."

"I'm okay," I told him, but he wasn't listening, so I grabbed a tissue and went over to pick up the gun. Ramsey didn't seem too anxious to get on his feet, so I left him where he was and stumbled back to my desk to call the police while Wally helped my sister stay dressed.

CHAPTER FORTY-FOUR

———

Curt arrived precisely on time for our date, and he brought chaperones in the form of the entire police department. While they hauled Mack Ramsey off the floor to slap cuffs on him, he pulled me aside and hugged me until the chill went away. Fortunately this took some time. Ramsey looked especially pathetic with his suit now rumpled and askew on his skinny frame and his eyes huge and confused, but this time his pathetic expression had no effect on me. The man would have killed me and my sister, and he'd already killed Dougie. I watched the officers lead him away and felt nothing but relief. That, and a growing awareness of how close Curt and I were standing.

"You should have seen Sherri," I said to him after Ramsey had been packed into the back of a squad car. His arm was still around me, keeping me steady on my feet, although the shot of brandy I'd pilfered from Ken's office had already done that job. "She was magnificent. She charmed him and distracted him and gave me a chance to—"

"Break his hip?"

I shrugged. "Whatever it took. I had no intention of missing out on dinner tonight."

"I'm flattered." He was also killer sexy in head to toe black. He'd probably dressed in five minutes flat and wound up looking that good, while I'd taken nearly an hour and now looked like I'd spent the day crawling through an alley. My hair needed combing. My brand new pantyhose were ripped. I was only wearing one shoe. If appearances were everything, I appeared to be a derelict.

"By the way," he said, his mouth close to my ear, "have told you how good you look?"

Sweet talker. It was enough to make me want to marry the man.

Curt glanced over to where Wally was still ministering to Sherri's torn spaghetti strap. "You know, I'm not surprised about your sister. I always had her pegged for something big."

"Like ten to twenty years?"

He grinned. "Not that big. Randall's gonna have his hands full with her, though."

"He could use the challenge," I said. If anyone could make the Boy Lawyer grow up, it was my sister. And it might be handy, having a lawyer around. Especially if she insisted on wearing clothes like that torn sundress, which was currently hanging off of one shoulder and dipping perilously close to her Wonder Bra. Wally was standing closer than he needed to, either surveying the damage or sneaking a peek at cleavage, but Sherri wasn't objecting. In fact, she looked pretty happy about it. "I don't think he'll be letting her go anytime soon," I added. I didn't even think he'd be letting her leave.

"I don't think I will, either," he said, his arm tightening around my waist.

I leaned into him. "She's a good catch," I said. "Don't you think?"

"Uh-huh." Curt nodded. "And he'll probably be able to keep her out of jail."

I caught Sherri's eye and smiled, and she gave me a wink and a nod that said: *Do not screw this up.* I nodded slightly. I had no intention of screwing it up.

"Come on." I slipped my hand into Curt's. "Let's go eat."

ABOUT THE AUTHOR

From her first discovery of Nancy Drew, Kelly Rey has had a lifelong love for mystery and tales of things that go bump in the night, especially those with a twist of humor. Through many years of working in the court reporting and closed captioning fields, writing has remained a constant. If she's not in front of a keyboard, she can be found reading, working out or avoiding housework. She's a member of Sisters in Crime and lives in the Northeast with her husband and a menagerie of very spoiled pets.

To learn more about Kelly Rey, visit her online at:
http://www.kellyreyauthor.com

Enjoyed this book? Check out these other fun reads available in
print now from
Gemma Halliday Publishing:

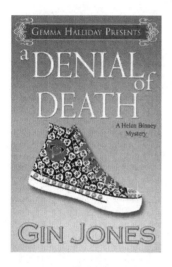

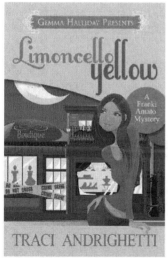

www.GemmaHallidayPublishing.com

Made in the USA
San Bernardino, CA
30 June 2015